DEATH TO DESERTERS

DEATH TO DESERTERS

A WESTERN DOUBLE

UZZIAH MOUNTAIN MAN
BOOK NINE

J.J. BONHAM

Death to Deserters: A Western Double
Paperback Edition

Wolfpack Publishing
1707 E. Diana Street
Tampa, FL 33610

www.wolfpackpublishing.com

Paperback ISBN 979-8-89567-361-4
Ebook ISBN 979-8-89567-360-7

DEATH TO DESERTERS

DEATH TO DESERTERS

1

Uzziah had gone off on some secret mission for Stonewall Jackson. Immanuel didn't know exactly what it was—he'd taken Abooksigun with him. Why Immanuel wasn't included, he did not know. What he did know was that the two scouts had left early—so early, it wasn't even false dawn—and nobody knew when they'd be back.

The valley campaign was still going on, and General Jackson had his boys marching every which way he could. If it was confusing to the enemy trying to figure out where Jackson was, then that was a good thing. When the Federals least expected it, he'd bring on his foot cavalry and see how they liked knowing where he was, then. The man sure enough stretched human limitations, both his own men and the Union forces.

Immanuel had made up his mind, he was leaving, that's all there was to it. He'd had quite enough of seeing men—men from the same country, mind you—shooting each other and running pell-mell into crowds with attached bayonets. It was sickening. No animal in nature did what man did, and that was one of the reasons Immanuel had left civilization, such as he had remembered it, and gone into the mountains. At least there, when danger appeared, it wasn't organized with cannons and grapeshot to tear you in half.

He and Uzziah had talked about it for several nights, but Uzziah's fascination with Jackson was just beyond Immanuel. He supposed it was the same thing that had happened with Porter Rockwell, he wasn't sure. Of course, then there was the fetching Mormon woman, Hannah, to lure him in, and lure him in she did. Died having a kid, and Uzziah wouldn't even so much as look at a squaw, saying he was celestial married, or some such shite.

Sometimes, he wondered how he and Uzziah ever got together. The two of them were about as different as two human beings could be, but still, even as he was packing up his meager belongings and making sure he had enough shot and powder, he was getting this pit in his stomach that he got every time he and Uzziah parted ways, didn't matter the reason. He contemplated what it meant. Two men, who worked well together, and lived and fought well together, giving up on each other and going their separate ways. It just was so much bigger than that, and it simply could not be explained.

Well, we all reaped what we sowed, and what this nation, these Confederates, were sowing was a mess of hurt that might just someday come back and call for the paying of the piper. In any case, he'd made it clear to Uzziah that he was fed up with the whole business and he was leaving. Uzziah, just like Uzziah always was, was willing to sit there and not ask Immanuel to stay.

The man, Uzziah said, was free to do what his conscience told him to do. If that meant leaving this mess of a civil war, then he supported him, but Uzziah could not, in all good faith, go with him.

Immanuel mounted up on Stygian this coolish morning in August, and quite frankly, he felt, if he never saw another uniform for the rest of his life, he would be happy. He rode away and wasn't looking back when a voice spoke to him from the darkness. He reached for his Walker Colt, but before he had a chance to draw it, he recognized Jackson's whiny voice. The man was from the hills, and you can take the boy out of the hills, but you can't take the hills out of the boy.

He turned his beautiful black horse toward the reed-thin voice, and there he was with a blanket, like some prayer shawl, over his head and shoulders, walking from the blackness of the fields.

"I thought that was you," Jackson said.

"Yes, General, it is me."

"Where would ya be goin' this hour of the morn?" Jackson asked, as if it were any of his business.

"Away from here," was all Immanuel said.

"I could always tell that this war did not suit you as much as it seems it does the O'Bannons."

"You're a keen observer, sir," Immanuel said as Jackson walked close to Stygian.

"This is a fine horse. I've always meant to tell you that. Too fine for the likes of me, I am a poor rider, and just keeping my seat seems enough for me."

When Immanuel didn't say anything, Jackson continued. "Yer probably wondering what I'm doing up at this hour," Jackson said, his hands gently caressing the nose of the great, black horse.

"We all know what you do at this hour, sir," Immanuel said.

"You do, well, why not? I don't make a mystery of my relationship with the Almighty. I have been in prayer with our Father. I do believe our Father is in absolute agreement with your feelings on this debacle called a civil war. Not a thing civil 'bout it, and it pains me a great deal to see so much death."

"Then, if I may be so bold, why do you command troops in these ignoble battles?"

"You surprise me, Immanuel, you really do. You believe in God, and in his Son, Jesus Christ, don't ya?"

"Of course, sir."

"Then you must know that when Jesus was in the Garden of Gethsemane, he prayed to have the cup passed from his lips. Did it happen?"

"No, General, it did not."

"So much pain that our Lord and Savior had to pass through, no way around it, over it, under it. He had to walk the walk through all that pain," Jackson said, and paused, his eyes looking toward heaven.

"And yet," Jackson continued, "it was a necessary experience of evil by the only son of God, so that we humans might be washed clean by his sacrificial blood, was it not?"

"That's what they say," Immanuel admitted reluctantly.

"You don't believe it?" Jackson asked, almost in childish disbelief that anyone could think such a thing.

"It's hard to imagine a father asking that much of a son."

"Yes, it is, isn't it? Yet Abraham placed his own son, Isaac, on the altar, did he not?" Immanuel kept quiet, knowing a rhetorical question when he heard one. "He put the son of laughter, that's what Isaac means, ya know, he put his own laughter on an altar and was prepared to kill the boy, to kill the joy...of his life, if that was what God wanted. Of course, a ram appeared in the bushes. Had it wandered there? I hardly think so, and God spared Abraham's son."

"I'm afraid there ain't no ram in these bushes, General, just a bunch of lambs in the fields, being led to slaughter," Immanuel said.

Those words sank in deeply with Jackson as he looked toward his muddied boots, and then back up into Immanuel's face.

"I take it you will leave us, now?" Jackson sort of asked.

"I am leaving, General, the slaughter is too much to witness."

"Yes, yes, it is," Jackson said, then added, "I will miss having *God with us* with us, if ya know what I mean?"

"It's been an honor serving under you, General Jackson, but I cannot say that it has been a pleasure," Immanuel said, and for the last time, he saluted the general, who saluted him back, the blanket falling off his shoulders and head as he did so. His appearance almost took the appearance of a boy, well, Immanuel could see the boy in the man when Jackson saluted.

Perhaps it was the conversation of sacrifices and war dead that had melted away the man from his face, but all Immanuel could see was the boy Jackson had once been. It was no secret among the troops that he was the orphan, the waif who had been raised by an uncle after his mother and father both passed. It must have been the loneliness that caged his heart and strangled his emotions. If Jackson were with the Mandan, they would build a sweat lodge, and in the heat of his suffering, he would gain a new perspective on life. But the white man's ways were different. Deal with what you've got, regardless, and the devil take the hindmost.

It was then that Immanuel saw the pain in the general's eyes. The moon broke through the cloud cover and shone just enough to put the catch light in the general's eyes. The grief that was being held there almost broke Immanuel's heart. How could any man begin to understand leadership in a war like this?

He brought his salute down and rode off, but Jackson wasn't through yet.

"If any enemy is spotted nearby, I do hope you'll consider having news sent our way," Jackson said just loud enough for Immanuel's departing ears to hear.

Uzziah and Abooksigun had been gone all morning before they saw the quartet of men. They were walking the road back down into the Shenandoah as if it were a lark, well, it could have been, but wasn't. None of the four men, nor the Algonquin Indian, nor Uzziah, a boy who had been raised in this very valley, knew exactly what would happen to these men.

At one point in Uzziah's company, General Longstreet had told Jackson that of the 32,000 men who were in his command, there were 7,000 missing from the camp. The rest, because it was harvest time, had gone home in order to do what men did every harvest time, bring in the grain. It wasn't like the women were going to be able to handle all of it. Some of it, yes, but the men left, they simply left and went to work their fields, their herds, their farms. Then, when the work was done, they would wander back into their regiments.

But recent events, recent scrimmages had left the Confederate high command with a bad taste in their mouths. More and more Confederate troops were leaving—away without leave, they called it—whenever the mood hit them, and there were no consequences. This would not do, it would never do, and the high command was determined to see an example set, and the one man that they knew who considered *duty* as high as a command from God himself, well, it most certainly was Jackson. Word had been sent him that he was to make an example, a terrible, deadly example, of what it could mean when men deserted.

That morning, when Immanuel had disturbed Jackson's prayers, he was in communication with God, the Father Almighty, about those very orders, and it seemed God had been mute on the subject. It seemed God had just reminded Jackson that even he had to sacrifice his only begotten son so that a greater good could be served. And then, there was the interruption of those prayers just as he was waiting for an answer.

Sometimes, God sent his answers through the voices of men. Immanuel James Jones had appeared and shown Jackson the other side of duty, the side that says, *this is too much.* He respected the mountain man's views and imagined for a man who was used to the relative peace and solitude of the mountains, all this blood and glory was simply too much. He respected the man for following his heart, as he respected all men who did so. And yet, hadn't he sent Uzziah, Immanuel's partner from the mountains, to gather up the four AWOLs who had been reported absent yesterday? There was part of him who hoped those men could not be found, but that part was a coward, Jackson was sure. Jackson knew there was a greater good to be served, he knew it as surely as he knew God above existed.

Wasn't the preservation of the Confederacy a greater good?!? Wasn't the northern aggression to be stopped and states' rights saved?

And so it was that Uzziah, who was as close to Jackson as any, had been invited into his tent, and told that there were four boys, yes, Uzziah knew the boys, well, they really weren't boys, they were more Uzziah's own age. He knew them, as he knew his brothers. They had worked farms north of where his father's place was, and there were these men that Jackson wanted brought back to the camp.

Uzziah had no idea why, he was simply ordered to do so, and he imagined, as he went after them, that they could have been his brothers. His brothers and father had certainly left without permission many times to gather in the wheat, plow the fields, and maintain the machinery and buildings required to run the farm.

Now, that's not to say that Uzziah did know many of those who left without permission, simply went to Richmond, and drank what they could, and caused trouble on the streets. This was the common problem, which the populace of Richmond had cried out against–something had to be done! It was a problem that grew, and to tell the truth, the people who thought of their military as something to protect them from the northern aggressors did not know what to make of this new type of slacker, stalking their streets, begging at their back doors, and not really caring what the population thought of their cowardice and desertion.

The need for Confederate soldiers came to such a height that the first conscription act came upon the south in the spring of 1862, in which males between the ages of 18 and 35 were required to give three-year service, unless of course, the war ended sooner than that. This conscription act also included those who were already soldiers in the war effort, conscripting them to an addition three years of service. As it might be imagined, this was not a popular act from the point of view of the common soldiers.

The other thing which this conscription act produced was the fact that those conscripted in 1862 were not the high-minded, blood-type who, when fighting, did so as if their own honor depended on it. That was not to say that the conscripts of 1862, nor those who had to sign on for additional years, were by any means cowards. However, their fervor was less than those who instinctually saw their duty was to the Confederacy.

It wasn't like the farms in the Shenandoah had slaves to work their properties, they did not, and so, their so-called *French Furloughs* were seen not as desertion at all, but as a necessity for the way of life being lived in the Shenandoah Valley.

But as Uzziah and Abooksigun rode up behind the four men, who were not brothers, but related as cousins and second cousins, the men turned and greeted them with smiles.

"Hey, Uzziah, where ya headed?"

"I think a better question would be where y'all headed?"

"Well, we read the new conscription act, and we're old enough not to be included, but we need proof that we're the age we know we are," said John Layman.

"Who's we?" Uzziah asked.

"Me and John here, John Rogers. He's in the same situation."

"What about you, ain't you James Roadcap?"

"That's right. Hey, I got me a four-day furlough from the 10th Virginia, but decided when it was done to go over and join Ashby's Cavalry," Roadcap said.

"Can ya do that, just change units like that?" Uzziah asked.

"Ifn ya want less constriction on ya, lots of fellas have done it," Roadcap said.

The fourth man had not spoken at all.

"Who are you?" Uzziah asked the man.

"I'm James Riddel Jr. Hell, I been bucked and gagged, horse whipped and just about everything else they can do to a conscript, but take a look at these shoes, will ya?"

Uzziah and Abooksigun both looked at what appeared to be shoes on the man's feet but were so full of holes that he'd stuffed newspapers in them to keep his feet off the rocks in the road.

"I gots me two good pairs of shoes at the house, and I'll be damned ifn I'm gonna go on another forced march like we just done and me be wearin' these broken-down shoes!"

Riddel's testimony about his shoes had the other three deserters laughing and holding their sides, but Uzziah wasn't amused.

"Well, you men got to come back with us, now," Uzziah said in a stern voice.

"What ya mean, them shoes aren't but three miles from chere," Riddle almost pleaded.

"Well, that's unfortunate, 'cause we are under orders from General Jackson to bring you back to the regiment," Uzziah said.

"And what's the Injun fer, ifn we misbehave, he'll scalp us?" Riddle was on a roll, and he wasn't going to stop joking. He was not taking this seriously. Uzziah knew Jackson's mind on this matter and was afraid that these men might be made an example.

"Here's the good news," Uzziah started in. "It ain't that far back to headquarters, and then ya can rest."

"Well, hell, it'll be just like ole John Casler. He left the brigade for some whiskey, and all he did was tell lies, and he got off with some stupid punishment," Riddel said, and the four turned around and started walking back toward the brigade headquarters.

2

After J.E.B. Stuart's ride around McClellan and his father-in-law being relieved of his Union cavalry command, because Stuart had literally run circles around the Union army, General Stuart rested his 1200 cavalrymen. Looking for their next adventure and waiting for their next orders, which would come from General Robert Edward Lee, the men relaxed and did what all men do between battles in war.

The camp where Stuart and his men lived had become a second home to many of the boys and older men who lived there. Quite a camaraderie grew up between all the men, as it always did when men risked their lives to further a good cause.

Sergeant Stark Simmons and John O'Bannon were fast becoming the friends that each of them, it seemed, had always wanted.

If there was one thing that Stuart believed in, it was drilling, and Hanna—a.k.a. John—had to admit, when you drilled as much as Stuart had his men drill, well, when things went south and to hell in a handbasket, it paid to be able to react, not think. Reacting was what drilling was all about. Men who stopped and thought were usually men who lay on the battlefield, having given up their seats on their mounts.

After drilling, this one particular evening, as they had indulged in whiskey, Hanna saw Stark tracing the wound on his scalp with his index finger and looking thoughtful. When he glanced over at her, for just a split second, he had the same look on his face that he had had that night. The night she had lied to him about being his wife, even used her own Christian name, Hanna, in doing so. What had she been thinking? For just that split second, the manner in which his head turned as he was looking at her, she thought to herself, *he must have remembered.*

It wouldn't have bothered her if he had simply gone on joking with his fellow cavalrymen, but he got up and walked over to where she was sitting. She didn't think it was wise to sit next to him all the time, though she always wanted to. When he came over, there was a peculiar expression on his face. She imagined she'd memorized all his ponderous glances, but this one was saying something different.

He plopped down beside her, the way he always seated himself, patted her leg as any man would do with a fellow cavalryman, then his head turned in her direction.

She didn't look to see that he had, but he had. She could feel his stare burrowing into the side of her face.

"Corporal O'Bannon, you look mighty pensive sitting over here, barely saying two words," he said, smiling that wonderful smile. That was the reason she had turned to him, she heard the smile in his voice.

"Well, as Mark Twain once wrote, *It's better to keep your mouth shut and be thought a fool than to open it and erase all doubt.*"

Sergeant Stark laughed, and when he was really tickled, which it seemed he was at this moment, he let it all out. Fairly soon, the conversations and falderal around that campfire ceased, and everyone looked at the sergeant and his corporal.

"So, Stark, what's so damned funny?" one of the officers asked.

He looked at John O'Bannon, whom he knew liked to keep a low profile, though he was certainly at a loss as to why. The young man handled himself like a regular in battle, and hadn't he saved the sergeant's life? Not to mention his comportment in the saddle, which outdid almost all the others.

"It was something personal," Stark said, and left it at that.

The conversations went back to where they were before he had interrupted with his guffaws, and he turned to Hanna.

"Thank you for that," she said, playing the bashful boy.

"Well, I just wish they all knew you as I do," Stark said, then added, "There's really no reason for your hesitance in showing how competent you are, really, Corporal, you are a most amazing companion and without a doubt, a fellow anyone one of these men would be glad to have fighting next to him!" Stark said and went back to listening to a story that one of the others was telling.

Well, if others knew her as he did, then she would be in trouble, she thought, *she'd be the entire regiment's trollop, wouldn't she?!* She had to chuckle to herself with that thought. Stark turned to her.

"Somethin' funny?"

"That story, even though I've heard it at least ten times, I like it," she said, referring to the story that was being told by one of the noncoms. Stark listened for a bit, then turned back to her.

"Yeah, heard that one a hundred times, count yer lucky stars that ya just joined up!"

That night, Stark got a bit in his cups, something she couldn't afford to do, well, she could, but then again, she couldn't.

Stark leaned into her as she helped him to the tent, then into his bunk. It didn't stop there, times like this, she also helped remove his uniform. He slept in just his long johns, and since it was so warm, nary a blanket covered him. As she put him on his side—she had heard stories of men strangling in the night if they vomited their drink—she looked him over and liked what she saw.

During the night, when she heard him muttering in his sleep, she looked over, and if he was on his back, his manhood would invariably be engorged. She enjoyed that, in her own way. Rahab had told all the girls the reason the boys didn't like to jump right out of bed in the mornings was their particular predicament with their manhood. Rahab knew that's what happened to their father when he dreamed and confessed that she had taken advantage of this *dream wonder*, as she called it.

She hadn't really believed her mother until this full-time bunk-mating with a grown man. Lord, it made her concupiscent just to lie that close to what she had had and obviously wanted again. Perhaps, her agony was enhanced by the fact that she had missed her monthlies, and that was worry enough. It had had a tardy arrival before, but never this late.

Add to that, she felt goatish most of the time. In the past, she had simply looked on when Stark had his man moments, but this particular night, before she knew where her hand was wandering, it had slipped beneath her clothing to her warm skin, and with her eyes glued on him and his situation, she'd wiggled herself to completion.

She moaned when it came upon her, and it did so without so much as a warning, and the moaning must have awakened Stark, because he turned to her just as she turned away.

"You all right?" he asked, with sleep dripping off his words.

She lay as still as she could, then finally, she heard him snoring.

Immanuel decided that if he was going to make it back to the Rockies, he'd better travel south first, then across Texas, and then dangerously up through Apache territory to the Rockies. It was well considered and made a lot of sense. Traveling straight to the Rockies would mean that he would be traveling through a lot of contested territory where Yankee and Confederate both thought they held sway. He simply wasn't up for continually trying to convince one group that he wasn't from the other group, and vice versa. That would have been Uzziah's job.

If Uzziah had seen how fruitless this Civil War thing was, but being a Virginian and all, well, he understood his partner's reluctance to leave his brothers, and perhaps he felt as if he didn't stay, it would send a message to his pa and his brothers that he didn't support them. Later, after this mess was over, Immanuel envisioned Uzziah having trouble trying to explain his leaving to his mother, Rahab, even if no other brother died, which was, he'd figured, against all odds.

With a family that big, there would be more death. Immanuel understood, but it didn't make it easier for him to agree with Uzziah. There were certain things that they disagreed upon, and those things stood until there was something bigger that both agreed on.

As he rode the flatlands that led toward Richmond, he appreciated the farming that was going on in the area. No wonder they used slaves, really huge plantations with cotton as far as the eye could see. Or at least, that's the way it had been. Now, once fertile fields lay fallow and unused. There was no way that white men could harvest such a crop and pay wages and come out on top. The slave trade had made this certain type of farming possible, and profitable. He was daydreaming when a rider came from the side of the road and challenged him.

"Halt, what are you doin' on this road?" the young boy, dressed in Confederate uniform, challenged.

"Ya know, I'm headed fer Texas eventually, why do ya ask?" Immanuel asked a question when questions were asked him, it threw the responsibility of the communication back on the one who had first spoken.

"There's a group—never ya mind why I wanna know, yer gonna come with me, now," the boy ordered, more than said. Immanuel recognized a Confederate cavalryman and wasn't going to object, till the next words escaped the boy's mouth. "Give me that blunderbuss, now!" he commanded.

My God, Immanuel thought, *this child thought his Hawken was a blunderbuss!? Now, he was sure that the Confederates were going to have difficulty winning a war, when they didn't know the names of respective firearms.*

"This chere is a Hawken rifle, son," Immanuel said, as he hefted the rifle from across his lap into the air.

The boy cavalryman fired his pistol at Immanuel, and thankfully missed, but the mount he was on reared up when the bullet had blown the tip of the horse's right ear off.

The horse took to bucking, and frankly, Immanuel didn't blame him. If someone shot his ear, he'd be way less inclined to let them ride him. The boy fought off the bucking fairly well, he survived the sunfish, the twist and shout, then left the saddle when the horse came down on stiff legs. The boy hit the ground badly and was out like a light.

Immanuel got off Stygian and tied the boy to the saddle on the Confederate's bleeding horse. He doctored the horse's ear with a poultice and a bright white bandage that he'd collected when he was with Jackson.

He scanned the horizon and noticed that off to the southeast there was a lot of smoke, probably from campfires.

Immanuel rode the dirt trail, with the wounded horse's reins tied to his D-ring, and when he rode into the campsite, there was quite a ruckus as other cavalrymen ran hither and yon, till a sergeant affronted Immanuel.

"Is he dead?" the sergeant asked, his own pistol drawn and pointing at Immanuel.

"Well, no, he's gonna have a hell of a headache tamarrie, but he ain't dead," Immanuel said.

"Get down off yer horse, sir, until we straighten this out," the sergeant asked with the pistol trained on Immanuel.

"I brought this youngster in 'cause in trying to secure me, he accidentally shot part of his horse's ear off, and then was bucked to unconsciousness," Immanuel said as he dismounted. "Would ya please point that Griswold somewheres else?" he admonished the trooper.

The trio—the sergeant, the unconscious boy strapped across his wounded horse, and Immanuel—walked to the general's tent. Immanuel was disarmed and put under guard while the sergeant disappeared inside.

It was suppertime, and from most of the fires there came agreeable smells, and Immanuel was getting hungry.

From one of those fires, Corporal John O'Bannon watched the sergeant take the mountain man and the wounded soldier to Stuart's tent.

"What's goin' on?" It was Stark, he had been taking a nap and came out. He knew when it was suppertime.

"Some frontiersman has been stopped by a sergeant. One of our men came in draped over his own saddle," Hanna said, as she stirred the concoction she was putting together for their supper.

Stark looked. It wasn't that far away, maybe thirty yards, and he saw the man that John was talking about, and seeing the body over the cavalryman's saddle, Stark pulled his suspenders up, grabbed his cap, and walked off toward them.

"I'll be back, don't eat without me," Stark said over his shoulder.

As Hanna watched Stark walk over to where the frontiersman was, she could hear some of what was being said, and by golly, she recognized the frontiersman's voice. It was Immanuel! What the hell was she going to do now?

By the time Stark got over to Stuart's tent, the general was out and inspecting the knocked-out cavalryman.

"How'd this happen?" General Stuart asked.

"He stopped me on the road, and wanted to take my Hawken from me, called it a blunderbuss," Immanuel said, smiling.

"So, you think this is funny?" the sergeant asked.

"Let the man finish," Stuart said.

"Yes, sir, sorry, sir."

"Well, I have this rifle in my hand almost every waking hour, and being a scout for General Jackson, I hardly thought it was worth me giving up something when the man didn't even know its proper name. So, when I refused, he brought his sidearm to bear on me. It went off, accidentally, I guess, but instead of doing me harm, he clipped the tip off his horse's ear. The horse did not take kindly to that and bucked his ass off!" Immanuel said, looking General Stuart right in the eyes.

"What's your name, scout?" General Stuart asked.

"Immanuel James Jones."

"Wait a minute, I believe my tentmate knows this man," Stark chimed in.

Immanuel turned to Sergeant Stuart and looked at him. "And who might that be?" Jones asked.

"John O'Bannon, Uzziah's brother," the sergeant announced proudly.

Well, Immanuel had seen John O'Bannon's dead body, helped carry it back to the farm, was there when they laid him in his coffin, so he knew something weird was going on, he just wasn't sure what.

"Bring Corporal O'Bannon over here so he can straighten out this mess, will you, Sergeant Simmons?" General Stuart asked.

Stark left immediately, and everyone watched as he walked the hundred feet to where his tent was. There was a brief exchange between the sergeant and the corporal, and both men began walking back toward the general's tent.

Immanuel didn't have the best vision at this point in his life, and he had a pair of cheaters which he used for reading, but there wasn't a dern thing wrong with his long vision. A young boy was walking beside the sergeant, and Immanuel wondered why he would use a dead man's name until they got closer, then he recognized Hanna O'Bannon. She looked like a young boy, the way her hair was cut, and her chest had, he imagined, been flattened out somehow, but there was no mistaking the henna hair!

As she and the sergeant walked up, she looked at him with trepidation. She was sure the jig was up!

"John, it's been a while, how are things?" Immanuel said, stepping forward and shaking Hanna's hand.

"You know this man?" General Stuart asked the corporal.

"Of course, he's been my oldest brother's partner for quite a while now, right, Immanuel?"

"Yep, me and Uzziah, we're like two peas in a pod," he said, trying to suppress a grin.

"Take the sentry to see the doctor, I'm sure he'll be fine," General Stuart said, but as he began to walk into his tent, he stopped.

"Is Jackson nearby?" Stuart asked.

"Now, General, you being the eyes of the army, wouldn't you know such a thing?" Immanuel asked, grinning from ear to ear.

"Of course," Stuart said and went on into his tent.

"You must come and have supper with us, Immanuel, I'm sure John has made plenty," Stark said, as the three men walked back together.

Immanuel knew a woman's cooking when he tasted it, and he couldn't understand why this yeawho didn't pick up on that, but he'd find out all about that later. He watched the two soldiers and realized that Hanna O'Bannon had completely bamboozled this cavalryman, the general, and the entire unit. He knew what an expert rider Hanna was, and he supposed that was part of it, no man wants to think a woman, or in this case, a mere girl, could ride better than they did.

After a few cursory questions from the sergeant, the rest of the, meal, and the smoking afterward, he was surprised that Hanna had taken that up, too, he was left to simply watch the couple, because he knew that's what they were.

Stark turned in early, and when they could hear him snoring there, in the tent, Immanuel turned to Hanna.

"Girl," he whispered, "what the hell are ya up to?"

She grimaced when she heard the word *girl*, but also knew she owed him somewhat of an explanation. He could never know the extent to which this charade had gone. Never know that her monthlies had stopped, and that it was only a matter of time before everyone would know that she was not a man!

"I am killin' Yankees," she said proudly.

"And yer ma, along with 'em," Immanuel did not hold back.

"I've written her," Hanna said proudly.

"I'll bet that was some consolation, taking yer dead brother's name." Immanuel was keeping it sotto voce and now listened once again to make sure the sergeant was still snoring. "Riding with the most flamboyant outfit in the Confederate army—"

"Isn't it great!" Hanna said, her eyes sparkling and her very soul aflame.

It was then that Immanuel knew it was hopeless. Unless he ripped her clothes off in front of the regiment, which, of course, was something he would ever do, but still, eventually, the whole thing was going to explode on her!

"How long?" Immanuel asked, referring to how long she thought she could keep this charade up.

She looked at him like he was a wizard. Maybe in the mountains, he'd learned more than how the animals reacted, more than simply how to exist in the middle of a freezing winter?!? Uzziah had gone on and on about all the things that Immanuel had taught him, but he'd never referred to this power of perception, the man knew she was with child.

She sat there way too long to answer the question that Immanuel had asked, and it was then that he knew, he knew, she had taken the *how long*? question the wrong way, and somehow, he had guessed her most terrible secret.

"Just a few months, not showing yet," she whispered.

"He knows, right?" Immanuel asked, nodding toward the snoring in the tent.

She shook her head *no*.

"How?"

"I tricked him," she whispered.

"How drunk was he?"

"Wounded, he was wounded," Hanna said.

Immanuel looked at her with disbelief.

"Headwound, he was confused," she said lowly.

"Ain't nothin' to how confused he's gonna be," Immanuel spat out.

My God, he'd stumbled into some shite before, but this was going to take the proverbial cake. He had wandered in way over his head, and he sure wished he hadn't. A pregnant girl, by her sergeant. He should have known, the way she looked at him when they ate. What the hell?

He knew now that he was not going back to the Rockies. He was going back to see Uzziah, he couldn't carry this burden into the mountains and not let his partner of all these years know, he was about to become an uncle. Damn! Life had ways of taking you by the ear and turning you back to where you'd just come from.

"Yer gonna tell, ain't ya, that's what yer gonna do?!?" Hanna asked in the most desperate voice he'd ever heard.

He reached out and touched her arm. "No, sweetheart, this ain't my secret to tell," he said in the gentlest of voices.

She began to cry, probably from relief, but she was crying nevertheless. He took her in his arms.

One of the cavalrymen from an adjacent tent looked over and saw him hugging her. He didn't care what that man thought. This young girl had herself into one twisted knot made of lies and love, and he wasn't sure what to do. One thing was for sure, Uzziah needed to know.

"I gots to tell Uzziah," Immanuel said, then added, "And I'm bettin' he'll tell yer ma."

That did nothing to stop her tears, nothing at all.

Immanuel could hear that the snoring had stopped, and he didn't want Stark to come out and find him holding John. He pushed her back and pointed with his head toward the tent. Hanna rubbed her face with her hands and dried her hands on her trooper's pants.

"John, what's wrong?" Stark's head was in the tent opening.

"Immanuel's just reminded me how much I miss my brother Uzziah," Hanna said.

"Oh, okay," the sleepy sergeant said, and ducked back into the tent.

Immanuel stared at Hanna and wouldn't have traded places with her for all the money, furs, or booty in the world. This girl had dug herself a hole which would be one hard place to get out of, of that, he was sure!

He filled his coffee cup, and as he sipped at the burned coffee, he thought how much better that tasted than what awaited Hanna.

By the morning, he was gone. He had watched her go into the tent with that man, and he didn't know how she'd gotten with child without Stark knowing she was a woman, and frankly, he didn't want to know. She'd said something about a head wound, good Lord! Women! They had their ways, and they would never be the ways of men, and he thanked the Lord for that!

By the time the sun was coming up, he was halfway back to Jackson's regiment, and running the conversation through his head where he told Uzziah what he'd discovered.

3

The road back to where Jackson was at Pisgah Church was uneventful. Thankfully, since Immanuel's arrival was in the middle of a hornet's nest. It seemed that when Uzziah and Abooksigun had gotten back with four so-called deserters, instead of them being slapped on the wrist as most of them had, there was a trial in session, a court-martial which had been going on for some time.

When Immanuel rode up, you'd have thought Uzziah had been waiting on something good to happen to take his mind off the trial.

"Immanuel," Uzziah said as the man still sat his horse.

"Yep, it's me, all right."

"I am so glad to see ya," Uzziah said. Abooksigun was sitting around the fire and was smoking.

"Abooksigun," Immanuel said, and the Algonquin grunted at him.

"Articulate as usual," Immanuel said. Abooksigun's expression didn't change at all.

"I've got some bad news fer ya," Uzziah said, and all the while Immanuel was thinking, *nothing to what I got, my old friend.*

Uzziah told him the story of the four men that they'd brought back.

"But two of these guys were goin' back to get proof that they were too old for the conscription act, right?" Immanuel said.

"Yeah, I know, I just hope they can make it clear to the officers on the panel."

"Well, they got lawyers and all, right?" Immanuel asked.

"Not exactly."

"And that means, what?"

"They're representing themselves," Uzziah admitted.

"I hate to remind ya, brother, but if we had done the same in Chicago, we might have hung like those negroes we saw on the island," Immanuel reminded his partner.

"Yeah, yeah, but nobody believes that anything will happen. Remember that guy who went away just to get whiskey, and when he came back, he kept lying about everything?" Uzziah asked.

"Yeah, ya mean Casler, so?"

"Nothin' happened to him, right?"

"There's only one problem with that kinda thinkin'," Immanuel said, pointing across the area where the regiment was camped. Uzziah followed his finger, and he was pointing at General Jackson's tent.

"That man has a lot of God in him," Uzziah said in his defiance.

"Need I remind ya of Sodom and Gomorrah?"

Immanuel said, pouring himself some coffee and wondering when he would have the opportunity to tell Uzziah his news.

"It'll be all right, I just know it. Jackson's got a big heart. At the most, they'll be bucked and gagged, or humiliated in some other way," Uzziah reasoned.

"Yeah, but Jackson's heart filled up pretty much with God, duty, and the Confederacy. And, if ya think 'bout it, there's no more humiliating a sentence as death, ya never get over that one."

It was the next day that the sentence was passed by the court-martial's board. All were found guilty of desertion and dereliction of duty on all counts. They were all sentenced to death by musketry—in other words, a firing squad. The men who had been brought back by Uzziah and the Injun weren't that worried, there had been other trials and other sentences, then leniency. Being away without permission just wasn't that big a deal, it wasn't. And yet, as the afternoon went on, the men got worried.

Usually, Jackson would have come forth to give his sentence of reprieve and have other punishments dealt out to them, but little did they know that inside his own command tent, Jackson was signing the death warrants on all four men. General Lee, himself, had granted Jackson permission to carry out such executions if he found them to be expedient in stopping the mass of desertions that were afflicting the Confederacy. All this had been decided on the 18th of August, but in the early morning hours of the 19th, all four men were informed that they would be put to death by firing squad. They were dismissed from the sentencing, and as the guards took them back, an argument ensued.

"Roadcap ain't no deserter, I tell ya," one of the guards from Company G argued. The other guards knew that James Roadcap was the only man accused of desertion who had not been conscripted, but enlisted when the war began. In the darkness of that early morning, Roadcap simply disappeared, and then there were only three men—Layman, Rogers, and Riddel, Jr.—who awaited the firing squad. There was a hubbub about the prisoner disappearing like that, but in the end, nothing was done about it. So much for military justice.

The reaction of the officers with Jackson's command were varied. Lieutenant Colonel Samuel L. Walker of the 10th Virginia, who was the commanding officer of John Layman and John Rogers, rushed to Jackson's command headquarters just hours before the execution. He met resistance when he tried to enter Jackson's tent.

Immanuel, Uzziah, and Abooksigun all witnessed this attempt at clemency by Colonel Walker.

"Sorry," said Staff Officer French, "the general does not want to be bothered with unimportant matters."

"Unimportant matters!" Colonel Walker protested, "My business involves life or death!"

The tent flaps had been rolled up because of the heat, and General Jackson was seen sitting there, doing nothing, it seemed.

He was then allowed into the tent. Jackson was not pleased to see anyone at this hour. He had been struggling for days with these matters, and his soul was troubled greatly.

"What is it?" he growled at Colonel Walker.

"I find it hard to believe that a fellow Christian would allow these proceedings to go on," Colonel Walker said with bated breath.

"And what proceedings would you be referring to?" Jackson asked.

"Why, the execution by musketry of the four men involved in these most recent trials of desertion," Walker pleaded.

"You'll be happy to know that there will be only three executions," Jackson told the colonel.

"You granted clemency, then, good. Can't you extend that same clemency to the other three?" Walker begged.

"Well, one of the four escaped, which only proves that we were on the right track all along," Jackson said.

"General, please, reconsider this most egregious mistake of judgment!" Walker said.

"Sir!" Jackson said as he stood from behind his desk and walked around toward Walker, "Men who desert their comrades in war deserve to be shot—and officers who intercede for them deserve to be hanged!"

Walker was staggered by this response and made an attempt to leave the command tent of Jackson's.

"What is your name, sir?"

"Lieutenant Colonel Samuel L. Walker of the 10th Virginia, sir," he said proudly.

"Mr. Walker," Jackson said, purposively leaving out his rank, "I advise you to resign!"

Colonel Walker saluted General Jackson, who refused to return the salute. Walker was waiting on the return salute, still holding the salute to his head. Finally, in somewhat of a disgrace, he turned and walked from the tent.

———

For the rest of the afternoon, as those who were in command of the executions made their preparations, the sides of the general's tent were raised even higher.

"He's just sittin' there," Immanuel said to Uzziah.

Uzziah looked up, and yes, General Jackson was sitting behind his desk.

"He's doin' a lot more than sittin'," Uzziah said in the general's defense.

"What, exactly?" Immanuel asked.

"Weighing the souls of the men involved in all this," Uzziah said.

"Hey, hey, here come a brave, approachin' the lion's den," Abooksigun said.

"That's the chaplain from the 10th Virginia," Uzziah said.

"How do ya know?"

"I know all the sky pilots," Uzziah said, and Immanuel just glared at him.

"Well, maybe a sky pilot is just what Jackson needs to hear from," Immanuel commented.

Most of what was being said between Jackson and the chaplain from the 10th Virginia was unintelligible until the end of the conversation.

"If those men are shot, they will certainly go to hell!" the chaplain said forcibly.

Jackson got up from behind his desk and, moving to the chaplain, he forcibly turned the man around by grabbing him by the shoulders, and then pushed him out of the command tent.

"This is my business!" Jackson yelled, then added, "The executions must proceed!"

Uzziah, Immanuel, and Abooksigun all looked at each other.

"Chief has spoken," Abooksigun said, and the two mountain men knew that their Algonquin friend was right. The executions would take place.

When the chaplain returned to where the prisoners were kept, he shook his head, and the effect this had on the three men was like a thousand-pound weight had landed on them. It looked to those who watched the prisoners that afternoon that their visages had changed, as if they had suffered months and months of a debilitating sickness.

Gradually, with the help of the chaplain, the three men reached a place of consignment. They knew it was going to happen, and that all hope of Jackson commuting their sentences was now removed. They cried with the chaplain, talked of their children, and never seeing them again. Some peace was brought into their world by the reading of scripture and the chaplain's prayers. But one officer noted that he could not look upon the three men without tears running involuntarily from his eyes.

Finally, in the afternoon, under a brutal sun, Taliaferro's division was formed into columns and marched through the woods until they reached a broad field near

Mount Pisgah Church. The various brigades formed a three-sided square.

The provost marshal appeared next, followed by the regimental band. They played the Dead March. Muffled drums were beaten out in a steady cadence, and a solemn atmosphere for death was sufficiently created.

Twelve men, carrying their loaded muskets—the firing squad—marched in, followed by the coffin bearers. These two groups followed directly behind the band.

At the very rear came the three prisoners and the chaplain who had argued so with General Jackson.

This entire procession marched in front of General Jackson and made the entirety of the three sides of the square before it came to a halt.

The drumming stopped. The three prisoners were placed in front of their coffins and told to kneel. As the crimes of these three were being read to the division, the chaplain from the 10th knelt with the three prisoners and prayed aloud.

Layman and Rogers were side by side. They had spent many Sunday afternoons at each other's homes, enjoying fried chicken and lemonade, but this Sunday gathering was entirely different. Both Layman and Rogers looked at each other and smiled as the chaplain's prayers ended and he got up and walked away.

The firing squad stepped to within six paces of the three men. They were composed of men from the companies in which all three had deserted. Half had balls and powder, and half only powder—they would never know for sure who killed the three.

There was a suffocating silence over the field, which was broken by a yell.

"Fire!" commanded Sergeant Charles Keller.

Volleys ripped through the three men. Two were killed instantly, but the third rose up. It was John Layman, he wasn't dead, but a second volley from all twelve muskets threw him back into the coffin that awaited him.

———

The soldiers marched away—they were not dismissed on the field—back through the woods they went to where they were camped.

Uzziah, Immanuel, and Abooksigun all stood off to the side watching the men march away, and then, they watched as other men placed the three bodies more or less correctly in the coffins. Holes had been dug, and they were carried off, ignobly, to their place of eternal rest. Uzziah wasn't sure how he felt about their souls. The chaplain from the 10th had yelled at Jackson that if they were killed like this, they would be in perdition and among the devil's angels, which seemed awfully harsh to Uzziah.

"Where do ya think those men went?" Uzziah asked the other two as they walked back to their camp.

Immanuel just looked at Uzziah and said nothing at first.

"Disgraced braves with no top knot, or having their eyes and ears broken, do not get to the hunting grounds," Abooksigun said.

"I do not know the answer about these men," Immanuel said, "but ask me the same question 'bout the one whose orders were followed, and I will answer with certainty."

Uzziah knew then how Immanuel felt about Jackson's part in all that occurred.

"Ya know his brother, Preston, was there," Immanuel said.

"Whose brother?" Uzziah asked.

"John Layman's."

"How do ya know that?"

"One of the guards pointed him out to me," Immanuel said.

"Where was he on the field?" Uzziah asked.

"Back in the ranks, but everyone faced the place of death."

"How terrible," Uzziah said to no one in particular.

"Mostly for Jackson, I would think," Immanuel said.

"Ya can't mean that."

"Think on it, partner, say that me, or Abooksigun was gunned down like that, what would ya be thinkin'?"

"But this is the Confederate army," Uzziah objected.

"And, young son, all sorts of shenanigans are taking place which ya have no knowledge of."

"And ya do?"

"I do."

"Name one, other than what we just witnessed," Uzziah demanded.

"Not till I get ya alone, back at the camp," Immanuel whispered to Uzziah.

"Don't worry 'bout me," Abooksigun said offhandedly.

"We don't, it's just a family matter," Immanuel explained.

"Not like I don't know the family," Abooksigun said, as they reached their tents and the fire, which had almost gone out.

"You care if he hears, or not?" Immanuel asked Uzziah, tapping him on the elbow as they sat by the fire and Uzziah threw more logs on it.

"He can hear, sure," Uzziah said.

"Fine. Thought I'd be discreet fer once, ya know? Not scream this thing from the highest mountain and all."

"*The time is coming when everything that is covered up will be revealed, and all that is secret will be made known to all. Whatever you have said in the dark will be heard in the light, and what you have whispered behind closed doors will be shouted from the housetops, for all to hear!*" Uzziah quoted from Luke, the twelfth chapter.

"Sometimes, partner yer sanctimonious ass is a pain in my ass, I ought to shout this shite right chere in camp, but in deference to our long relationship, I won't."

"Just spit it out!" Uzziah said, tired of Immanuel's rantings.

"Yer sister Hanna's fighting as a man for General Stuart's Cavalry and she's using the name John O'Bannon!"

"What!? Ya've got to be kiddin' me!" Uzziah protested.

"And ifn that don't take the cake, she's with child!" Immanuel said, then picked up the coffee pot and poured some into a tin cup.

Uzziah sat there mildly smiling as if this was a joke

being perpetrated by his older partner. Abooksigun got up and walked away. He was the smart one.

"Yer jokin', right?" Uzziah finally said, looking at his partner sip lukewarm coffee.

"I wish I was, partner, I wish I was."

"And how, pray tell, do you know these things?"

"Well, I left yer arse, again, as ya may remember, and thinkin' about how I was gonna go back, and decided that goin' west was not as safe as goin' south, then west."

"And?"

"And I got sort of caught up with this sentry from Stuart's command and—it's a long story—anyways, I got taken back to Stuart's tent when this sergeant walked up, and all of a sudden he says he has a tentmate who knows me." Immanuel stopped and, realizing how difficult this was to explain, he took more of the lukewarm coffee, which he felt like spitting out, but he was delaying the story.

"Who was that?" Uzziah asked.

"Yer dead brother, John," Immanuel said.

"And since we both know that John is moldin' in the ground, who the hell was standin' in fer him?"

"Yer very much alive sister, Hanna," Immanuel said, and moved the coffee pot over to where it would actually get hot.

Uzziah sat back and reached for the coffee pot.

"Don't, it needs some heat," Immanuel said.

"Yer either lying to me, or just tryin' to upset me, and I'm not sure which," Uzziah said.

"Trust me, the coffee's lukewarm, at best."

"Not 'bout the coffee, 'bout all this shite with Hanna, and did ya say she was also in a family way!?!"

Uzziah said, standing up and pacing back and forth in front of the fire.

"Yeah, she is."

"And how did you find that out? I mean, how does that come out in casual conversation?"

"When I confronted her 'bout not being her dead brother, John, the conversation got anything but casual!" Immanuel said, and hearing the coffee start to jump in the pot, grabbed the handle, burned himself, cursed, then, taking a glove, poured himself what looked like scalding coffee. It sure smelled scalded.

"We have to go get her," Uzziah said.

"After what ya just witnessed, ya wanna go traipsing off to get Hanna?!?"

"Yeah, there is that, ain't there," Uzziah said, his mind going a million miles an hour.

"Look," Immanuel started in, "ifn it's any consolation at all, she's in love with this Sergeant Stark Simmons."

"And he knows that he's a she and that she's with child?" Uzziah asked.

"Not exactly."

"What's that supposed to mean?"

"It means, she done tricked him—"

"Tricked him!"

"Now, just let me finish, okay? I don't know how she done it, or why, but obviously, ifn she's in a family way, then they did the deed, right?"

"And he don't know?" Uzziah said in disbelief.

"She mentioned somethin' 'bout a head wound," Immanuel said, not enjoying the scalded coffee, but drinking it anyway, sorta went with the conversation.

"A head wound?"

"Must've been how she tricked him and his johnson—"

"Stop! I don't wanna think of Hanna like that," Uzziah said, pouring himself some bitter coffee, and making a face when he took a drink.

"So, mastermind, what's we gonna do now?" Immanuel asked.

"I'll talk to Jackson, tell him there's a family emergency, and it will take the two of us to bring it around to right," Uzziah said.

"Thank the spirits, yer leavin' me outta this," Abooksigun said, as he walked in, emptied the scalded coffee, and started making a new pot.

"Yeah, well, he'll need a good scout, and ifn I tell him yer stayin' then we can straighten out the situation," Uzziah said.

"There is charm among the twisting path in the hills, but no one dares follow the trail of a young girl in love," Abooksigun said.

4

First, Uzziah met with Jackson, who was in a foul mood. He and Jackson prayed together, and that seemed to ameliorate Jackson's mood somewhat. When Uzziah presented the problem he and Immanuel had to take care of, Jackson sat with his mouth wide open, not sure that anyone could lie this well. Jackson figured no one would make up such a disgraceful story about their own family, unless it were true. He granted them a leave of absence, just so they left the Algonquin Indian to scout. Uzziah had figured on that. Jackson even gave the two scouts passes, so that no one would be able to question, as if they were away without some sort of honorable leave-taking.

Next, they visited his pa, Sean, and his five brothers. They were happy to see both mountain men, but overjoyed to see Uzziah. It had been a while since they had visited.

"What ya think of that awful thing we had to witness?" Sean asked the other brothers sitting around a common fire and listening.

"Pa, never in my wildest dream, did I imagine that it would come to that," Uzziah said, and he sort of summed up every one of the O'Bannon men's feelings.

There were *uh-huhs*, and *oh yeahs*, and a few *Amens*, which went around the campfire.

And reminded Uzziah of church meetings they had been to, when something notable was said.

"Pa, me and Immanuel got a special mission we're gonna be on for General Jackson," Uzziah said.

Immanuel looked up, surprised that the man's oldest son was outright lying about what they were up to, but considering the fragileness of the issues involved and the fact that three men had just been gunned down for desertion, Immanuel figured Uzziah knew what he was doing.

"Is it dangerous?" Sean asked. A silly question in times of war, but a father can be excused for being silly when it comes to the health and welfare of his oldest son.

"No more dangerous than sitting around here," Uzziah said, then added, "Anything we do within the confines of this conflagration could be the end of us, but neither Immanuel nor I expect to be in any real danger."

"Will ya have a chance to see our ma?" the black Irish Raymond asked.

"We might, ya got any letters or anything ya want me to tell her?"

The boys scattered and came back with a few more letters than Uzziah imagined that they were able to write.

"Somebody's been busy," Immanuel said, taking the

letters and putting them into his saddlebags, which hung from Stygian's rump.

"Well, the mail service is awful," Obadiah commented.

"Hell, before all this with the deserters, Obie, was thinking of taking the mail to ma, hisself," Hank commented.

"Well, don't do nothin' stupid," Uzziah said to Obadiah.

"That's gonna be hard for the cave dweller," Zachariah said, and he and Obadiah got into a wrestling match, and the boys took up encouraging one or the other of them, then Obadiah got his older brother, Zach, in a head hold, and that ended it.

"Don't be callin' me names," Obie said, and that comment showered Obadiah with more names than he could react to.

They all ended up laughing and jostling each other around, and Obie blushed like he did in the old days, before he'd taken to prayer and Jackson.

"I think the general done right by us all," Obadiah said, and the other brothers just looked around, knowing that Obie had a religious thing for the general. He had never failed to kneel beside Fancy, the general's horse, when the battle was raging.

As the night lingered on, and the brothers of Uzziah went off to their bunks, there came a moment in which the eldest son wanted to tell his pa what he was up to. But good sense dictated that he not do so.

"Is there anything else on yer mind, boy?" his pa asked as he rubbed Uzziah's head the way he used to do when he was but a pup.

Uzziah leaned into the rub and yearned to unburden himself, but one look from Immanuel sold secrecy to his heart.

"No, Pa, it's just these uncertain times, and not knowing, ya know, who's goin' to catch a Minie ball, or who'll get blowed up, ya know?"

"I do, son, and believe me when I tell ya, it's on my mind constantly. That's why I'm glad I'm chere. I tell the boys to pray often as they can and take the most care that anyone can in battle, but the odds, I'm afraid, are stacked agin us."

"We'll be leaving too early to say our goodbyes," Immanuel said as he stood and shook Sean's hand. "Ya take care, sir, ya hear," Immanuel said, and Sean nodded and was unable to speak.

Uzziah got up, and the eldest son and the father hugged, and as it lingered on, Immanuel wished he had that kind of relationship with his pa.

The next morning, as promised, they were up and away before reveille. Even though they had ridden for more than forty minutes, the winds must have been just right because they could hear the bugler faintly.

"What exactly did ya tell old blue lights?" Immanuel asked, using one of Jackson's many nicknames.

"Pretty much the truth."

"What?!?"

"Nothin' sells like the truth, ya know/"

"About her being with child and all, that, too!?"

"Well, let's just say that ya don't know that fer sure, okay?"

"But she told me!" Immanuel insisted.

"Yeah, I know, but ya didn't grow up with Hanna, she has a way about her of stretching the truth, no matter how insignificant it is," Uzziah tried explaining.

"Ya don't believe it, do ya!?!"

"Well–"

"Either ya do, or ya don't!" Immanuel insisted.

"When a young woman speaks about such things, her language may be confused and muddled," Uzziah started to explain.

"Yer amazing!"

"Well, thank ya," Uzziah said, smiling.

"It weren't no compliment. I tells ya what I done heard, ya take it in, then turnin' it 'round in yer head somehow ya come out on the other side, with a completely different story!"

"Hanna had a beau early on. She weren't more than twelve, but she sure looked older. She developed..." Uzziah was moving his hands around his chest area.

"Yeah, yeah, I get it," Immanuel said, worried that Uzziah would start blushing talking about his sister's tatas.

"So, this chere fella was visitin' from Richmond, and the family had money, and he done asked her to this fancy dance and she'd said *yes* without even consulting Ma and Pa–"

"Previews of what was to come, no doubt."

"Yeah, maybe," Uzziah said as he kicked Shadow up from a walk into a dog trot. "Anyways, she said, she was goin' to a friend's farmhouse, and a bunch of girls would be there and they'd be spending the night."

"And she stayed out all night with this bounder from Richmond!?!" Immanuel asked.

"Well, she done forgot her pajamas, guess she wasn't plannin' on wearin' any, and Ma and Pa drove all the way to that girl's farm. The family was embarrassed, there weren't no slumber party, no buncha girls gathered all around, just the girl who lived there, and when she got pressed by her own pa, she fessed up and told."

"So, what happened?" Immanuel was into this story of deception that Hanna had woven when she was a mere child.

"Ma and Pa rode to the big house, and they—well, they, I guess ya'd say they crashed the party in their farm clothes. Hanna saw them, well, she heard 'bout them first, some older couple had arrived without being properly dressed up, and she thought it was real funny, till those around her were pointing to her ma and pa!"

"Good Lord!"

"To say the least, so she could see what a mess she'd made and wanted above all to spare herself this embarrassment which seemed about to overwhelm them, so she screamed bloody murder!

"Then, started goin' on and on, how she had been abducted by this young man from Richmond, and thank God her parents had come to save her! She rushed into their arms, and as they privately scolded her, she fainted, or pretended to, and did not wake up till they got her back to our farm."

"And the consequences of all this?" Immanuel asked.

"Ma and Pa laughed about it, and neither of them were willing to admit that she'd faked the fainting," Uzziah said, shaking his head.

"Well, there it is," Immanuel said, like he'd ridden up on something that they had been looking for.

"There what is?"

"The reason she's the way she is."

"Immanuel, sometimes, ya make no sense atall!"

"Ifn, they had tanned her fanny when she lied like she did, then this impersonation of yer dead brother would never have happened," Immanuel said, satisfied that he had come up with the explanation of everything about Hanna.

"Apples and oranges." Uzziah spoke the words softly.

"What!?"

"They are not the same thing, right? Apples are apples, and oranges are oranges," Uzziah elucidated.

"Orange is a color as I remember it," Immanuel said.

"Ya know it's a fruit and oranges and apples are vastly different."

"So, yer tellin' me that the lie which Hanna perpetrated at that party, then pretending to faint, so she could be removed from an embarrassing situation, is not similar atall to what she has done now?"

"Not the same, as ya told me she wanted to avenge her brother, John, and in some ways, what she's done is noble," Uzziah said, his nose higher in the air.

"Noble or not, lying is lying!" Immanuel nearly shouted.

"Do ya want to bring every vagabond on the road toward us?" Uzziah asked as he looked around.

"Yeah, like we're worried about that," Immanuel said as he raised his Hawken from off his lap.

Just then, from back in the woods, off on what

seemed a side road, a female voice could be heard, "Help, help, help me!"

Both Uzziah and Immanuel took off down the sideroad, and not two hundred yards off the road lay a woman, rather nicely dressed, and her hands and feet were tied, a kerchief had fallen down from her mouth and was still knotted.

Immanuel was the first one off his horse, as Uzziah's head was on a swivel. There had been reports of a rise in crime in Richmond, and the thieves, this time, the story went, were white females.

"Oh, thank goodness, you are here!" the woman said in exaggerated tones. Once her hands were free, one of them went to her forehead as she leaned back against Immanuel's arm.

"What happened to you?" Immanuel asked.

"My name is Susan Smith, and I was walking in Richmond, that's the last I remember," she said, looking around, totally disoriented.

"But this is miles outside the city," Uzziah reminded her.

"Yes, yes, of course, wait, I do remember, this nice gentleman offered me a ride. It was cold last evening, and he also offered me a drink," she said, blushing. "I know I shouldn't have taken either, but the times have been so hard on everyone."

"You just rest up, while my partner and I decide what to do," Immanuel said as he brought the rather well-dressed lady to her feet.

"Immanuel," Uzziah said, and he came over to where Uzziah had not dismounted from Shadow.

"Yeah, partner?"

"This woman just being out here, it seems all too

convenient," Uzziah whispered as he kept one eye on the woman, who seemed to be fixing her hair.

"What ya mean, she's a lady, and she's in distress." Immanuel begged to differ.

"She might be...lying," Uzziah suggested.

Immanuel took another look at her. She was pretty as well as dressed for the city.

"Really? She don't look like a liar," Immanuel whispered.

"If she were ugly, would she look more like one?" Uzziah suggested.

"We're not that far from where General Stuart has his men encamped. We'll take her there and figure out what to do with her then. That all right with ya, or do ya wanna leave her out chere to fend fer herself?" Immanuel said, and before Uzziah could answer, Immanuel had helped the lady into the saddle on Stygian and had mounted up behind her, riding the horse's rump.

It took them the rest of the day to get to where General Stuart and the 1st Virginian Cavalry had encamped, but all that was left of the camp were smoldering fires and the detritus of war. As they rode around, they noticed an old Negro going through some of the trash that the 1st had left behind. They rode over to where he was scrounging.

"I didn't mean nothin', I didn't," the old man said, as he pocketed something and held his arms up to defend himself.

"We don't mean ya no harm, uncle, just got a question fer ya," Uzziah said, as the old man looked between the two mountain men and the woman riding with one of them.

"Found yerself a woman, did ya? Scrounging must be better in yer neighborhood, yes sir, must be!" the old man said, then added, "What ya wanna know?"

"How long have these men been gone?" Immanuel asked.

"Oh, jeez, they done pulled out maybe two days ago," he said.

"Two days!" Uzziah said, exasperated.

"Which way they go?" Immanuel asked the old Negro.

"Don't know, just got chere myself," he said.

"We can scout around and find out which way," Uzziah said.

The sun was sinking fast in the west, and the chill in the air wasn't getting much better.

"I'd sure like to get warm," Susan said.

"She's cold, Uzziah. Let's take one of these camp spots and rebuild the fire. We can start out in the morning," Immanuel said as he pushed himself off the back of Stygian. Susan Smith, seeing that she was mounted on this fine animal all by herself, kicked him up and was riding away from Stuart's old camp.

Immanuel whistled, and the horse turned and came back.

"That was a neat trick," Susan said.

"Yeah, train all my horses like that, saves me havin' to fetch 'em when I want 'em," Immanuel said, as he reached up and took her off the horse.

The whole time, Uzziah was watching this and having thoughts of his own.

Immanuel started placing logs and twigs on a smoldering fire, and in no time at all, there was a nice blaze going. He found an empty ammunition box and set it up for her to sit on, and Uzziah, being Uzziah, began cooking something for their supper.

"I need to use the facilities," she said as she got up and walked toward the bushes.

They both watched her walk off.

"She was stealing yer horse, fool," Uzziah said.

"Was not, he got the wrong signal when I got off the back, and took off with her," Immanuel said.

"Then, why was she clicking him up, and driving her heels into his side afore ya whistled?"

"Was she doin' that?" Immanuel asked.

"Ya know she was. Now, fer me, this is a case in point. Yer believing this woman ya don't know, but thinkin' Hanna—my sister, and a woman ya do know—might be lyin'. That don't make sense."

"Shh, here she comes," Immanuel said, nodding toward the bushes from which she was walking.

They had a meal of bacon, beans, and Uzziah's cornbread, which Susan swore was the best cornbread she had ever had. He was not warming up to her. To his way of thinking, she was a thief, a desperate woman, who either wandered out on the road by herself or was brought out there to lure unsuspecting men into compromising situations. As far as Uzziah was concerned, and he kept feeling this, there was someone watching them. For his money, it was the man, or men, that she was in cahoots with, and come bedding down time, and maybe before, they were going to come down on the two partners like flies on shite!

It was Immanuel's blind spot—women. They sensed it about him, and whenever they were around the two of them, they always, no matter if it were a saloon girl or some really nice lady, like his own ma, they always drifted in his direction. He did not hold them accountable, nor did he suspect anything might be up, except what was going on.

Uzziah had to wonder how a man like that could listen to his sister, Hanna, tell her story and not be sympathetic. Perhaps it was the fact that she was with child that put Immanuel off the scent. Uzziah couldn't figure it out, and this woman showing up as she had wasn't going to do anything but slow them down, and it was imperative that Hanna be found and brought back home, especially if she were in a family way.

She did offer to clean the dishes after the meal, tin plates and cups, and a few forks, and she did a fine job down by the creek.

When it came to bedding down, she borrowed some of Immanuel's blankets, he had a nice buffalo robe that she could wrap up in, and she bedded down a respectable distance from both men.

Uzziah barely got any sleep because every noise he heard, he thought that they were being set upon by her unsavory friends. Two mountain men making it through all those years of being in the snow, cold, and grizzly bears everywhere, just to have their throats cut by some two-bit bandits in the middle of the night.

The morning came, and Uzziah was bleary from having no sleep, well, a wink here and there, and the two of them, Immanuel and Susan, seemed to have slept like babies, and she hadn't even tried to crawl into Immanuel's bedroll. Well, that didn't prove anything. Maybe she was playing a long game on both men? Uzziah would have to wait and see.

Immanuel left and was gone for a bit, leaving Susan and Uzziah alone there after breakfast.

"You don't like me, do ya?" she asked.

"I don't know ya," Uzziah admitted.

"Still, ya don't like me."

"Jury's out on that one."

"Ya got any idea how bad it is in Richmond?"

"Haven't been to the capital in years."

"Ya wouldn't recognize it. All these women without men, and half of 'em depended on those men for their livelihood," she said, wringing her hands.

"How'd ya get out to that side road, all tied up like that?" Uzziah asked her.

"I believe I told that story, sir," she said, giving him the stink eye.

"Yeah, and quite a story it were."

"What's that supposed to mean?" she asked, standing up and acting insulted.

"Did he do anything to ya, afore he tied ya up?" Uzziah asked, not being very gentile about it.

"I was drugged, how would I know?" Her voice was getting strident, and her posture more aggressive with every word.

Uzziah was, without trying to make it obvious, scanning the nearby woods. This opportunity of her accomplice could not be ignored. There was only one man with her now. He had all the food supplies, a good damn horse, a rifle, and other weapons. This would be a cache well worth taking.

"Ya insult a woman, then ya won't even look at her! What kinda man are ya?!?" Susan was yelling now, trying, it seemed, to pull his attention away from where he was looking, those damned woods. He was about to go back to her when, from the corner of his eye, he saw something coming from the woods.

It was three men, and they were riding horses. They looked like mounted city trash, and all three were armed. *Well, I'll be damned*, Uzziah thought, *this was a hell of a time for Immanuel to leave.*

Uzziah figured this was as good as any Injun attack, and he was going to treat it the same way. His attention had been drawn to the three, screaming maniacs firing their weapons and coming fast, but instead of concentrating on them, he turned toward the woman!

She had pulled a derringer from her reticule and was in the process of pointing it at him. She fired, and he fired at the same time. It was a 54-caliber round shot versus a 41-caliber, and when the ball from the derringer went into his chest, he saw the shock and awe of the Hawken blow the woman back into the fire. She was dead, he hoped, because now she was starting to burn.

Uzziah fell down, which kept him from being clipped by rounds being fired from the three riders, who were screaming like Injuns and coming closer with every stride of their horses.

Uzziah cross drew his Walker Colt from its holster and fired it three times at one of the riders, the closest, and he went backward off his horse. The next rider came in, expecting to finish off Uzziah, and was rewarded with a tomahawk which tumbled end over end till it implanted itself deeply into his face. He never saw it coming. The third and furthest rider grimaced when he saw his second partner cleaved with the tomahawk, his bloodied head as good as divided against itself, and reining around, headed back for the woods.

Uzziah stood, gritting his teeth with the 41-caliber in his chest, and taking careful, raised aim, fired off the last two shots in the Walker Colt. It seemed both missed as the rider made it to the edge of the woods, then slid off his horse.

Uzziah made sure the two men were dead. They were. Susan was cooking nicely in the fire, her dress flaring up when the flames reached that low. He should have kicked her out of the fire, but let her burn, damn sow!

Mounting up, he rode toward the man who was now crawling toward the woods. Dismounting, he took his bowie knife, and pulling on the man's long hair, scalped him, then cut his throat, breaking his wind off mid-scream.

Immanuel must have heard the shots, he came riding up with another horse in tow, and seeing the woman burning, and all the other carnage, followed the scream to the edge of the woods, where Uzziah had collapsed beside the exsanguinated body of the third male thief.

———

"I ain't seen nothin' like this, ever! That there white man must be part Injun the ways he treated those bastards. The woman acookin' and the three mens thinkin' they's got the upper hand, but no! Mr. Injun there, he just kilt two, then getting up with the bullet in him yet, he raised up that Colt and brought down the other man. Ain't nobodies gonna made a hundred-yard shot like that with no handgun, no sir! I swear, I ain't never gonna see nothin' agin like that if I lives to a hundred! Four to one, shot in the breast, and he still come out on top! Lord, have mercy!"

Uzziah had opened his eyes and listened as the old Negro was telling Immanuel the blow-by-blow in the fight he had with the four bandits.

Immanuel served up the Negro his dinner, and then saw Uzziah watching.

"Don't worry, young son, we got plenty fer ya!"

"Mr. Uzziah, I am Adam, named after the first man, and you's be the fiercest fighter this nigger ever saw, yes sir!" Adam said, taking a big spoonful of what looked like rabbit stew.

Immanuel came over with a bowl for Uzziah.

"You doin' all right?"

"Is the slug still in me?" he asked.

"No, I dug it out while you drank the majority of the whiskey."

"Good, didn't want to die from that cow's bullet," Uzziah said.

"He's right," Adam said. "The womens from Richmond soon as cut yer throat as look at ya."

"Well, she got well done afore I picked her off the fire," Immanuel said, smiling to himself. "Smelt like good barbecue, tell the truth," he added.

That got Adam laughing, so he choked, and Immanuel had to pound his back as a piece of rabbit flew into the fire from the old Negro's mouth.

"Thank ye, laughin' and eatin' don't goes together," he said as he continued to eat and chuckle.

"Adam thinks he knows where Stuart's goin', so I figured we got an extra horse, he ain't got nothin', so he's ridin' with us," Immanuel said in explanation.

"Ifn that's all righteous with ya, Mr. Uzziah, don't wanna make ya mad, no sir!"

"It's fine with me, I grew up in the Shenandoah, so yer as welcome as can be," Uzziah said as he ate the rabbit stew.

"Thank ye," Adam said.

"We're gonna rest a few more days, had to dig pretty close to yer heart. That wound needs to heal more afore ya go ridin' into the sunset," Immanuel said.

"Can I sleeps here tonight?" Adam asked.

"Sure," Immanuel said.

Adam finished his bowl of stew and got up.

"Gots me some hidden things in the woods," he said as he walked off.

As they watched him walk off, Uzziah got up on one elbow to finish the stew.

"Ya sure it's a good idea, takin' the old man along?"

"He probably ain't got no place else to be. Hell, Yankees done burned down the plantation he worked on, besides, we've had stragglers afore," Immanuel said, helping himself to another bowl.

Uzziah held out his empty bowl, and Immanuel filled that, too.

"Leavin' a smidgen for the old man, too," Immanuel said. As he looked up, he saw the old Negro reenacting the scalping of the White man at the edge of the woods. He was grinning like a fool when he went through the motions.

"Uzziah," he said, pointing to where the old Negro was acting out the third bandit's death, "think ya got yerself a hero worshipper."

5

Immanuel thought a five-day rest would be enough for Uzziah's wound near his heart. Adam agreed. Evidently, the old Negro had helped treat many a gunshot wound for those who had tried to escape from the plantation they worked on but couldn't run faster than a bullet.

By the time they were ready to go, Adam suggested they go back by the plantation and see if there were some supplies, since they had fed three for five days, and they were short.

They rode east toward the coast, and Adam knew his directions like Abooksigun knew his. They arrived at the plantation where he and his family had worked for three generations, and Adam was mighty glad to be home.

There was a light burning in the south wing of the mansion, which had mostly been burned down, and Adam ran into the portion of the mansion that had survived. He wasn't gone but ten minutes when he came back smiling.

"Mr. Yates, hisself, is hold up in that ramshackle place, and he wants ya both fer dinner tonight," Adam said.

"I don't think I'd taste too good, but Uzziah's younger, he may be an agreeable meal," Immanuel said, and left Adam scratching his head before he started in laughing.

"Ya some of the funniest Whites, I ever knowed, where ya from, Immanuel, not the valley?"

"No, raised by Injuns way out west," Immanuel said.

"They must be a happy people. Now, come on, I'll walks ya in," Adam said.

They entered through the main door, and immediately, they could see the burned-out north wing. They walked down a hallway and to a library, where Adam opened the door, and Mr. Yates, who was no younger than Adam, had fixed a few steaks, and some potatoes were burning in the fire.

"Massa Yates, this be Immanuel and Uzziah, my friends," Adam said as Yates stood, and putting his hands to his back, extended one of them to shake.

"My congratulations on killing the riffraff! Adam told me all about it," Yates said in a deep Southern accent as he shook hands with both mountain men.

Immanuel shook his hand, then said, "I best pull them taters off the fire, sir, they's burnin'."

"Well, leave one in, that's the way I like them," Yates said, then added, "Check on the steaks, some of the slaves slaughtered a cow for me, and I'm anxious to taste the old girl."

"Ya like the steaks burned, too?" Immanuel asked.

"No, just knock the horns off is good for me," Yates said, then turned to Uzziah.

"You must be the Viking that slaughtered the town trash?" he said in great admiration.

"Well, sir, I do not like a pushy woman," Uzziah said, and Yates started laughing so hard that Adam had to pound him on the back to get him to stop.

"The old nigger said you were funny, and you're not a disappointment. Please pull up some chairs, and let's eat." Yates gestured with his aging white hand.

"There's only three steaks, sir," Immanuel said.

"Adam will be eating with the other slaves," Yates said as Adam left the library.

Adam smiled at the two mountain men, then left the library. The food looked good, and it had been a while since the boys, either one of them, had had steak.

The conversation between the three men dropped off significantly as they ate, as it usually did when men ate.

About halfway through his steak, Uzziah turned an odd color and looked between Yates and Immanuel.

"You all right, son?" Yates asked Uzziah.

"Don't know, feeling kinda odd," Uzziah said.

"Did you happen to save the slug you took from your partner?" Yates asked Immanuel.

"Save it fer what?"

"Did it look whole?"

"It was all tore up, must have ricocheted off a rib or somethin'," Immanuel said.

Uzziah had stopped eating, and his color wasn't good.

"Go get Adam and have him bring a pot of water in for us to boil," Yates said.

"What's goin' on?" Uzziah wanted to know, even though he'd lain back in his chair and his color was worsening. Immanuel had run from the library to get the slave.

"My full name is Bertram William Yates, M.D. I was a surgeon before the war. If I'm not mistaken, there is a part of the bullet fired by that pushy woman still in you. And even though it missed your heart, that fragment will kill you if I don't get it out!"

By the time Immanuel got back, Adam had a pot of water on the fireplace in the library, and the fire built back up nicely.

Immanuel was pacing around, worried. "What can I do?" he asked Yates.

"As I told your partner, I am a surgeon, and had practiced till the war came along. You can assist me if you're not bothered by the sight of blood."

"Just as long as it ain't my own, it don't bother me," Immanuel said as he looked at Uzziah, whose color was turning gray. Uzziah smiled at him, but the grin was wan and lacked conviction.

In the meantime, Dr. Yates had pulled his medical bag from a closet in the library.

"I'll get the whiskey ifn y'all tell me where it's at, suppose Uzziah will need plenty of that," Immanuel conjectured.

"Got something better, it's called chloroform, synthesized by Dr. Samuel Guthrie from New York," Yates said as he held up an innocuous-looking bottle.

"When the water's boiled, I want you to wash your hands and put this on," Yates said as he threw a white operating gown to Immanuel, "And you might as well take off the deerskins, if you don't mind."

Immanuel began to strip, while Uzziah was taking everything in.

"So, that little bit of liquor gonna make me not feel ya cuttin' on me?" Uzziah asked.

"Oh, you're not going to drink this, that would kill you. No, no, we're going to put it on a rag and hold it over your nose and mouth."

"Immanuel, ya sure he's a doctor?" Uzziah asked.

"Or a madman, eh?" Immanuel said, and Yales chuckled.

"Always good to have a sense of humor when it comes to these things, but you'll see, it works like a charm," Yates prattled on as he donned the white surgical gown and looked over at Immanuel, who was dressed in the same manner.

"What do I need to do?" Uzziah asked weakly.

"Survive what I'm about to do to you," Yates said, taking his arm and sweeping everything off his desk. "Do you mind, lay up here for a little nap, okay?" Yates requested.

Immanuel helped his partner up on the desk, and no sooner had he lain back than Yates placed a rag soaked with the chloroform over Uzziah's face. He struggled for a bit, then went limp as he continued to breathe in the fumes.

"That works faster than any pop skull I ever saw," Immanuel said.

"Well, we don't want him to awaken while we're cutting him, do we?" he asked Immanuel with a certain gleam in his eye.

"You've done this afore, right?" Immanuel asked.

"Psshaw," Yates said, then added, "let's take off everything on his chest."

They stripped Uzziah down to his leggings and then, with iodine, he washed the area he was about to open up.

Dr. Yates looked at the incision which Immanuel had made, and looked up at the man, "What kind of knife did you use to do this?"

"A Bowie knife," Immanuel said.

"You have amazing control of things in your hands, don't you?"

"Guess," Immanuel said.

"I'm not going to reopen the same incision, but cut here instead," Yates offered, and no sooner had he said that than he drew what looked like a reddish line on Uzziah's chest, then went deeper with the scalpel.

"Use the gauze to staunch the bleeding, please," he asked Immanuel, who was on it, wiping away the blood so Yates could see what he was doing.

Just outside the half-burned mansion, the Union cavalry had a squad of men who had been to the campsite of General Stuart and found the burned body of the woman, who called herself Susan. They thought that the crimes against humanity which were perpetrated there were some of the worst they had seen, but they had no idea that just one man had done all that damage. When they found the scalped thief, they made up their minds to track these marauders and bring them to justice.

"Corporal," a private said, "there seems to be lights on in part of the house."

The corporal, still mounted, swiveled in his

McClellan saddle and saw the lights. It was his first rifle squad that he had been allowed to mount up and command, and he didn't want to mess things up.

"Yes, I see, but," he continued, looking down at the private who was the tracker, "are those the same tracks that surrounded the dead back at the camp?"

"They are, Corporal, they lead back behind what remains of the house, probably to a barn."

Back in the library, Yates had found the shrapnel that had broken off the bullet that almost killed Uzziah. He took it out and showed it to Immanuel.

"There's our culprit," Yates said.

The doctor had no sooner plopped the fragment into a metal bowl than Adam came into the library.

"Massa, those blue bellies are back," was all he said.

"I'll grab his feet, you take his torso, we'll move him into the wine cellar," the doctor said.

The wine cellar happened to be a secret room off the library. When Adam pushed on a section of books, a door opened, and they carried Uzziah in there.

They laid him on a table in that room.

"You'd better get those Union cavalry to leave here, if you can. I'll close up your friend," Dr. Yates said, and as Immanuel came from the wine cellar, Adam pushed the door closed, and essentially, the room disappeared.

The Union cavalry should have gone to the barn first, because that's where Immanuel was going, being shown the way back there through the kitchen. Instead, they bashed in the front door and stormed the library, which was where all the lights were blazing.

The corporal and the seven privates with him had seen the skullduggery which had been perpetrated on the three men and the burned woman back at Stuart's old campsite, and they weren't about to run afoul of whoever had done those things. They ran down the hall toward the library, and when they forced that door, too, they were confronted by an empty room with a nice fire going.

Immanuel mounted up on Stygian and thought about running the Union cavalrymen's horses off, but if he did that, then they would be stuck there with the doctor and Uzziah. Instead, he gathered up the reins of half the horses, and as he was riding off, fired his Walker Colt several times into the air.

By the time he made the woods, he let the horses go, and they immediately began cropping grass just off the road.

The corporal and the seven privates ran from the burned mansion and were faced with too few horses and too many men. Immanuel fired more shots, this time, at them, and got those with horses mounted, and galloping his way. He put Stygian into a run and knew for a fact that no one on earth would ever catch him.

What he imagined would happen, happened. When they came upon the rest of their mounts munching away on the roadside grass, someone gathered them up and brought them back. Soon, the entire squad was after Immanuel and Stygian.

Every ten minutes or so, Immanuel would stop to make sure they could still see him and were still in pursuit, then he'd kick up Stygian again and give them the slip.

———

It was in Verdiersville, Virginia, that Jeb Stuart and part of his 2000 cavalrymen were nearly captured by Union cavalry.

How those Union cavalry had snuck up on such a large body was not understood, neither at the time, nor later. But in his haste to retreat and avoid capture, Stuart's infamous plumed hat, his haversack, containing important Confederate maps and locations of Lee's troops, all those things were captured.

Stuart rode right for Lee's camp to warn him that his position might have been compromised by the Union's retrieval of those maps.

Lee sat in his command tent and was quietly reading his Bible when his adjutant flipped back the tent flap.

"General Lee, I am sorry to bother you, but General Stuart is here, and he's in rather a tizzy," the adjutant said.

"Please, show him in," Lee said, putting the Bible to one side and standing to greet his favorite cavalryman.

"General Lee!" Stuart said as he came to attention and saluted Lee.

"There is no need for that. You seem a bit distraught, what has happened?" Lee asked, gesturing to the seat across from him. Stuart sat down, and immediately Lee realized that he was not wearing his plumed hat.

"Have you resigned yourself to more traditional wear? I don't see the peacock," Lee said, smiling. It was a name that Lee used to refer to the plumed hat.

"That's why I'm here, General Lee, my hat has been captured!" Stuart said, not realizing how foolish that statement sounded.

"*Quel belles chapeaux*," Lee said in perfect French, and both men laughed.

"I'm sorry, of course, it's just a hat, but my haversack and maps inside were also absconded with."

"Then, you yourself, we're also in danger," Lee said with real concern. After all, the Confederate cavalry was the eyes and ears of the Confederate command.

"Perhaps, but we escaped. My fear now is that General Pope will know exactly where you are encamped," Stuart continued.

"Yes, yes, but now that I know that he knows, we shall move, and perhaps you can pay him a visit before he moves on me?"

"That's an excellent idea, General Lee. But is it too bold, after having just been saved from capture?"

"I do not think that anything that is properly conceived and carried out can be too bold, especially for such a man as yourself, do you?" Lee asked as he stood and walked to the map table that was on the other side of his command tent. "I do believe that Pope and a lot of Union supplies are here, don't you?" Lee asked as he pointed to a section along the Orange and Alexandria Railroad known as Catlett's Station.

"Yes, General, that is where we believe he is," Stuart said.

"Those supplies are needed by the Union armies, are they not?" Lee asked another rhetorical question.

"Of course, they are, General Lee."

"And what a pity if they should fall under the care and protection of someone who did not want them to resupply Union troops. What a disaster that would be," Lee said, smiling his mischievous smile.

"Oh, General Lee, are you suggesting what I think you're suggesting?"

"Maybe, and there's always the chance that amid those vast supplies and supply trains, Pope himself may be encamped thinking he is safe from intrusion, eh, General Stuart?"

On the outskirts of Lee's encampment, 2000 plus Confederate cavalry were still mounted, having just made their escape from their Union foes.

"What do ya think Stuart's gonna do?" Hanna asked. She was still posing successfully as John O'Bannon, and her episodes of sickness, which came on each morning, she carefully took care of when she did her latrine. Once in a while, during a hard ride or in battle, her stomach did anything but cooperate. But throwing up in the face of an oncoming Union cavalryman was a tactic that she found worked wonders.

She was still worried about what Immanuel James Jones would do with the information she unwittingly gave him when he showed up at Stuart's camp. She knew the mountain man had been partners with her brother for many years, and the chances of him not telling Uzziah were more than likely nil.

She did worry about the baby, but her loose-fitting clothes hid from wondering eyes any hint that he might be a *she* and that she might be in a family way.

Her love and concern for Sergeant Stark Simmons had done nothing but grow, and her admiration of his fighting skills and tactics left her at times breathless. She had learned so much from the man, and in their endeavors with General Stuart, they had—as the Injuns say—counted coup many times and delivered some to the other side of the veil.

"About what?" It was Stark and his usual manner, he did not answer a question right after it was asked but waited in his own good time to reply.

"About what just happened, his plumed hat stolen, his haversack taken!?"

"Well, that, my dear boy, is exactly why he's in General Lee's tent this very moment," Stark answered. And no sooner had he spoken than General Stuart emerged from the tent smiling.

"Well," Hanna said, "the corners of his eyes are smiling, and I think that portends well, don't you?"

"Indeed," the sergeant said, as commands were given to the officers who were passing them down to the noncoms, and soon, both he and John O'Bannon would be on their way to a new adventure.

They were told to muffle their horses' hooves. Cloth was handed around, and each cavalryman made soft cloth wrappings for the shoes of their horses. They had a way to go before these coverings would be used, and they made good time, until they got close to Catlett's Station. It was there that the command came down to muffle their horses' hooves. Captain W.W. Blackford rode up to where Stark and John O'Bannon were wrapping their horses' feet.

"You two come with me," he ordered from atop his mount.

Hanna's gut twisted as she realized that the only reason Blackford was going anywhere was to check on the Union supplies at Catlett's Station. So she and Stark would be with Blackford as he did his reconnaissance.

It took the greater part of an hour and a half for them to encircle the Union supplies there. There was no large body of troops present to protect anything. All they found were wagons stuffed with supplies. There was a small camp guard at the crossroads, but they rode by with their muted shoes.

When they rode back and Blackford reported to Stuart, the general seemed very pleased.

Stark and John O'Bannon rejoined their rifle unit, and the entire party began. The first to fall to the raid was the small camp guard at the crossroads. Those men were quickly captured and, under the circumstances, more than happy to surrender.

They were questioned for intelligence, and Stuart soon found out that: one, they either didn't know much, or two, they were lying!

"We're going to set our sights on General Pope's headquarters. It has to be within the perimeters of this encampment, now strike out, and find it!" Hanna heard General Stuart give the order.

An hour later, they had come no closer to finding Pope's headquarters than when they first arrived. It was a huge encampment, and it looked very much like Pope had hidden his needle of a headquarters within his haystack of an encampment.

It was then that Corporal O'Bannon spotted a Negro, a contraband of the Union as they were called. She rode over to where the man was sitting, sipping some coffee.

"Where's the boss's headquarters?"

He looked up, surprised anyone would ask him a question that he, indeed, knew the answer to.

"I'll show ya," he said, smiling, and led Stuart's men straight to it.

Once they found the headquarters, the bugler gave the call, and they attacked. There were three parties to the attack: one group attacked the headquarters, one group plundered the camp, and the final group, which contained Sergeant Simmons and his boy wonder, John O'Bannon, attacked the depot. There was firing and yelling all over Pope's camp as each group did its job.

Sergeant Simmons's group of mounted rifles met with little to no resistance at the depot. In fact, sooner than later, most Union blue bellies were glad to throw their rifles down and their hands up. Within the depot itself, there was a cache of monies in the coffers, and a great many mules and horses were taken from stock cars and along the sidings. They set the Union supply bridge on fire, but it had rained so much in the past few weeks that the fire was soon diminished to a smoldering mess, and nothing more.

Among the 300 prisoners, there were also 500 mules and horses, and then someone found the

Yankees' payroll safe—$500,000 in greenbacks and $20,000 in gold, which went to supply the Confederate war effort.

As they were leaving the depot area, a soldier discovered a lot of Union baggage, and within those bags was one with a tag on it which read: ***John Pope, Major General***.

The bag was delivered to Stuart, who found within it the best of General Pope's uniforms, including his best cloak and hat. Both of these made the rounds as various members of General Stuart's staff tried them on, to the hilarious laughter of those who stood by and watched.

Finally, Stuart sent the coat and hat to Governor John Letcher of Virginia, and they were displayed in the capital building as one of the Confederacy's great prizes of the war.

Before sending the coat off to the Governor of Virginia, Stuart took the opportunity to write General John Pope a short missive. It read:

General:

You have my hat and plume. I have your best coat. I have the honor to purpose a cartel for the fair exchange of the prisoners.

Very Respectfully,

J.E.B. Stuart

Maj. Genl. C.S.A.

6

It was false dawn when Immanuel made it back to the half-burned mansion, and the Union cavalry patrol was somewhere miles away still trying to track him. He had made sure of that by taking streams in both directions, then doubling back. When he rode back to the barn, Adam was out there sitting on a stump, enjoying his pipe.

"Give them blue bellies the slip, did ya?"

"Oh, yeah," Immanuel said as he dismounted, and Adam took the reins.

"How's my partner?"

"Why, it'd take more than a nick off a bullet to kill that Injun," Adam said, laughing.

Immanuel opened the door, and he guessed that Uzziah was so used to Adam's comings and goings that he didn't even look up from the book.

"What ya readin' there, partner?"

"Hey, Immanuel!" Uzziah said as he started to get up, but Immanuel put his hand on Uzziah's shoulder.

"Don't get up. Adam says you're doin' fine. How ya feel?"

"Gettin' better with every day. Why were ya gone so long? Started thinking those Yanks had a horse faster than Stygian."

"Are ya kiddin' me. No horse is as fast, unless it's Shadow," Immanuel sat down in the other overstuffed chair in front of the fire. He reached over and took the book from Uzziah, "*Tale of Two Cities*, by Charles Dickens. Never heard of it," Immanuel said, handing the book back to Uzziah.

"Listen to this," Uzziah said as he opened the book to its first page and read. "*It was the best of times, it was the worst of times, it was the age of wisdom, it was the age of foolishness, it was the epoch of belief, it was the epoch of incredulity, it was the season of Light, it was the season of Darkness, it was the spring of hope, it was the winter of despair, we had everything before us, we had nothing before us, we were all going direct to heaven, we were all going direct the other way—in short, the period was so far like the present period, that some of its noisiest authorities insisted on its being received, for good or for evil, in the superlative degree of comparison only.*"

"Wow, it sounds like today, doesn't it? I mean like this war and everything that goes along with it," Immanuel said.

No kiddin'," Uzziah agreed. "God, it's good to see you alive and well."

"Same goes fer me, but ya know that, already."

The door opened, and it wasn't Adam, but Dr. Yates.

"Gentlemen, Adam told me you'd come back, finally," Dr. Yates said.

Immanuel stood up and shook the doctor's hand.

"I wanna thank ye for doin' such an excellent job on my partner."

"Well, there's nothing like operating on someone who is hale and hearty."

"When will he be ready to ride?" Immanuel asked, looking at Uzziah.

"Another few days should do it, if he doesn't ride too hard, or too far, all at once."

"Good, I shot a deer on the way in, thought I'd treat you, Doctor, to a meal that we love."

"I love venison, too," Dr. Yates said, his eyes growing bright, then added, "I'll have Adam dress the meat."

They stayed with the doctor another month. Uzziah just didn't look right until then, and Immanuel had his own problems with his heart, so he understood. A slug that close to his heart might have caused some damage, and Immanuel wanted to make sure his partner of all these years was really ready to travel before they took off.

Finally, the day arrived, and their horses had been saddled, their supplies resupplied, thanks to the doctor, or maybe more especially thanks to Adam, who had packed them with enough grub to make a month's journey.

When they went back inside to say goodbye to Doc Yates, Immanuel had a special request. "Say, doc, before we take off, I think I should tell you what mission we were on afore Uzziah took that slug," Immanuel said.

"Go ahead," Yates said, knowing that just about anything could come from either of their mouths at any time.

"Uzziah?" Immanuel was giving his partner a chance to tell the first part. They had discussed the subject between themselves, and Uzziah knew what Immanuel was going to ask.

"My sister's in a family way," Uzziah began, and the doctor picked up his tea and took a sip. "It ain't normal that she's this way," Uzziah continued and didn't really know where to go from there.

"Son, nothing's normal with this war. I'm sitting in a house which the Yanks tried to burn down and might have succeeded if the rains hadn't come and saved the place."

"She's in General Stuart's Cavalry," Immanuel injected.

"I didn't know the Confederacy was conscripting females," Yates said, now really interested.

"They're not. She cut off her hair when her youngest, well, also my youngest brother, was kilt at First Manassas, and she can ride like the wind—"

"She took her brother's name and fooled the whole unit," Immanuel added.

"Very interesting. And she's married, that's why she's with child?"

"Not exactly," Uzziah said.

"This is where it gets real interestin', Doc," Immanuel added.

"Her sergeant impregnated her when he had a head

wound, and he don't remember the act, but what's growing in her belly is testimony to it," Uzziah finally spat out.

"And there's a question, or request in here for me, is there?" the doc said, looking at both the mountain men.

"Can we borrow some of that chloroform that ya used on Uzziah?"

"I see, she won't come easily, is that what you're saying?"

"Most definitely," Uzziah said.

"Well, yes, I have plenty, and the chances of me doing another operation at my age, well, to tell the truth, I wasn't so sure I could pull the one off on Uzziah," the doctor said.

"Now is definitely the time to tell us that," Immanuel said.

"Yes, didn't want you doubting me from the beginning now, did I? So, if she's pregnant, the chloroform won't hurt her, unless...you give her too much. If you're just going to knock her out to take her some place where she can have the child, I would say, it's safe, just a little, though."

Both men relaxed, and Dr. Yates continued, "It seems to me that this sister of yours, what's her name?"

"Hanna," Uzziah said.

"Hanna must be an extraordinary young woman, and if she's still pregnant by the time you find her and she's been riding with General Stuart's Cavalry this entire time, nothing will stop that from being a healthy baby."

The weather had turned cold for this early in the fall. It was nearly December, and to tell the truth, Uzziah and Immanuel had no idea where either General Jackson or General Stuart was. The first thing they decided to do was find a store and see if a newspaper had been printed recently, which might give them some information on where either, or both, units were.

As they rode out away from the nearly burned-down mansion, they encountered a mercantile store that was still, unbelievably, doing business. They tied their horses outside and went in to see what they could find out.

The man behind the counter had a Navy Colt lying on the counter, and when they entered, he picked it up. Both Uzziah and Immanuel raised their hands as if they were surrendering.

"It ain't funny," the man said.

"We ain't laughin'," Immanuel said.

"Whatcha lookin' fer?"

"Information?" Uzziah said tentatively.

"Leave!" the man shouted.

"He's kiddin', we need baccie and lucifers, ya got any?" Immanuel said.

"Yeah, but they ain't cheap, ain't nothin' cheap these days," the man said, reaching beneath the counter, and bringing both tobacco and lucifers up from down there.

"Life," Uzziah said.

"Say what?" the man asked.

"Life is cheap these days," Uzziah repeated.

"You two look like yer scoutin' fer somebody," the man said as he made change from the money that Immanuel had put on the counter.

"We do, we scout fer Jackson," Uzziah said.

"That right," the man said, not sounding impressed.

"Yes, it is right," Immanuel said, as he gathered up the matches and the tobacco and put them in his possibles pouch.

They started to walk away when the man spoke up.

"Been a lot of activity along the Rappahannock, there has," he said as he lit a pipe.

"That right?" Uzziah said.

"A lot of Federals, damn their hides, goin' toward Fredericksburg."

"Thank ye," Immanuel said. The man nodded.

The boys walked from the store and mounted up.

"Do ya know which way that river is from here?" Immanuel asked Uzziah.

"Sure, I do, this is my state, partner."

They rode to Richmond, it was a lot closer than Fredericksburg. When they got to the train station, Uzziah dismounted and went to the man at the depot window.

"Can ya get us on a train with our horses to Fredericksburg?"

The man leaned nearly out the window to see who the other part of *us* was.

"Ya ain't from around chere, are ya?"

"Shenandoah Valley," Uzziah said.

"Like I said, not from around chere. I can get ya on the next Richmond/Fredericksburg Potomac train, but y'all have to ride with yer horses," he said, smiling, showing the few teeth he did have.

"That's fine. How much?"

When the depot man told him, Uzziah whistled, "Ya sure we ain't goin' all the way to Canada?"

"Very funny," the man said as he made the change and pushed it across the counter.

It was a few hours before the train was scheduled to leave, so they rode into Richmond, and were amazed at how many Confederate soldiers, if you could call them that, were wandering the streets. They found a restaurant called *The Red Fox Inn & Tavern*.

The place looked like it had been there quite a while, and when they entered, they were greeted by a young woman who took them to a table.

"This might be too expensive," Uzziah whispered to Immanuel.

"Nothin's too good fer us, partner," Immanuel said.

The waiter brought the menus.

"Do ya have a venison stew?" Immanuel asked, not looking at the fare written on the menus.

"We do, sir."

"Bring us two big bowls of that and some hot, fresh bread," Immanuel said.

"To drink?"

"Cold beer," Uzziah cut in on the ordering.

"Very good, sirs," the waiter said and walked away.

Immanuel looked at Uzziah and raised his eyebrows.

Another gentleman walked over and stood beside their table.

"Can we help ya?" Immanuel asked.

"I'm interested in how the war effort is going. Do either of you gentlemen have news?"

"Well," Immanuel said, "we're on our way right

now to join Lee's Army of Northern Virginia at Fredericksburg."

"That's what all the movement has been about, near and around the Rappahannock, then?"

Immanuel nodded in agreement.

"I'm the owner of this fine establishment, ya know, we had George Washington in here before he was President."

"Ya don't look that old," Immanuel quipped.

The man laughed.

"Well, now ya can tell people that ya had Immanuel James Jones and Uzziah Ferguson O'Bannon in here during the current unpleasantness," Uzziah said confidently.

"Which is which?" the owner asked.

"I'm Immanuel, that's my partner, Uzziah."

"I've heard of the O'Bannons, they're from the Shenandoah, aren't they?"

"We are, sir, glad to make yer acquaintance," Uzziah said, extending his hand.

"I'm Jeremy Reutter," he said, then shook Immanuel's hand.

The waiter appeared with the bowls of venison stew, hot bread, and cold beer.

Jeremy looked at the food, "Excellent choices, and our beer comes up from the basement. It's so very cold."

Jeremy stood, "And please, this meal is on the house, the news about General Lee is most appreciated," he said, and walked off.

"Guess we came to the right place, huh, Uzziah?"

"We don't really know that Lee will be at Fredericksburg," Uzziah scolded Immanuel.

"Well, let me tell ya, if large Union forces are gonna

be there, so will Lee!" Immanuel said, as he took a bite of the venison stew and burned his lip, "Careful, young son, it's piping hot!"

They had another beer and then thanked Jeremy Reutter before they left the Red Fox Inn and Tavern.

Riding toward the train station, they were both in very good moods.

"Yer feelin' better, ain't ya?" Immanuel asked Uzziah.

"Yeah...yeah, I am, think I'm on the complete mend," Uzziah said.

"Hope that stock car ain't crowded, would love to take a nap on the way to Fredericksburg, those two beers got me groggy," Immanuel said.

The train was full of steam and getting ready to go when they got there. It just so happened that the stockcar that was assigned to them was nearly empty, two other horses at the other end. They loaded up Stygian and Shadow and laid down in the haystack that was on their end. Both knew better than to smoke, although they both wanted to. As the train began to rock its way north, they both fell asleep as Shadow and Stygian enjoyed the hay.

7

The train stopped short of Fredericksburg. The brakeman from the caboose came up the line and banged hard on the stockcar. Uzziah opened it to find a man who was rather excited beyond his experience.

"There must be over 100,000 blue bellies on the hills across from Fredericksburg! Look!!" he shouted, as if they weren't standing right up there in the doorway.

They leaned out, and sure enough, what the man had said was correct. Fires from the different divisions under whatever general that Washington had there were burning brightly into the coming night.

"Ifn yer gonna go there, ya better get off chere," the brakeman said. "We ain't gonna go into that mess. Besides, they probably already burned down the bridge across the Rappahannock!"

"Thanks, we'll get off, just like ya said," Immanuel said. They tightened up the cinches on their saddles, and, giving both horses a look at the jump they were about to make, jumped them from the stockcar to the easement.

The two mountain men had exited the train on the side of the river where Burnside, the Union general, had occupied Stafford Heights. He had been waiting there for weeks, since November 2[nd,] for pontoons which were to arrive so he could ford the river with all his men and cannons. Unfortunately, this gave Generals Lee, Jackson, and Stuart enough time to occupy the heights on the east side of the Richmond, Fredericksburg, and Potomac railroad line, the very line that Immanuel and Uzziah had exited from, north and east from Burnside's position.

The two partners forded the Rappahannock River at a spot north of Fredericksburg, which Burnside had been advised of but decided not to take his army across. He had planned on the pontoons, and by golly, he was going to wait until those damn pontoons showed, then go about his attack on the Army of Northern Virginia.

It seemed all the pieces were coming together for Immanuel and Uzziah to find Hanna, and do something about that tomboy, and get her with-child arse back home. They had a plan, but they weren't sure how to implement it. It's one thing to think about chloroforming someone and another one to figure out when to do it.

"All we gots to do is get her alone, and put that chloroform rag over her face, and the next thing she knows she's back home," Immanuel said.

"She won't be out that long."

"How do ya know. When Doc Yates operated on ya, ya was out the entire time, and I had to wait what seemed like an awfully long time afore ya woke up," Immanuel said.

"But we're taking her from wherever we find her to back home, and I think ifn we use enough to keep her passed out that long, then it might have an effect on the baby," Uzziah complained.

"We gots to come up with a concrete plan," Immanuel insisted.

"I think ifn we get in the vicinity of where she's at, then God will provide," Uzziah reasoned.

"Now yer soundin' like Jackson, depending too much on divine intervention, it ain't a good idea."

"So, I'm waitin', what's yer concrete plan?" Uzziah asked.

"It ain't that simple," Immanuel complained.

"Right, I know, we gots to wait till the opportunity presents itself, then we jump into action."

"Uh-huh."

"Well, give me a concrete plan we can go with, and I'll stop dependin' on God," Uzziah said.

"Sometimes, yer ridiculous, ya know that?"

"I know."

"Well, just so's ya know."

Stuart had received orders from General Lee to bring his cavalry to Fredericksburg, where he was sure Burnside would attack. Lee had wanted to engage Burnside in a different place, a place of his own choosing, but Burnside had decided to ford the Rappahannock at Fredericksburg, and that was that. The time it took to get the pontoons allowed the Confederate generals to find good places to receive Burnside's attacks, and Lee was pleased enough with that.

Stuart and his cavalrymen camped back away from Lee's position at what became known as Lee Hill. He told his subordinates to let the men relax, for they were, it seemed, all waiting on Burnside to ford a river which was more than fordable a few miles northeast of his position.

Tents were put up, and the familiar interiors of the tents appeared in unfamiliar surroundings, but that was the life of a cavalryman.

"Corporal O'Bannon, do you call that an organized bunk?" Sergeant Simmons asked his favorite trooper.

Hanna was tired as hell, and she did not want to put up with Stark giving her a lecture on her bunk. She had stopped throwing up, and that was good, because throwing up was hard to hide, not the vomit itself, but the gagging and all, usually drew attention.

"Look, Stark, I ain't in the mood fer this, ya got it?"

Stark had started his teasing in good humor, but this insubordination from a corporal would not do.

"Either fix the bunk, or I'll make ya fix it," Stark said.

Hanna turned to Stark, really, after the ride they had made to get here, he wanted to play soldier. The man was insufferable sometimes, as all men were.

"Make me!" Hanna said, and before she could say another word, Stark tackled her, and they both fell upon the cot, which collapsed, and Hanna turned to keep the big sergeant from falling on her belly, and when she did so, her shirt ripped, and loosened the bindings that kept her chest secured.

As she tried to wrestle away from Stark, he grabbed

at her and pulled the bindings off her left teat, and there it was, exposed for him to see.

You'd have thought the man had never seen a breast, or that Hanna's guts had somehow suddenly appeared outside her body.

Stark jumped up, not sure what to do or say.

"Yer a..." he stammered.

Hanna covered herself up and scampered out of the tent with Stark on her heels.

"John," Stark said, then reconsidered, "whoever you are, you're a woman!"

Hanna looked around, and there weren't any cavalrymen nearby, so she took off away from Stark and the rest of the outfit, and he was right on her heels.

"Slow down, we gotta talk," Stark shouted, but Hanna just kept on walking as fast as she could without being noticed, as she would have been if she had broken into a run.

Burnside was the latest of all the reticent Union generals, and he did not want to seem to wait. But wait he did because of the late arrival of the fording mechanisms.

Lee knew that Burnside had to attack, no matter where his army was situated, and they were definitely in the catbird's seat. When General Jackson arrived with his foot cavalry, Lee placed him south of him at Hamilton Crossing. The Confederates were entrenched when the pontoons did arrive, and even though there was a heavy fog for days, it did not keep the Confederate sharpshooters under General Barksdale, including Uzziah and Immanuel, from picking off the Union engineers who were trying to place the pontoons across the river.

Burnside became so frustrated with having his engineers shot that he ordered the city of Fredericksburg bombarded, even though the majority of the enemy were out of range, secured in the heights around Hazel Run and Telegraph Road.

And yet, his bombardment did have an effect. For Uzziah and Immanuel were hiding in one of the houses, up in the attic, getting easy pot shots at the engineers.

"This serves us right," Uzziah said, as the house next to them was blown to smithereens.

"And how do yah figure that?" Immanuel said as they scurried down the stairs from the attic, trying to get out of the house, which was in the range of the Union artillery.

"Shooting fish in a barrel ain't exactly my notion of being brave," Uzziah said as he made the ground floor, and the next cannonball fell on the very house they were trying to exit.

Everything seemed to be momentarily thrown into the air, and all Uzziah could see of Immanuel was him being tossed up with timbers, settees, books, part of a fireplace, and then everything came back down in a big crash!

"Immanuel! Immanuel!" Uzziah was screaming at the top of his lungs as other shells bombarded the town of Fredericksburg. If nothing else, Burnside sure knew how to scare away the sharpshooters who were giving his engineers so much deadly trouble.

"Over chere, young son," Immanuel said, and his voice sounded weak.

When Uzziah threw the rubble away, he found his partner, who was covered in white dust and looked like a spook.

"You okay?" Uzziah asked as he got closer to where his partner was half-buried.

"Yeah, but my leg's trapped under this truss," Immanuel said.

"Is it crushed?" Uzziah asked as he got enough of the rubble away so that he could finally stand near Immanuel.

"No, no, don't think so. Try and lift this bitch off me," Immanuel said.

Uzziah got down and grabbed the truss, even putting on his gloves for a better grip, but it must have weighed a ton, or it had so much other crap piled on top that it wouldn't budge.

Other blasts from Burnside's canons threw cannonballs into the houses next door. Terrific explosions, but no damage to where Immanuel was trapped.

"Well, at least they've changed their range," Immanuel said. "That's a plus."

"I gotta get help, or you'll be trapped down chere when the Yanks come through the town," Uzziah said.

"Well, what are ya tarryin' fer, go! Go!" Immanuel shouted.

Uzziah made his way back to the entrance, or what was left of it, climbing over all sorts of rubble, then found the main street and ran toward Lee's position. That's where they had left both their horses, with soldiers joking that if they didn't make it back, those two horses would be taken care of.

General J.E.B. Stuart had delivered a package to Jackson the night before the pontoons finally arrived. When Uzziah made Lee's camp, Jackson had just ridden up and dismounted. He was resplendent in a new uniform. It had the requisite stars on the collar, the spaghetti on the sleeves, as the troops called it, and he finally looked like the amazing soldier that he was. As Uzziah walked up to get some help, he overheard Stuart say something, it was a compliment, but the way he said it, Jackson remounted his horse, Fancy, and rode back toward where his men were stationed along Hamilton's crossing.

"I think you embarrassed the general," Lee said as Uzziah came up.

"I need help," Uzziah said frantically. "Immanuel's trapped under some rubble in one of the houses!"

"I'll send men to help, don't worry," Stuart said, then as he mounted up and rode back toward his regiment, who should come running down the road, but Corporal John O'Bannon, and behind him Sergeant Simmons.

"Just the people I need," General Stuart said. "Come with me!" he said, as he turned his mount around and headed back toward Lee's headquarters.

Uzziah waited near Lee's command tent. The general looked the mountain man up and down.

"It got rather unpleasant down there, didn't it?" Lee asked Uzziah.

"Ya might say that, yes, General, unpleasant is exactly how it was."

"Still, the shooting of the engineers bought us a little time, and was unnecessary. Though if Burnside hadn't begun shelling, I do believe General Barksdale would still be down there, plunking away," General Lee said, chuckling. "He does enjoy shooting Yankees."

"My feelings exactly, General Lee," Uzziah said as General Stuart came riding up with two cavalrymen scampering behind him.

"Come with me!" Uzziah said as he ran toward the town, not noticing who they were.

Hanna didn't know why General Stuart had sent her and Stark over to General Lee's tent, but now, it was obvious. Someone was stuck in some rubble, and the man they were following needed their help. The only trouble was, that man was none other than her brother, Uzziah Ferguson O'Bannon! How in the world? What were the chances?

There were still cannonballs falling and exploding in the middle of Fredericksburg, and a couple of times, houses they had just run by were demolished, and timbers, killing timbers, were thrown into the streets behind them. They ducked, bobbed, and weaved, till Uzziah thought he'd found the right house.

"Immanuel!" Uzziah yelled, "Immanuel!"

They were a half block off, and when they heard Immanuel yelling, they ran into the mess that was once a house, a home, and found him.

"Nice of ya to drop by," Immanuel said, he had a lit pipe in his mouth, and was smiling.

Stark and Uzziah got a hold of the truss beam and,

grunting with all their might, managed to get it lifted just enough for Immanuel to wriggle from under it. Just as that happened, Hanna got under Immanuel's shoulder to help him, another cannonball hit the house, and with the fire and smoke, it was lucky that Stark and Uzziah made it out at all.

By that time, the fires which had started up had made it to that block, and between the continual firing of Burnside's cannons and the smoke from the fire, it was impossible for Sergeant Simmons and Uzziah to see anything.

"We've got to get them! We can't leave them inside that inferno!" Stark shouted at Uzziah, but the flames blocked the entrance they had used, and to stay would have meant their certain deaths.

"Come on, they're gone!" Uzziah said, a lump in his throat, knowing that the young boy with Stark had to have been his sister, Hanna.

More shelling, and Stark and Uzziah ran for the hills, being chased by explosions and fire.

By the time they made it back, Stark and Uzziah were beside themselves with anxiety and fear.

"Where are the others?" Lee asked, he'd been waiting for Immanuel's rescue as if he were his very own brother.

"Shelling got them!" Stark said, his heart as heavy as he could ever remember it. Now, he would never know the what and wherefore of Corporal John O'Bannon's secret, and he had a niggling feeling that some things that had happened in the past that he thought were dreams, may not have been!

Uzziah had not completely given up. The manner in which the house exploded, and he had seen Hanna being used as a crutch by Immanuel before the last shell hit, and it looked like she was leading him out a side door. Perhaps both had been killed, but then again, perhaps both had been saved?

Sergeant Simmons, devastated by two things now, first the discovery that O'Bannon was a woman, and not ten minutes later, her gruesome death in a federal shelling, excused himself and walked back to where Stuart was supporting General Jackson.

When General Lee turned to say something else of condolence to Uzziah, the man wasn't there. *Strange that,* thought Lee.

When Uzziah got back to where they had set up camp, Hanna was there, passed out. Immanuel was gathering up all their supplies and packing up his saddlebags.

"What happened?" Uzziah asked, checking to see if Hanna was still breathing.

"We made it out the other side, and when she thought she was helping me up the hill, I slipped the rag over her face."

"How did ya get the chloroform on the rag?"

"Very sloppily! Now, get yer stuff, and I'll hand her up to ya, and yer gonna hafta ride double with her in front."

Uzziah got Shadow saddled, and there wouldn't be any trouble with the extra weight. Heck, when Immanuel handed her up to him, and he readjusted her in front of him, she hardly weighed anything.

As they rode off from what would be one of the south's greatest, if not the most ignoble, victories of the

War Between the States, the two mountain men started in.

"She's like a rag doll. How much chloroform did ya give her?"

"Stop it, Mother O'Bannon, I did what I did, she's here with us, now let's get the hell away from chere!" Immanuel said, as he kicked up Stygian and the two dark horses rode away from the battle and off to the east.

They rode toward the Shenandoah Valley. They had to get Hanna O'Bannon back home so she could have the baby she was carrying without the war interfering.

They weren't five miles from the raging battle when Hanna awakened. She was disoriented at first, since anesthetic has that effect.

"What in the name of God!" Hanna said as she turned and looked at Uzziah.

"Hey, sis," Uzziah said, then Hanna saw Immanuel riding abreast.

"So, this is the way ya pay me back, ya bastard," she spat at Immanuel.

"Listen, I—"

"What the hell was that awful-smellin' stuff ya covered my face with!?! If ya hurt our baby, I swear to God, I'll have yer balls on a platter."

"Well, her speech patterns have certainly changed since joining up with Jeb Stuart," Immanuel said, and laughed.

"There's nothin' funny 'bout any of this," Hanna screamed, and she writhed in the saddle trying to either get off the horse, or force Uzziah off. When it didn't work, she burst into tears, and perhaps because it was the first time she'd relaxed since she became a young boy, instead of a young girl, she fell into a troubled, deep sleep.

They camped that night at the half-burned mansion of Dr. Yates, and he was delighted to see them. Hanna was sullen and almost insulting to the man, and she refused to eat. It wasn't until Adam was introduced to her that she seemed to come alive.

"You 'member me?" Hanna asked the old Negro.

Adam looked at her and turned his head almost like a dog.

"No, ma'am, am I supposed to?" Adam asked in all sincerity.

"The last time I was here, Jeb Stuart, the general, was burying an officer in yer front yard. I had a wounded man under my care, and ya showed me a place in the barn where he could recuperate.

"I 'member that, yes ma'am, but ya wasn't there, I'd 'member a good-looking woman like yerself," Adam said.

"I was a young boy, then," Hanna said.

"Y'all have to excuse me," Adam said, "I's gettin' too old fer these times." Then he left the library.

"I didn't meet you, then," Dr. Yates said, "but Adam told me the story about the sergeant and the private he gave shelter to. My, my, those Federals showed up, right after that, it's amazing that you both weren't caught and put in irons," Dr. Yates said.

"You'll have to excuse me," Hanna said as she started to walk from the library.

"Where ya goin'?" Uzziah asked her.

"Don't worry. Just afore yer so-called rescue, the gig was up," she said and left.

"Don't ya think we should foller her?" Immanuel asked.

"No, ifn this was where what I think happened happened, then she don't need us now," Uzziah said, accepting a glass of merlot from Dr. Yates.

Hanna walked out into the moonlight. Yes, it was the place, she could see the marker there in the front yard, where the gallant Southern general had buried his fallen comrade. She couldn't remember the man's name, but so many had fallen, how could she remember any of them?

She walked around to the back, where Adam was sitting smoking a pipe. When he saw her, he smiled.

"I understand now, ya was the boy who was really a girl, that was you, right?" Adam said in his convoluted way.

"Yes, that was me," she said, glad that the old Negro had not forgotten her, and Stark.

"I thoughts that man was gonna die, that's what I's thought," Adam said, puffing away on his pipe.

"Me, too," Hanna said, looking longingly toward the barn where she had posed as Sergeant Simmons's wife and they had coupled that fateful night.

"Go on in, it's all right," Adam said, knocking the dottle from his pipe.

She walked through the door, which made the same squeaking sound it had made that night, and with the moonlight scattering itself over the floor of the barn, she was transported back to that evening, when she had taken a bath, and Stark had wandered out and discovered her.

"Who are you?" he had asked her, and she had lied, oh, how she had lied.

"I'm yer wife, Hanna," she had told him, and then they had lain on the small bed, and intertwined as only couples can do. They jokingly call it the beast with two backs, but there was nothing bestial about that coupling, that lovemaking. She and Stark had become one, so much so that that evening marked the one and only chance she had ever had to be with child, and now, she was.

He knew her secret of not being a young man, and she was sure he had felt violated in some way, but now, she wondered if the memory of that evening had come back to him since she had been kidnapped from his presence. She was sure that he thought she was dead, and maybe that was for the best.

She would go home, reconcile with Rahab, her mother, and what a reconciliation that would be. Her sisters fluttering around her, her secrets openly exposed, and the whole family standing with her.

She would have the baby, and he would think she was dead, and perhaps that was the best of all possible worlds in this war-weary world. For her to be dead to him, and he, well, he probably would be killed also, but she would never know. Best for everyone, yes.

She resigned herself, lying on the bed where her child had been conceived, lying there, and remembering his touch, the roughness of it, the gentleness of it, and the way they had breathed together, breathed a new life into being, breathed a new world into possibility.

"Hanna," the voice was her brother's, Uzziah. It was just an inquiring voice, not harsh, not too concerned, just enough so that she knew, if he hadn't come along, then only God would have known what she would have done.

At that moment of Uzziah standing in the darkened barn with the light scattered in spiderweb configurations on the barn floor, she realized that God must have sent her brother, her blood, to rescue her from what?! She could not imagine, and that's why she relaxed into her rescue as something desirable, something preferred over riding into battle carrying a mute and unseen burden that should have been a blessing.

"Uzziah?" she whispered, and it must have been just the right whisper, because he ran to her, and they embraced, and she cried, she cried the tears of her death, of her being separated from the father of her child, the tears of joy that now, she could blossom forth and be pregnant, be with child, be—in a family way and not care who saw. The blessed joy of relaxing into herself overcame her in those tears, and she realized that Uzziah was weeping, too. He felt her joy, pain, struggle, triumph—all of it, and accepted it, because she was blood of his blood!

8

Dr. Yates had a horse for sale, but he wouldn't take any money for it. He tried to explain it to the two mountain men, how pleased he was that in the confines of that old, broken-down barn, a new life had begun. So, now, Hanna had her own horse, a roan, and she wasn't that old. Immanuel complained that it wasn't good for Stygian or Shadow to have a mare with them, but he was overruled.

They no longer had to worry about Hanna running away. Somehow, the few nights at Dr. Yates had changed the way she felt about what the boys had done. Immanuel was especially happy about that, since he was the one who had chloroformed her.

It took them a few more days to get to the valley. They had to avoid the home guard, who had become a problem of their own. Men who had not qualified for service, but who now thought they had the right to do all sorts of stuff to whoever was left behind.

Uzziah worried that Rahab might be having trouble with them, and couldn't wait to find out. He also worried about his brothers and his pa, whom he'd left at Fredericksburg, and he prayed that no matter what happened that they would be safe from the Federals and make it through another huge battle.

They came in from the south, and the whole way, all either of the two, brother and sister, could do was dredge up old memories of what the Shenandoah Valley had meant to them, and how it would always be a part of their lives. When they came to the farm road that led to the O'Bannon farm, it was no good trying to tell Hanna that she couldn't ride pell-mell down that road at a gallop. The girl was incorrigible.

Uzziah stopped Immanuel from riding after her.

"We'll let her have this," he said, and Immanuel pulled Stygian back. The stallion had grown quite fond of the roan mare, and perhaps that was one of the reasons Immanuel's horse had taken off like it did.

By the time they got within sight of the house, there was a clothes line nearly full, and a turned-over basket of wet clothes that their ma had dropped when she spied her red-headed child who had come back from God knows where. They were still hugging, and the rest of the girls had spilled out of the house, no doubt hearing the squealing sounds that women make when they are overjoyed.

Uzziah and Immanuel sat their horses, there on the road, not twenty feet from where all the goings on were going on, and finally, some of the girls came running over, particularly Sally, who, in a moment of drunkenness, had once asked Immanuel to marry her. She ran right to his horse, and he got down before she got there, and you would have thought that they had been married and she was welcoming him home.

The other sisters, Sarah and Faith, were congregating around Uzziah, and he was receiving hugs and kisses galore.

Then, Rahab came down with Hanna holding onto her, and hugged both the men, both the mountain man partners that she loved. She had in her heart of hearts accepted the fact that Immanuel, probably closer to her age than Uzziah, was really a long-lost brother, and a child of her heart. They hugged, and she kissed him on the mouth just as she did all her children, and the gathering of love and reunion was taken into the house, into the home, where the smells were just as they had always been in Uzziah's mind, and he wondered why, why, had he ever left? Why had he ventured forth to become what—a mountain man, or was the journey itself what he was entertaining? He wasn't sure, but all he knew now was he was glad to be back, glad to be in front of the fireplace where so much had happened in his life.

That night Rahab made his favorite, a pork loin, even though the pig wasn't yet full-grown. It was lean and tender, and the mashed potatoes were fluffy, and the gravy from the drippings off the pig meat was delicious, then there were her homemade yeast rolls. The kitchen seemed to be more a church than any church Uzziah or Immanuel had ever been in. They worshipped the way the women went about their work, and the communion they had there, the supper of love was blessed as Uzziah prayed over the food that would nourish the girls, the mother, and his pal, Immanuel—God with us!

———

As was not uncommon, when one part of a family was enjoying the felicity and good humor of a reunion, another part, all the remaining brothers, plus their father, were in the grips of the final day of the Battle of Fredericksburg.

Jackson had noticed when he was inspecting his lines that there was a gap, there just below Prospect Hill, but he felt, as did General Hill, who had seen the same gap, that the area was too low and swampy for any Federals to make headway, and it was summarily forgotten.

During the artillery battle between the Federals and the Confederates, Lee had advised, rather ordered, that Jackson's artillery, some sixty-three pieces, remain quiet during the barraging. Jackson was lying down while Minie balls buzzed overhead and enjoying a rest when a message came from Lee. Jackson advised the messenger to lie down beside him while he read the message and wrote a reply to Lee.

Federals, thinking that all the batteries of Jackson had been decommissioned by their ferocious firing, and that Jackson's batteries had been stuck and were out of commission, were about to begin an attack which they believed would be unopposed by Confederate artillery.

Jackson had been advised by Lee to keep his artillery silent, and it wasn't until Meade had advanced way too far forward that all Jackson's cannons opened up. The battle, which looked like it might take a turn for the Federals at this point, was suddenly thrown into confusion, and Meade's troops ran helter-skelter to avoid the Confederate bombardment.

What they saw was a copse of trees at the base of Prospect Hill, and being men of considerable self-survival instincts, they ran for those trees. Finding no Confederate troops within those trees, they continue to steam forward up Prospect Hill and then right into General Greggs's Carolinians, who were so relaxed that they had their rifles stacked. Gregg was mounted at the time and took a ball in his left side and fell to the ground mortally wounded. His men fled in confusion, but when Jackson was advised that this had happened, he showed no concern because he knew he had brigade stacked upon brigade behind Gregg's Carolinians.

These brigades were eventually brought into the battle, and among them were Sergeant Sean O'Bannon and his five sons. They ran into the Federals, who imagined that they had a full ticket to the back of Lee's army and, pushing hard, drove the Federals back, but all this occurred within heavy musket fire, some of it sounding as if all the men possessed repeating rifles, which they did not.

At one point, Sergeant O'Bannon looked down the line of his men and saw two of his sons fall and not get up again.

But these things happen in battle, and being the sergeant in charge of a troop, Sean O'Bannon continued to press with his other three sons and the remaining troop. They pushed the Federals back out of the copse of trees, there at the base of Prospect Hill, but the whole time, Sergeant Sean O'Bannon hoped and prayed that those boys of his that he'd seen fall were merely wounded. He would have to wait until this part of the battle was over and Meade and his Federals had been driven back to where they belonged before he could be sure!

The night of the 13th of December 1862, Sergeant Stark Simmons sat in his tent. He was proud of the job that Stuart's Cavalry had done, pushing back General Meade's advance up Prospect Hill. The Federals had run amuck and overextended their line, and pushing them back was relatively easy.

But as he sat on his bunk and could hear the other men talking and some even laughing, he was reminded that his bunkmate was missing. The person he had known as John O'Bannon, the young presumptuous boy who could ride like the wind and had a sense of humor which Stark loved, was gone.

And yet, he could not get over the fact that shortly before he was killed in a cannon blast from Burnside's artillery, he had suddenly become a woman. How could Stark reconcile that? Who would he tell, who would believe him? Or better yet, why had the young girl who had posed as John O'Bannon done what she had done?

What kept haunting him was the dream that he'd had after he'd been wounded. The O'Bannon boy had brought him to safety and even taken care of the head-wound, but there was the space between getting shot and waking up the next morning and remembering who he was.

In an effort to remember, he laid on the bunk that the young girl had occupied all the months they had known each other. He buried his face in her pillow, and the smell of her skin, just that, and nothing more, transported him back to that barn behind where they had buried the only casualty of that ride. He had missed the burial because he was being so tenderly attended to by

John O'Bannon. And yet, the dream he had, the dream of the beautiful, young girl, standing from the water trough, perhaps that wasn't a dream? What had she told him when he asked who she was?

"I am your wife," she said as the beaded water stood upon her gooseflesh.

They had coupled that night, or at least, there was a strong memory of something like that which involved a young girl, moonlight, and a barn. Of course, he wasn't a virgin when the war began, and there had been other girls in other barns, but the smell trapped in the pillowcase of his bunkmate, that smell told another story.

He got up. He couldn't sleep anyway. The dying and wounded out below Marye's Heights were caterwauling and calling for their mothers, water, and just plain help. How could anyone stand to listen to that!?!

He walked up to the stonewall behind which 5,000 Confederates had repulsed 12,000 Federals. There were still men standing guard there. At the ready in case—he wasn't sure why.

Stark looked over the wall and could see a man with many canteens moving among the dead and wounded on the darkened battlefield.

"Who is that, and what's he doin' out there?" Stark asked the nearest Confederate soldier.

"A man who proves that officers are crazy," the man standing behind the man he asked said.

"What's he mean?"

"That's Second Lieutenant Richard Kirkland, Sergeant," the man he asked answered.

"And he's doing what?"

"It's amazing, Sarge, he's giving water and succor to those wounded out there."

"And the Federals aren't shooting at him?"

"No, sir, it's just too brave," the Confederate soldier said as Stark vaulted the wall and walked out to where Kirkland was giving water to the wounded.

"I wouldn't do that, sarge, one man's a humanitarian, two an invasion!" the soldier yelled.

As Stark got closer, he could hear the mumblings of the federal to whom Lieutenant Kirkland was giving water.

"You're a Reb," the wounded soldier whispered.

"No, I'm just a man," the lieutenant said, then looked up as Stark got down and crawled toward him. "Ya want to help?" Lieutenant Kirkland asked.

"Sure, have ya checked the town itself?" Stark asked.

"Sergeant," Lieutenant Kirkland said, "they occupy that ground, this, this is no man's land, and it's as far as we dare go."

"So, ya ain't been down into the rubble of the town?" Stark asked.

"No, they would take me prisoner, and I'd spend the rest of the war in Camp Douglas," the Lieutenant said, and got up to move on.

"Thank you, Lieutenant," the wounded man whispered, "I'll never forget yer kindness."

Stark watched as Lieutenant Kirkland continued, his canteens jangling as he walked not that far to the next man who needed water.

Sergeant Stark looked down into the town of Fredericksburg and made up his mind, when Burnside retreated, he would check to see if he could find her body.

Off to the southeast, nearly three miles away, Sean O'Bannon with his sons Hank, Short Samson, and Obadiah were walking through the marshy ground at the base of Prospect Hill. Above them, the aurora borealis shimmered green and red, lighting up the entire battlefield. Some had said that it was a good omen for the Confederates, but Sean O'Bannon would only believe that if he found his two missing sons, Zachariah and Raymond, alive, then there might be luck.

They had checked at the barn near Bernard's Cabins, where there were so many wounded. They were lined up almost entirely around the barn. Neither of his sons were there. It was then that the father, Sean, and his other sons had taken to the base of Prospect Hill to see if they lay among the dead.

"Pa!" It was Obadiah, and the way his voice sounded, it wasn't good.

Sean, Hank, and Short Samson ran further up the hill, where they found both of their dead.

From the way the bodies were situated, Zachariah had died first, since Raymond was holding him. Both were stone-cold dead.

The brothers began silently weeping, and Sean just sat there and looked at the colors of the lights reflecting in his two dead sons' unseeing eyes. He did not close those eyes, and when Hank tried to, Sean reached out and grabbed his son's arm.

"What do we do, Pa?" Hank asked.

"You boys go up, get some supper, and come back at dawn with some shovels."

"Shovels!?! Ain't we gonna take 'em home?" Obadiah asked.

"We can't, son, ya saw what happened to those three from the valley. Deserters are shot."

"So, we gonna bury 'em here!?!" Hank asked incredulously.

"For a while, after this is all over, we'll come back and get 'em."

"But why, Pa, why?" Obadiah sincerely asked.

"Ifn we don't hide 'em, they'll throw 'em in a common grave, we'll never find 'em again. Now, go, eat, come back at dawn, hear!"

Hank gathered up Obadiah, who couldn't stop staring at the dead bodies of his older brothers. Obadiah might have gotten away from Hank if Short Samson hadn't gotten Obadiah's other arm. They literally dragged him up the hill.

When the war was eventually over, Sean O'Bannon framed a poem by the Yankee poet Walt Whitman. Sean figured by that time, it didn't matter if the man had been fighting for the north. It was hung on the wall in the parlor so everyone, if they wanted to, could read it. Sean said that Whitman had caught the essence of that night he spent with his two dead boys, and that's all he ever said about it.

Vigil strange I kept on the field one
night:
When you my son and my comrade
dropt by my side that day,
One look I but gave which your dear
eyes return'd with a look I shall
never forget.

One touch of your hand to mine O boy,
reach'd up as you lay on the ground,
Then onward I sped in the battle, the
even contested battle,
Till late in the night reliev'd to the place
at last again I made my way.
Found you in death so cold dear
comrade, found your body, son of
responding kisses, (never again on
earth responding.)
Bared your face in the starlight, curious
the scene, cool blew the moderate
night-wind,
Long there and then in vigil I stood,
dimly around me the battlefield
spreading,
Vigil wondrous and vigil sweet there in
the fragrant silent night,
But not a tear fell, not even a long-
drawn sigh, long, long I gazed,
Then on the earth partially reclining sat
by your side leaning my chin in my
hands,
Passing sweet hours, immortal and
mystic hours with you dearest
comrade—not a tear, not a word.
Vigil of silence, love and death, vigil for
you my son and my soldier,
As onward silently stars aloft, eastward
new ones upward stole,
Vigil final for you brave boy (I could not
save you, swift was your death,
I faithfully loved you and cared for you

living, I think we shall surely meet
again.)
Till at latest lingering of the night,
indeed just as the dawn appear'd,
My comrade I wrapt in his blanket,
envelop'd well his form,
Folded the blanket well, tucking it care-
fully over head and carefully under
feet,
And there and then and bathed by the
rising sun, my son in his grave, in his
rude-dug grave I deposited,
Ending my vigil strange with that, vigil
of night and battlefield dim,
Vigil for boy of responding kisses, (never
again on earth responding.)
Vigil for comrade swiftly slain, vigil I
never forget, how as day brigthen'd,
I rose from the chill ground and folded
my soldier well in his blanket,
And buried him where he fell.

9

As soon as Burnside had slipped away in the fog from Fredericksburg and the disastrous decisions that had not only lost him the Battle of Fredericksburg, but also inevitably the command of the Army of the Potomac, Sergeant Stark Simmons rode down into the rabble and confusion of what was left of the town.

Stark remembered, sort of, where he had been when they had lifted the truss off Immanuel's leg. And yet, the continual bombardment of Fredericksburg had rearranged most of the neighborhoods, and in the end, he was simply guessing. He searched around for an hour, looking for the body of John O'Bannon, knowing, of course, that it would be the body of a young woman who had posed as John. He found nothing.

He had to return to his command with J.E.B. Stuart, and as he was riding back up to where the Confederate cavalry was saddling up, he couldn't help but think. Who would have impersonated John O'Bannon? The impersonator had known so much of the O'Bannon family and had had the confidence of Immanuel James Jones, the man known to be the partner of Uzziah O'Bannon, that it could only have been one of the O'Bannon family. It had to be! And since the impersonator had been a young woman, she would have been one of O'Bannon's sisters, and there were only four sisters—Sally, Hanna, Sarah, and Faith. And because of their ages, the one who pretended to be John, the brother, had to be either Sally or Hanna.

He knew from all *John* had told him that Sally had been married and moved to Harper's Ferry, had a child, who had died, then left her husband, who had turned into a drunk after the daughter's death. Simple elimination made it obvious that the daughter of Sean O'Bannon who had decided to become John O'Bannon could only be the middle daughter, Hanna. Of course, it came to him, then.

In the dream he had when he was wounded, he was married to a woman, and her name had been, yes... Hanna! Then the final and most important part of the dream rushed in on him—they had made love! He and Corporal John O'Bannon, a.k.a. Hanna O'Bannon, had made love that night. He remembered it quite distinctly now.

"Sergeant!?!" It was Jeb Stuart, and he'd ridden up beside him.

"Sorry, General, I was lost in thought," Sergeant Simmons said.

"Well, if my thoughts were that engaging, I'd be lost in thought, also. We will follow General Lee and continue to be his eyes and ears. Join your troops and prepare to leave," General Stuart said.

Sergeant Simmons rode over to where his men had gathered and were about to mount up.

"Where's O'Bannon?" one of the men asked. Well, of course they would want to know, he was popular with his troops.

"I'm afraid he was killed when we went down into the town to rescue one of the scouts," Stark said.

The men looked around as they always did when a death was reported. They had grown close to the young boy and liked him, and now, he was gone. Such were the fortunes of war, but still, it hurt. They would probably never mention John O'Bannon's name to their sergeant again, they knew how fond of him the sergeant had been.

Back at the O'Bannon farm, the home guard had checked in with them several times, but since the two scouts weren't officially enlisted in the Confederate army, there wasn't anything they could do about them being there.

The months flew by as Hanna's belly got bigger and bigger with each day. Immanuel and Uzziah worked the fields, plowing and making them ready for the spring planting. Each night, they had supper with the five women—the four daughters and the mother, Rahab. They hadn't eaten that well in they couldn't remember when? Many of those during the war were deprived of their livestock and went without, but Rahab, remembering where Obadiah's caves were, had taken many of the livestock there and penned them in. There was plenty of forage in the area, and because of that, there was a constant supply of meat, both pork and beef, for the greater portion of the war.

It helped when Immanuel and Uzziah were there because they could see to the care of the hidden livestock.

By the time spring came along, Hanna was beginning to look like she might have the baby at about any moment. Enough time had passed that she had not only forgiven Immanuel and her brother for what she had imagined that they had done to her, but knew now that they had rescued her, truly. On her own, would she have left her true love? Probably not. Then, what would have happened to their baby?

"Uzziah?" Hanna asked as he came down for breakfast one morning.

"Hanna, how are you?"

"I'm sorry," Hanna said.

"For what, sweetie?" he said, taking a fresh biscuit from the basket on the table. Rahab slapped his hand as she placed the fried ham slices on the table.

Hanna watched her mother chastise her oldest brother and realized that no matter how old someone got, they were beholding and belonging to others. This made her think about the baby that she was carrying.

"For being such a shite," Hanna said.

"No swearing," Rahab warned her middle daughter.

"You were angry. We took you against yer will, I understand."

"But it saved my bacon, didn't it?"

"Maybe," Uzziah said as Immanuel came into the kitchen.

"Who saved whose bacon?" Immanuel asked as he

reached for the biscuits and was given a double hit by both Rahab and Hanna.

"No fair, both of ya!?" Immanuel protested.

"I was just tellin' Uzziah how you and he saved my bacon," Hanna said.

"Oh, that, well, what was we to do?" Immanuel asked, stealing a biscuit when Rahab went back to get the eggs.

"Immanuel, while yer eatin' that biscuit ya think ya stole behind my back, go to the foot of the stairs and yell for the other girls, will ya?"

"I'll go up and push 'em outta their beds ifn ya want me to," Immanuel said, walking toward the stairs.

"Just a hollerin' will be plenty," Rahab said.

"Y'all get yer arses down chere!" Immanuel yelled.

"No swearin'!" Rahab said, then added, "This family's gonna sound like a bunch of sailors when you boys leave!"

"Mama, that reminds me, we are leavin'," Uzziah said.

"When!?!" Rahab seemed genuinely surprised.

"Today."

"Today!" she said and came over and grabbed both mountain men and kissed them both.

"Promised General Jackson we'd be back afore long, and it's already been too long," Uzziah said.

"I personally think we should stay," Immanuel said, as Sarah, Faith, and Sally joined them around the table.

"You're leavin'?!?" Sally asked. "I thought ya were gonna stay on and marry me?"

"Sally, stop it, that talk will get ya nowhere with that man!" Rahab warned.

"Never know, Mama," Immanuel said, he had taken to calling her that. "I might just oblige her."

"Over my dead body!" Rahab said, "Now, Uzziah, bless this food and this family."

"Heavenly Father, we gather this mornin', not knowin' how the other children in this family are doin', or how their father is. What we want to thank ya for is this day, this food, and the fact that we can gather here under this chere roof, and commune with one 'nother and be blessed by all of us being chere. In yer son's name, Amen."

The *Amens* went around the table, and they started passing the food.

The boys had pretty much sprung their leaving on the women, but it was necessary. They didn't want to see the long faces as the time drew near for them to leave. They both knew it was better this way.

As they mounted up, the girls gathered around, and more hugs leaning from horses were had, and Mama Rahab got kisses again, too, by both men. They said their goodbyes, and looking at Hanna, Uzziah knew the next time he saw any of them, if indeed he would survive the rest of this dab-blamed war, that he'd be an uncle and Hanna would be a ma. Strange how things just kept mounting up if enough time went by.

They were riding down the road that led to the main road when Uzziah heard Hanna screaming.

"Uzziah, wait! Wait!"

When they both stopped and turned in the saddle, a very pregnant Hanna was wobbling down the road.

She was out of breath when she made it to Shadow's side.

"What is it, sweetheart?" Uzziah asked.

"I truly am glad ya did what ya did, both of ya," she said, as she looked between Uzziah and Immanuel.

She dug into the pocket in her dress and pulled something out.

"I know, if he's still alive, that y'all probably see Starkie again. When ya do, he'd owed this chere letter," she said as she reached up with it for Uzziah to take. Right before he took it, she drew it back.

"Don't read it! Understand?" she was being adamant.

"Yeah, I got it," Uzziah said as he reached for it the second time.

"And not you, neither!" Hanna said, looking at Immanuel.

"We got it, missy, we won't read it," Immanuel said.

"Even if, by God, he turns up dead, it ain't yer letter, got it?" She held the letter out and her hand was shaking.

"Ya sure ya want me to deliver it?" Uzziah asked, holding the letter so she could take it back, if she wanted.

Her movements belied the fact that she was thinking about taking the letter back, but then, she stuffed her nervous hands into the pockets of her dress.

"No, I wrote it fer him, he needs to read it," she said and turned around and started walking back to the house.

"Love ya, both, ya know that, right? Mama don't need any more graves chere, understand?"

They both waved, and Immanuel blew a kiss her way. They turned and started for the main road.

"What was that all 'bout?" Uzziah asked.

"What, what ya talkin' 'bout?"

"That blowin' a kiss thing?"

"It was exactly that, just that," Immanuel said.

"You are so weird sometimes."

"Me?!? Young son, ya take the cake fer weird."

"Why would ya say that?"

"I done read ya from the Daily Richmond Examiner how many passed at Fredericksburg, right?"

"Yeah, so?"

"Nearly 15,000 died there, and ya wanna go back to see more?"

"It ain't 'bout the dead," Uzziah said.

"Then, who is it 'bout? Ya tell me and tell me true," Immanuel demanded.

"It's 'bout that baby boy or girl that's livin' inside Hanna. It's 'bout the future of this country, whether we let big business, and industry run us over, or whether there's still a place for men and farms, and babies, and all the things I grew up lovin'!"

"Ifn ya loved 'em so much, why'd ya come to the Rockies?"

"My education wasn't done, ya've been my educator, ya know that, right?"

Immanuel was a little taken aback by this admission of Uzziah's.

"Don't ya?" Uzziah insisted.

"Yeah, yeah, I know. But it ain't like I've been the onliest one teachin' here, pard, ya done showed me some stuff I never woulda experienced without ya, and ya know that, too, right?"

Uzziah looked at the older mountain man, and his breast swelled with the love and admiration he had for the man, and it looked to Uzziah as if Immanuel were feeling the same.

"I'll race ya!" Immanuel said as he kicked Stygian into a gallop, and Uzziah was right behind him on Shadow.

As they raced down the country road that would lead them further south to where they suspected General Jackson's foot cavalry were, they could have cared less who won, or who lost this simple race between excellent horses. What they wanted to avoid, well, what Immanuel wanted to avoid, above all else, were his deep, deep feelings for a younger man, which could only be couched in the terms of *son*. The older Immanuel got, the more obvious it was, or at least it seemed that way to him. Uzziah had been under Immanuel's wing for a long time, but as Uzziah's strength and wisdom increased, Immanuel could see there in the shadow of his strong friend, a place to hide, a place of safety, a place a whole lot like home.

They smiled as their speeding horses were neck and neck, and looking ahead, they realized they'd have to slow for a wagon approaching. They both reined in as the wagon passed.

"Do I keep goin' this way?" the older man asked as he pulled some straw from his mouth.

"Whacha mean?" Uzziah asked.

"Well, ifn you fellas is runnin' from somethin', then maybe I should turn 'round and go withcha!?" the old fella said.

"Nah, we just racin'." Uzziah said.

"Young people," he said, and spat some tobacco juice on the road as he shook his head.

They turned in their saddles and watched him go off, still talking to himself, but too far away to understand.

"He called us young people!" Immanuel said.

"Yeah, well, he's probably half blind," Uzziah came back, and the two mountain men laughed heartily, as they continued on down the road.

10

It was reported that the name for whores given after the Civil War, that name being *hookers*, came from the fact that General Joseph Hooker, of the Army of the Potomac, President Abraham Lincoln's next gamble for leader of his huge, but inept army, was smart enough to let a bevy of women follow his troops. It had always been a custom to let drovers drive cattle behind troops, simply because, as Napoleon had so well stated, *An army marches on its stomach.*

And yet, old Joe Hooker must have surmised that if an army couldn't march without food, then perhaps it was best if they also didn't march without having at their disposal some sort of cranny hunting available.

Regardless, sutlers, cattle drovers, and madams with their entourage in tow followed one of the biggest armies ever toward Chancellorsville, Virginia, in Spotsylvania County. After all, there were within the Army of the Potomac over 133,868 *present for duty equipped,* as the army put it.

Fighting this mass of humanity were about 60,298

Confederates who may never have been, as stated by the Army of the Potomac, *present for duty equipped,* since a lot of those present for the Confederates were still looking for a decent pair of shoes to wear into battle, not to mention a musket with plenty of powder and shot.

The threesome who represented the Confederacy were General Robert Edward Lee, who still dressed as if he might have been an older private, General Thomas Johnathan Stonewall Jackson, resplendent in the new uniform offered to him by J.E.B. Stuart at Fredericksburg, and of course, the gift-giver himself, General Jeb Stuart, the Confederate cavalry Cavalier.

These three, plus General Longstreet, had taken on General Burnside, and thrashed him soundly at Fredericksburg, and that was the main reason, General Joseph Hooker was now in command of the Army of the Potomac.

Lincoln kept finding generals who looked good on paper, but when it came time for them to act, they either hesitated, as McClellan always did, with Pope and Burnside following suit, the one being timid as McClellan, the other audacious to the point of lunacy as he sent fourteen charges at the sunken stonewall across from the Fredericksburg highlands.

The point being, at this juncture of the War Between the States, the Federals had all the men, but the Rebels had all the generals. This would play out again at Chancellorsville as General Hooker thought he could put a pincer movement on Lee and catch him from the south, with Major General Sedgwick coming up from Fredericksburg, and General Hooker attacking from the north.

Everyone in the state of Virginia knew where these armies were, it wasn't exactly a surprise, and when Immanuel and Uzziah caught up with General Jackson, he was with Lee's Army of Northern Virginia, still at Fredericksburg. Lee, having the excellent eyes and ears of Stuart's Cavalry, already knew what Hooker was planning, and he was ready for it.

Uzziah and Immanuel found the teepee that only Abooksigun could have erected, and they joined him there.

"Boy, thought maybe ya two forgot 'bout the war," Abooksigun said in his understated manner.

"How has it been?" Immanuel asked.

"Teepee's warmth helps me sleep."

"They don't care?" Uzziah asked.

"Many visit, like."

There was something cooking on the fire in the middle, and Abooksigun spooned out portions into wooden bowls.

Uzziah took his offered bowl and smelled it.

"Rabbit stew," Abooksigun said.

They sat and ate in silence. Bowls were emptied, and Abooksigun filled them again.

"Knew you coming," he said, as he handed the second bowls to them.

"How?" Immanuel asked.

"Sean got a letter."

"From Ma?"

"Yes," Abooksigun said.

"He write back, right?"

"He wait," the Algonquin said, spooning more stew into his mouth.

"Why?" Uzziah wanted to know.

"You see him," was all Abooksigun would say.

After the supper, Immanuel and Uzziah found an adjutant and found out where Stonewall's men were camped. They heard the harmonica before they saw the O'Bannon family.

When they saw the fire, Hank was dishing up supper, and Sean, Uzziah's pa, was sitting back smoking. Obadiah was playing the harmonica, and for some reason, Short Samson was dancing to the Irish tune that Uzziah recognized. It was the anti-recruiting, anti-war ballad, *Arthur McBride*. The song wasn't exactly a jig, but Short Samson was putting some good moves on it. The dance, like the song, was a melancholy affair.

At one point, Hank put down the serving spoon and sang the ballad. When that happened, all of the O'Bannons joined in, even Uzziah. They hadn't seen the two mountain men till that moment, and Sean went to Uzziah as they sang and put his arm around his waist, as they glided up the scale in one particular point in the song.

When it was over, Uzziah spoke up.

"Was that in honor of the Irish that fell at the sunken wall at Fredericksburg?" Uzziah asked.

"Them, and others," Sean said. "Ya want some supper?" he asked, looking at both the men.

"No, Pa, Abooksigun fed us," Uzziah said.

"Good man," Sean said.

Uzziah noticed the others had gone to eating without the food being blessed, and that was a strange thing. He couldn't remember a time when Sean did not want his boys to bless their food and say their prayers at night. Sean took up a bowl that Hank had handed him and began to eat.

Uzziah and Immanuel pulled their pipes out, packed them, and lit up.

The night was warm, and the last of the sun's rays were leaking off to the west, and the stars, the stars with their magical ability to guide any man who knew them, began to appear against the backdrop of purple.

Uzziah looked at his pa, Sean, and his one thought was, the man had lost some weight. The other boys looked good, but then there were only four of them, Sean, Obadiah, Short Samson, and Hank. Counting Uzziah, there were seven brothers. John had died at Bull Run, and now, it seemed the company of brothers had been further compromised.

Sean pulled out his pipe, lit up, and stared at the two mountain men.

"Pa?" Uzziah said, and with that one word, Sean pulled a folded piece of paper from his wallet and held it out toward Uzziah.

"What's that?"

"Take it," Sean said.

Uzziah took it and unfolded it. It was a crude map. Evidently, Sean had drawn it, but things were labeled. At the bottom, it said, Fredericksburg, then there was the one word, Lee, above the left-hand section of the map, and Burnside on the right, and a wiggly line showing the Rappahannock River.

Then, down from where Jackson had been stationed, there were crude drawings of trees, and above it the words, Prospect Hill. There were two Xs beside one tree.

"That there tree is a huge weeping willow, huge. Off the western side of that tree, there's a treasure," Sean said, his voice choking up.

"Raymond, Zachariah?" Uzziah whispered, not believing what he was saying.

Sean nodded, and when Uzziah looked around the fire, all the other brothers were busy doing something else. Finally, Sean found his voice.

"We all saw what happened to deserters. You two pretty much come and go at will. So, afore we leave this area, appreciate it ifn ya could go get them two, and take 'em home."

"Pa, I..."

Sean held up his hand. He had talked and thought about those boys' deaths for the past four months, and he was at his wits' end with it. Uzziah looked around, and all the remaining brothers, Hank, Obadiah, and Short Samson, were looking at him with pitiful eyes.

The next day, May 1st, General Hooker advanced from Chancellorsville toward Lee at Fredericksburg. This was where Lee showed his superior generalship. He split his army, leaving a small force to fight Major General John Sedgwick, or at least keep him from advancing on Lee's flank. He then advanced on Hooker's army, his huge Army of the Potomac, and once again, Lee split his forces, sending General Thomas Jonathan Stonewall Jackson's entire corps flanking the entire Union XI Corps.

No one would have suspected that General Lee would divide his Army of Northern Virginia, not once, but twice. The flanking movement by Jackson was by pure stealth, and no one in the Union XI Corps had any idea that Jackson was coming up from behind. Not to mention the fact that most of the XI Corps was made up of German and Central European conscripts, and they had no battle record to speak of. In fact, General Hooker had planned on using the XIth as a mopping-up Corps that would come after the battle was over and clean things up. Imagine their surprise when, just as supper was being served, Jackson and his flanking movement descended upon them. It happened with such rapidity that General Hooker, himself, was caught unawares, barely escaping capture at the place where he'd set up his headquarters.

Uzziah and Immanuel had been with Jackson the entire way and marveled at the general's composure, especially when the rout began. No federal soldier knew what was happening. It was a great victory, which Jackson should have relaxed into, but Jackson always wanted more, more from himself and more from his men.

Against all advice from scouts, Jackson rode out on the Plank Road to reconnoiter the Union positions in the dark. Uzziah was supposed to be with General Jackson, but he got lost in the wilderness area, as it was known, and by the time he found Jackson, he was on his way back. Immanuel was coming from a different position, and when the firing broke out from the picket lines of the 18th North Carolina, Immanuel was coming up behind them. It was dark by then, and he pulled Stygian to a halt behind a large tree, and as he sat there, not sure who was firing and in which direction, he saw Preston Layman of Stonewall's brigade, the brother of

John Layman, who had been executed for desertion at the Pisgah Church.

Preston Layman ran directly past Immanuel, and he was wearing a smile that Immanuel thought, at the time, was unusual in the middle of a battle.

It was only moments later that Immanuel was joined by Uzziah, who was frantic.

"Jackson's been shot, the 18th North Carolina pickets thought he was a federal coming at them," Uzziah said as he and Immanuel rode back toward where most of Jackson's men had stopped after their rout of the XIth Corps.

Jackson was spirited off to a small white office building on the Chandler plantation at Guinea Station. His wife Anna and their baby daughter joined him after he became sick with pneumonia. He was being given laudanum and whiskey, which essentially made General Jackson fade in and out of consciousness. The self-assured man and leader of the Confederacy was no longer himself.

On the 3rd of May, the second deadliest battle of the Civil War occurred when Lee threw his Army of Northern Virginia into Hooker's positions at Chancellorsville. There were heavy losses on both sides. On the same day, General Sedgewick defeated the small Confederate force at Fredericksburg at Marye's Heights in what would be called the Second Battle of Fredericksburg.

Lee's victory at Chancellorsville was the greatest of all his military victories. Not only because he faced a much superior foe, in numbers, but also because General Lee had had the gumption to split his forces not once, but twice. The backside of that was Stonewall getting shot, but even with that, a great military victory. The little office opposite the Chandler plantation was not that far from Lee's headquarters, where Jackson lay dying. Lee had been asked if he wanted to see General Jackson, but his fear was that he would lose his composure and break down in front of the dying man, so he stayed away.

Of course, the hopes of all the south was that he would live to fight another day, but the inclement weather, continually raining, and Jackson's use of a water treatment on his side when he was in pain, a water treatment that his own doctor, Dr. McGuire, would have forbidden, if he hadn't been getting some necessary sleep, pushed the man toward pneumonia, and his breathing became much more labored.

A week later, Sunday, the 10th of May 1863, as General Thomas Jonathan Stonewall Jackson was dying, Immanuel and Uzziah rode onto the battlefield at Fredericksburg and down to the copse of trees at the base of Prospect Hill.

"This must be the tree," Uzziah said, as he pulled the wagon they had *borrowed* from an abandoned farmhouse, up and along the vast weeping willow which Sean O'Bannon had described to Uzziah. Both Stygian and Shadow did not care much for wagon duty, but they put up with it.

Taking the shovels from the back of the wagon, they

dug up Raymond and Zachariah O'Bannon. They wore their bandanas tied around their faces as both brothers had begun the process of returning to the earth. Inside the wagon, they had also procured two coffins from a mortuary in Fredericksburg, which had been shelled by the Federals. Uzziah had also taken a large amount of potpourri, which he scattered around the blanketed, wrapped bodies of his two brothers once they had been coffined. He had no desire to see their remains, knowing that Sean had made a battlefield identification of their dead bodies.

Making the main highway between Fredericksburg and the Shenandoah Valley, the two mountain men made their way north toward the O'Bannon farm. But first, they had a letter to deliver, if it were deliverable. They asked some soldiers along the road, and they were told that General Stuart and his cavalrymen were hanging around Lee's headquarters, and they headed there.

11

They saw General Lee around his command post, but traveled on to find General Stuart's men. His headquarters were not that far away, and, asking around about Sergeant Simmons, they found the man sitting outside his tent, enjoying some coffee. As the two rode up, Sergeant Stark Simmons jumped up and ran toward the wagon they were riding.

"But sir," he said to Immanuel, actually grabbing his shirt sleeve and tugging on it, "I thought you'd been kilt along with..." He didn't know exactly how to refer to John/Hanna O'Bannon, but looking into the back of the wagon, he said with a heart-wrenching voice, "Is this her body ya've come back with?!?"

"These are the bodies of two of Uzziah's brothers," Immanuel said, and Stark gave a sigh of relief. Uzziah and Immanuel could see the agony of not knowing fall from the sergeant's shoulders.

"So, she's alive!" he said without thinking, and both mountain men nodded their heads in agreement.

"This is fer you," Uzziah said, as he dug into his vest inside pocket and handed the letter across.

Sergeant Stark Simmons took the letter, recognizing the handwriting right away, he had always thought John O'Bannon's hand was more like that of a woman. He tucked the letter away.

"Oh, are ya goin' back that way?" Stark asked.

"Yes," Uzziah said, his head pointing back to the two caskets, "taking these boys back to their ma."

"I am sorry. We lost a lot, but they lost a whole lot more," Stark said.

"Any word on Jackson?" Uzziah asked.

"No one thinks he's gonna make it," Sergeant Simmons said, and Uzziah's head hung for just a moment.

"Stay here," the sergeant said as he ran off.

"Where's he goin'?" Immanuel asked.

"Got me."

Within five minutes, they saw the sergeant leading a horse, it was Mandy, Hanna's horse.

"I think she'll be wantin' this," Stark said as he tied Mandy to the back of the wagon.

"Very thoughtful of you," Uzziah said. "Ya know where we live, right?"

"Can't be that many O'Bannons in the Shenandoah Valley," Stark said, as he reached up and shook hands with both men.

They rattled down the road, the traces on Stygian and Shadow making the requisite noises which nearly always put Uzziah to sleep.

"There's something ya got to know," Immanuel said.

"Well, fess up, what is it?"

"Back at Chancellorsville, when the North

Carolina pickets opened up on Jackson's scouting party..."

"Yeah?"

"Well, right after the shots were fired, I was coming up behind the 18th, and y'all never guess who I saw," Immanuel said, hoping that Uzziah would believe him.

"Who, for God's sake, spit it out!"

"Preston Layman."

"Who's that?" Uzziah was confused.

"'Member the executions back in the summer?"

"A course," Uzziah said, racking his brain for what Immanuel was driving at.

"Well, John Layman was one of the executed, and his brother Preston was there, 'member?"

"Oh yeah, and none too pleased," Uzziah said, thinking about the executed man's brother, "And ya saw him where?"

"Runnin' from the back of the 18th's pickets."

"What the hell was he doin' there?"

"Well, that's what I have been wonderin' ever since," Immanuel said.

"And yer just now tellin' me this!?!"

"Well, it took a while fer it to fall together in my brain."

"Really! That man looked like he could shoot Jackson right after his brother's execution, and it's just now congealin' in yer brain?"

"It's kinda serious, even thinking somethin' like that," Immanuel said.

"Not to mention doin' it! Really, Immanuel, ya should have stopped the man right there and then! Why didn't ya!"

"He had this maniacal smile, and he was just a flash as he ran by."

"So, Stonewall was shot by Preston Layman?" Uzziah asked no one in particular.

"Preston wouldn't have had to actually shoot Stonewall, Uzziah, ya know. Just firing on the scouting party, and the 18th Carolina would have done the rest, right?"

"I can't think that way. I just can't! Stonewall was too good a man, and the thought of someone actually carrying a grudge and carrying out something like that, well, it's despicable."

"Yeah, but look what happened to us when there was a price on our heads. People we thought was friends, come after us, 'member?" Immanuel said.

"I'm gonna ride Mandy, don't think she likes it back there, the smell of my dead brothers and all," Uzziah said as he climbed back past the coffins, and got on Mandy and rode on ahead of the wagon. *Mandy did seem to like that,* thought Immanuel, *but he reckoned he knew better why Uzziah didn't want to ride the wagon, what with all the talk of Stonewall being murdered!*

Sergeant Stark Simmons looked for things to do. He polished his brass, his boots, curried his horse, even though there was a man hired by the cavalry to do just that. The letter in his pocket was burning a hole in him. More than anything, he wanted to hear news of the boy/young woman whom he had learned to love, and possibly had done other things with, which turned his head around, and he didn't even want to consider.

Still...he was glad she wasn't dead, he still hadn't washed the covering for her cot, and when he was overcome with sadness, he'd literally wallow in her bedclothes. He hated himself for that, but often people did things in private that they would not like to admit in public.

He was invited over for supper at another troop unit, and he accepted gladly. He hoped they would have some pop skull at the meal, and they did. He drank way too much, and talked too much, and he thought he saw some of them looking at him strangely, like you look at someone who's lost someone. He didn't bother to tell them either that John O'Bannon was still alive, and he certainly wasn't going to tell them that the young boy was really a young woman, and she'd pulled the wool over his eyes for all that time. What was he thinking? She'd pulled the wool over all their eyes, and in his cups, he was about to tell them all, but he fell down from too much drink, and one of his friends assisted him back to his tent.

"Which one is your'n?" the man asked Stark as he pushed back the flap and they were standing in Stark's tent.

"That un," Stark said, as he pointed to Hanna's bed.

The man dropped him onto the bunk, said his goodbyes, and was gone. The tent flap folded back, shutting out the firelights and giving the tent a smallish, cozy feel.

Stark rolled over on the pillow that *John* had used all the time he was there, and he inhaled deeply. Yes, he could still smell her, and the memories of what they might have done when he was wounded came rushing back in on him, but he fought it, rolled over, and stared instead at the firelights playing on the canvas.

He reached into his pocket and pulled out the letter. It was still sealed. Of course, it was, he hadn't opened it, he hadn't dared to open it. He tore it open, and later regretted not having the envelope in one piece so he could put it back in there for safekeeping. Then he read:

Dear Starkie: I know you don't like being called that, but that's how I think of you. I wish there was some way to explain to you just what happened. I wanted more than anything to avenge my youngest brother's death. I was afforded that opportunity by you, and for that, I shall always be grateful. As long as I live, one of my fondest memories will be you and I shooting into a group of Yankees, and seeing them fall off their horses! A sight for these vengeful eyes, believe me.

Now, about me being a woman. That certainly wasn't yer fault, and I wasn't about to let ya know that I was, even when it became obvious that we was becoming best friends. Ya taught me a whole bunch, and our time together meant more to me than you'll ever know, truly.

When we was tussling about and ya saw what ya saw, I shoulda stood my ground, and explained, but after so much lying, the truth seemed hard pressed to be talked about.

I did not run away, but was spirited away by my brother, Uzziah, and his pal, Immanuel. They feared for my life, and in so many ways, I am glad not to be a part of the killing anymore. I'm sure I will face other trials, but this being away from you is hard. I think of ya often, dream 'bout ya more often, but mostly hope and pray y'all fergive me fer being a liar, and lettin' ya believe me.

I pray the Lord God Almighty will protect and keep you, and pray so ever night. Forgive me, if ya can, forget me, if ya will.

Hanna O'Bannon

Without thinking, he kissed her signature, then folded the letter back up on itself, and tried to stuff it back into the torn envelope. He cursed himself for ripping into the letter like he did, and before much else happened, he was asleep.

In the morning, his head throbbed from the pop

skull, and then he remembered the letter. Frantically, he searched for it in his tent. The wind was flapping the sides of the tent like crazy, and he rushed outside looking for the letter, which, to anyone else, would simply be trash.

Across the way, two cavalrymen were looking at something written on a piece of paper and laughing. He ran over there, and tearing the paper from their hands, discovered he was holding a new limerick which one of the camp bawdies had written.

The two soldiers looked at him like he was crazy, as he handed the limerick back to them. Walking back to his tent, he saw the letter blowing toward his now smoldering fire and grabbed it just before it had made the hot coals. He looked at it. It was her letter. He went back into his tent and put the letter safely in his Bible, which his mama had made him carry to war. It would be safe there.

12

They made up their minds on their way back to the O'Bannon farm. They would bury Uzziah's two other brothers and then go back to the Rockies. Immanuel had had enough of the war for some time now, but with this rumor that Stonewall might have been killed with purpose by his own troops, and any wind that Uzziah had in his sails to maintain his presence in that war, disappeared.

As they rode the dirt road to the farm, no one came running out. No one came to greet them. It seemed, all of a sudden, as if the farm had been deserted. They pulled the wagon into the barn, where Uzziah was sure that his ma, Rahab, would want to actually see their decomposing bodies and make them more presentable to her daughters, their sisters.

Immanuel was taking the harnesses off Stygian and Shadow as Uzziah walked to the darkened house. It was a sunny day, and in the valley, to keep a house cool, you had to keep the drapes shut. As he walked in, there was no one in the kitchen or parlor. Strange that. Then he went upstairs, and all the bedrooms were darkened, but the door to the balcony off Rahab and Sean's room was open, and a triangle of light was spilling into the neatly kept bedroom, the bed always made, and Uzziah could see his ma's feet setting up on a settee. She was asleep.

He gently opened the balcony door and slipped into the chair across from her. The summer wind was playing with the trees out by the creek, and he watched as they turned their silver bottom sides up in the wind. His ma had always told him that that meant there would be a storm, and looking off toward the western mountains, he could see the cumulus clouds billowing up, trying to make a thunderclapper.

He wanted to wake her, but more than that, he wanted to nap there with her, nap as if there was nothing at all wrong in the world, nap as if he was a boy again, and this sacred moment of napping could be indulged in, and they would wake finding the world had set itself right again.

He guessed he was more tired than he imagined, because when he awakened, she was sitting there with a cup of tea in her hand and smiling at him. She sipped the tea, and he sat up in the comfortable chair and started to speak.

"I know," was all she said as she sat there sipping her tea.

"How?"

"Immanuel was in the kitchen looking for something to eat. He told me."

"I'm sorry."

"It weren't yer fault, son."

"Sorry, I didn't wake ya and tell ya."

"Don't ya worry, sometimes, it's best to hear from

unconcerned parties, not that Immanuel don't care, but he didn't grow up chere and all," she said, finishing off the tea.

"What ya want me to do?"

"You and Immanuel can dig the graves a course. The girls are in town and will be back later. Ya can help me clean them up and get 'em dressed properly for the Second Coming."

"They been dead some time, Ma," Uzziah said.

"Saw 'em, boy, the odor, but we can do it. Ya will help, yes?"

"A course," Uzziah said.

They did just that. Immanuel dug both graves, and when the girls, Hanna, Sally, Sarah, and Faith made it back, all they had to see was the graves, and they knew someone had died. Not seeing Uzziah, they thought it was him, and the wailing that went on, till Immanuel tried to explain. They came running into the barn and hugged Uzziah like he'd just come back from the dead. He sure smelled like it!

The smell drove them out of the barn, and so did Rahab.

That night, supper was a somber ordeal, but Uzziah marveled at how his ma, Rahab O'Bannon, kept her eye on the living and moved like that was all that mattered. Sure, she didn't love or even like the fact that her sons, three of them, were about to be in the ground, but she thanked God that night when she blessed the meal that her husband and four other sons were still alive and fighting the northern aggressors.

After supper, Uzziah read from the Good Book, and prayers were said around the parlor, even Immanuel joining in.

The next day, they put the two boys, Raymond and Zackeriah, into the ground with a good service. They didn't invite the neighbors, they had their own crosses to bear, literally.

Later that night, everyone in the house was awakened to the sounds of Hanna screaming. She went into labor and gave birth to a healthy baby boy, who had red hair like Hanna, but a nose, she swore, that was the spitting image of his father, whom only Uzziah and Immanuel had met. They agreed, but truthfully, they were men and saw little to no resemblance between that new life and a grown man.

After the excitement, and Uzziah was back in bed, he thought about the cycle of life which had been admirably displayed by two going into the ground, and a third coming from the womb. He thanked God, the Father, that things were as they were. If we didn't end up killing everyone, the world would inevitably go on, and that was a fact.

A week later, Uzziah and Immanuel left for the Rockies. Everyone seemed to understand. Their place had been in those mountains all along, and this war was winding down, or so it was said.

As they rode down the road, they waved and yelled until they were almost on the main road, and then settled into going west, away from the battles, away from the killing, and toward their life elsewhere.

TWO YEARS LATER

Rahab received many letters from Uzziah explaining their return to the mountains and the trials and tribulations they had on their way. Sometimes, when you want to leave a war, the war may not be willing to let you leave.

The two armies' Generals, Grant and Lee, met at Appomattox, Virginia, and they signed a treaty which ended the War Between the States, which had 618,222 men laid in their graves, and Rahab and Sean were glad that only three had fallen from their family.

Obadiah started a mercantile store not far from their entrance off the main road. He sold vegetables and meats from the farm, and took in all sorts of arts and crafts that were made by the locals. The Shenandoah was touched little by reconstruction. The people who ran the reconstruction government were pretty much the same who had run the government during the Civil War. Andrew Johnson was a Southerner from Tennessee, supported leniency because he knew the political realities of needing the south if he were to be reelected President.

Short Samson ran off to Richmond and was reported to have become a gambler, while Hank married a girl he'd been sweet on before the war, and they built another smaller house back in the hills behind the main house.

The bond between Rahab and Sean grew stronger after the war. Sometimes, children's deaths did that, and sometimes, they didn't.

The baby, named John, they called him Johnny, after her dearly departed youngest brother, grew healthy and strong, and one afternoon, when Hanna was hanging up laundry in the side yard, and little two-year-old John was playing nearby, a stranger rode up the road.

Hanna thought she recognized the way the man sat his horse, and as she continued to put clothespins on damp sheets, he left the horse ground-tied and walked toward where she was partially hidden by the still-wet sheet.

When she looked up, she saw the man she had fallen in love with when she was thought to be a boy, then, looking down and blushing, waited for him to speak.

"Hanna?" he said tentatively.

She looked up, but did not speak. Perhaps the length of her hair had thrown him off. Certainly, she was only a few years older, and her face had maybe matured.

"You lookin' fer Hanna?" she asked, and you could see his body change as he recognized her voice.

"Yes, ma'am, would she be about?" he asked politely.

Just then, a little toddler ran between the sheets, screaming with joy. He stopped at her leg and pulled the wet sheet to one side. His red hair sparkled in the sunlight.

"Mama, who dat?" he asked Hanna.

The man looked at the boy and knew, for the first time, who both he and the boy were.

UNHINGED

1

They traveled mostly by night, like they would if they were in the desert. They were. They were in the desert of human kindness, the desert of men feeling brotherly for each other, the desert of bullets which knew no bounds, horrors that escaped men's demented minds and found their way onto the plains of their existence.

It was almost dawn, they would be camping soon, and he could see Immanuel looking for a spot along the river where they could get back under an escarpment, and the smoke from the breakfast Uzziah would make would disappear into the ledge and the trees surrounding the river.

In some very real ways, he felt as if he had deserted his pa and his remaining brothers, but Rahab had gone out of her way to help him get over that, through that, beyond that. And he had felt good for about the first day, but the further he got from the cannon smoke and the firing of the muskets, the more he felt like he had run from a fight.

So, he had taken to praying at night, speaking the words. The first few times he did it, Immanuel looked around like, *what the hell are you saying*?

"Just talkin' with Father," Uzziah whispered a bit louder.

"Well, mention me, ifn yer inclined to," Immanuel had said.

Of course, Immanuel was always in his partner's prayers. He, Uzziah, felt a bit bad about the way he prayed. He sort of—well, to tell the truth—he always repeated about the same thing every time he prayed. He had this order that he went in, and it helped him to remember what came next. He prayed for his family, and naturally, Immanuel was the first one on that list, then he went to the Shenandoah Valley, and the families there, then to those he met by accident or otherwise who had stayed with him.

He always prayed for Porter Rockwell and wondered how it was going in Salt Lake City. Porter was the Deputy Marshal there, and Uzziah found himself thinking that maybe the two of them could go that way, and stop in and see him, and Hannah's parents, the Larues. He prayed for them, too, and the younger daughter, who had just about assumed he would take her for a bride. Sometimes, when he lay awake and couldn't fall right off to sleep, he wondered what it would have been like if he had taken the youngster into his bedroll and just continued on. How many kids would they have by now? How high in the church would he have risen? Then he thought about Immanuel, and those houses of cards came tumbling down!

What in the world was he thinking like that for!?!

He would remind himself of the hunt, and the chase, and the men he had put beneath the grass, as they had tried to put him there. He would not have changed any of that for anything.

This war business was like trying to cram into a few years a lifetime of killing. Killing that couldn't be avoided. Not men lining up in straight lines and walking toward each other, with the opponent's artillery throwing grapeshot and ball into your midst, just to see whose head they could lob off!?!

"This is good," he heard Immanuel say, not really a whisper, not really in everyday talk.

Uzziah looked, and sure enough, there was the escarpment, and the stream flowing easily to the next place where water gathered.

They pulled their horses in and tied them just down from their camp, along the stream, where they could chomp grass and get fat. Well, this trip across country was going to take that fat off real fast.

"What ya want fer breakfast?" Uzziah asked.

Immanuel just looked at him and laid down on his bedroll.

"Well?"

"We are not married, need I remind ya?"

"It's polite to ask."

"Just make it. I always eat it, don't I?"

Uzziah really did want to please too much. He knew that about himself. It wasn't one of his better qualities. He wanted to make Immanuel what he liked, and hell, he knew what his partner of all these years wanted. He wanted crisp bacon, boiling beans, cornbread, or johnnycakes, and plenty of coffee. He'd start with the coffee.

By the time they'd finished what Uzziah had made, Immanuel was down at the stream, scrubbing the tin plates with sandy river bottom. It was then that they came out of the east, and they weren't interested in being welcomed at a homely fire. Their horses were lathered up as they came riding down the stream. Stygian and Shadow disappeared, which was the smartest thing they could have done if there hadn't been others up on the top of the escarpment who grabbed them easily.

The first shots threw the water up in front of Immanuel. The man just didn't go and do anything without his Hawken. He rolled to one side, picking up the weapon in one easy grasp and firing through two of them, who were almost on top of him. Their blood and guts flew back out of them, and Uzziah had already taken another close one with his Hawken, and then it was just a matter of who had a Walker Colt, and who didn't. They did, both of them.

By the time the horses ran up the rise to avoid the running horses and the firing guns, Stygian and Shadow were being escorted out of there by two hombres. All these men had on tattered Confederate uniforms of butternut or gray. Deserters, deerlicks, malcontents who were meeting the fate they deserved.

As fate would have it, they had tied Shadow to Stygian, and one whistle from Immanuel brought Stygian to a halt, which pulled the horseman from his saddle, and the other one just kept riding.

Immanuel had already reloaded his Hawken, and he laid up on a big flat boulder and took his time sighting the man in as he rode into the sun. That sort of thing never bothered Immanuel, enhanced his shooting, he'd say. Outlined the man, so to speak.

The shot rang out, and a good three to five seconds later, the man disappeared off the horse, which just kept right on running.

"Yes!" Uzziah said, pumping his right arm and looking at the man who had made the shot.

Immanuel just rolled to his side and smiled that goddamn smile of his, which basically said whatever you were thinking.

The boys gathered up their horses, and when they got back to the camp, one of the men was trying to crawl back from where he'd come from. Immanuel just checked his Walker and nonchalantly fired into the back of the man's head, blowing his Confederate officer's hat off him, and the process ending his life.

"Damn!" Immanuel said.

"What?"

"Jackson was right, every one of them deserting sons a bitches deserve to die! Everyone of 'em!"

Uzziah smiled to himself. It wasn't often that he was proved right in such a dramatic way, but there it was.

They had to move their camp, which was a pain. Packing back up, and riding during the sunrise, and being watched by God knew whom.

"Let's just go all day and night, then stop. We'll rest the horses plenty, and water 'em often, what say?" Immanuel asked.

"Best idea I heard," Uzziah said, knowing that if these six had come along, they probably belonged to a much bigger crowd who would be looking for them to return, and when they didn't, they would go looking for them. Traveling away from the place was the only idea worth considering.

———

When they finally did stop, both horses, after having their saddles removed, rolled in the sand next to the river. Immanuel was good at finding water. Uzziah cooked a deer that had been out early for their convenience, and both men enjoyed the venison steaks. Uzziah found some wild onions and stole a couple ears of corn from a field early that morning, actually four ears. They roasted those in the fire, and the deer meat and that popped corn with the wild onions were great.

They slept all day and part of the evening before they rubbed down their mounts with wheatgrass and saddled up. Both the blacks were ready for something, that was for sure.

"Maybe we should run 'em a bit," Uzziah offered after the horses had warmed up.

"Let's go!"

They raced down a back road, and the only sounds in the night were the sounds of their thundering hooves and the breathing of the horses. Yes, they wanted to run, and run they did. Finally, the men had to pull them back, and they laughed like two boys who had stolen their pa's horses and taken them for a joy ride.

"I was thinkin'," Uzziah said, as their horses walked along. They were getting their breath back.

"Uh-oh!" Immanuel said.

"Ya always say that."

"Because when ya say ya been thinkin' it's usually some harebrained idea. What is it this time?"

"Let's go through the Salt Lake, whatcha say?"

"Ya wanna see yer bulletproof friend, huh?"

"Yeah, yeah, I do," Uzziah admitted.

"Well, okay, that's what we'll do," Immanuel said, smiling.

"Really?"

"Ya act like I never wanna do nothin' ya wanna do?"

"Well?"

"Okay, let's just say, after all we just been through, maybe a good dose of Mormons would do us some good!" Immanuel said, laughing and barely able to actually get the words out.

Uzziah joined in, they had a good laugh. Yeah, a good dose of Mormons was just the thing to balance three years of bloodshed.

By the time they got to Tennessee, they could hear off in the distance some fighting, some big fighting. There were clouds floating close to the earth some miles away, down in a valley, and both of them knew that they weren't clouds but smoke from all the cannons. They could see the men, and they looked like ants from their perspective, and they saw the lines advancing and the cannons blowing their death, and they just sat there for the longest time and watched.

"Like we needed reminding, huh?" Immanuel finally said.

They turned their backs on what would have been quite a spectacle for ordinary folks and rode away, glad that the sounds of the battle receded as they rode.

Off in the coming distance, there was a bunch of buildings, and a lot of barrels stacked all around. Armed men carrying rifles and wearing bibbed overalls, like they were farmers, walked from the bushes along the side of the road.

"The battles that way," Immanuel joked, and neither of the two who looked like they might weigh in at 275 a piece cracked a smile.

"I don't think they care," Uzziah said to his partner.

"Guess not."

"Ya can't come through chere," the smartest one said. They figured he was either the smartest or the only one who could actually speak.

"What ifn we wanna buy whiskey?" Immanuel said.

Whiskey, what gave the man the idea that there was whiskey around? Then, it hit Uzziah, and all the barrels made sense.

"Ya got money?" the smart one asked.

"No, we're gonna sing and dance fer a jug," Immanuel said, always ready with a quip.

"Ya dance good?" the one they thought was smart asked.

At that point, Immanuel pulled out his pouch in which he had, evidently, during the skirmishes and fights of the past three years, gathered quite a bit of loose Yankee coin. Independent of anyone seeing him, of course.

Uzziah just looked at Immanuel, who shrugged.

The rifles, actually, there was *a* rifle, the smart one carried that, and the one who hadn't spoken carried a scatter gun, a Greener, Uzziah thought. Guess he spoke with that.

They rode in front of the two, who they imagined kept their guns trained on them in case they what? Who knew?

They were taken to a house, a little log cabin, where there were more than a couple of children running around outside. When they went inside, a man was sitting, eating a bowl of stew.

"Mr. Daniel, we caught these fellers on the road, didn't figure they was Yankees, but it's gettin' so ya can't tell," the smart one said.

"Hell, Williams, them is sure 'nuff mountain men," Daniel said, then added, "Get back on the road and keep watchin'," Daniel said, in a thick Scots-Irish accent.

The two men left, and Daniel looked at the boys.

"Ya hungry?"

They looked at each other.

"Pull some chairs up. Matilda, two more bowls, please."

As the boys sat down and leaned their Hawkens against the table, Daniel whispered.

"Do ya mind, the wife don't like the firearms at the table," and then he winked.

Uzziah got up and took both Hawkens to where another rifle hung over the fireplace.

"Thank ye," Matilda said, as she brought the stew to the table.

"Now, I'm Job Daniel and that there is me wife, Matilda," he said, reaching across the table and shaking their hands.

"I'm Uzziah O'Bannon, and this chere's my partner, Immanuel James Jones."

"An Irishman and an Englishman as partners, you two must have had some fights in yer time!" Job said.

"We have, sir," Immanuel offered.

"Now, why would this be Irish stew, huh, O'Bannon?" Job asked.

"It's got mutton in it, not beef," Uzziah said, spooning a goodly portion into his mouth.

"Have ya had much trouble with the Federals?" Immanuel asked.

"Well, when they occupy this area, which I sincerely hope they never do, I've heard stories, so I'm takin' precautions," Job said.

"What kinda stories?" Uzziah asked as he spooned in more of the delicious mutton stew.

"As early as last year, a new Union General by the name of Grant moved against two different forts with their naval forces. He took Fort Henry on the Tennessee River, which is south of us, and Fort Donelson on the Cumberland River, which is way north. They've mainly been interested in the big cities, Nashville, Middle Tennessee, Memphis. Even though they've taken most of them, and basically driven the Confederate government from the state, they're playing footsie with us, mostly."

"I don't understand?" Immanuel said.

"Well, they wanna win our hearts and minds, and not bludgeon us to death," Job Daniel said.

"Well, what's the best way to travel to avoid the kid glove Yankees? We just left General Jackson's brigade, we'd been scouts with him since Manassas," Uzziah said.

"It's awful him gettin' kilt by his own men," Job said.

Uzziah and Immanuel just looked at each other, they didn't want to open that can of worms.

"Yes, sir, it's why we's gonna go back to the Rockies, that's our home," Immanuel said.

"Can ya tell us how best to avoid them Federals as we make our way west?" Uzziah asked again and was certainly hoping to find out.

"No, but one of my oldest, well, he's only fifteen, but he can lead ya, ifn y'all pay him," Job offered.

"How much?" Immanuel asked.

"A few dollars oughta do it," Job said, then added, "Matilda, where's Jack this time a day?"

"Ya know he's working at Preacher Call's grocery store."

"That's right, if the boy is anything, he's outrageously productive," Job said.

One of his children ran into the house to grab something and Job corralled him.

"John, saddle me the mare," Job said, and the boy ran back outside. "I'll take ya to Call's, it ain't that far."

They finished another bowl of stew, and then the boys went outside where they had tied their horses, and Job's mare, Belle, was standing, all saddled, waiting for him. The three men mounted up, and both Uzziah and Immanuel noted that Job pushed a rifle into the boot on his saddle before they took off.

The road was wet from the dew and rain, but the scenery was magnificent. The rolling verdant hills, and down from them, little rivulets which ran away, making wonderful musical sounds. They rode without talking until they turned a bend in the road and Job stopped Belle.

"That's it. The store. Call will know where Jack is," Job said, and shook hands with both the mountain men, "Safe journeys, ya hear!" he said playfully, and turned and rode back a bit faster toward his home.

Uzziah dismounted at the store and went inside. They both thought it was best to keep watch on their two good-looking horses in the middle of horse country.

Uzziah came out in a minute, and mounting back up, said, "The boy's down at the barn, working. We can go see him there."

The barn wasn't that far from the store, but it was back in the trees, and sort of out of sight.

They walked in and were, to say the least, surprised. There was a huge distillery in the barn. In fact, the entire bottom floor of the barn was nothing but tubes, vats, and other distilling machinery.

A negro, not that old, was showing the boy, whom they imagined was Jack Daniel something, and for a minute or two, neither of them even knew that the two mountain men were watching.

Finally, it was the negro who turned and saw them.

"Can we helps ya, gentlemens?" he asked in a very convivial way.

"We're looking for Jack Daniel," Uzziah said.

"That'd be me," the young boy said, as he walked over and extended his hand, "And who might you interestin' men be?"

"I'm Immanuel James Jones, and this is my partner, Uzziah Ferguson O'Bannon."

"Well, well," said Jack Daniel, "this chere is Nathan Nearest Green, and I am, as you surmised, Jasper Newton *Jack* Daniel. How may I be of service?"

Nathan Nearest Green had nodded when he was

introduced and extended his hand for the mountain men to shake. This was not a common habit of slaves, and both the boys thought that the man must be more than chattel, perhaps even the man who ran the distillery for Call.

"How come a preacher runs a distillery?" Uzziah asked.

"Now, I can answers that," Nearest said, "Ya sees every man gots two sides to him. Yes, sir, there's the devil's side and then the angel's. Now, each of these are interested in different things. The angel side likes church and Sunday dinner with the church folk. The devil likes spirits. So, as ya can see, Preacher Call services the whole man, not just part of 'em."

Immanuel and Uzziah liked that explanation. It fit the way they looked at things, the two of them, in fact, almost being the embodiment of either side, from time to time.

"Yer pa said ya'd help us navigate Tennessee and not run into Yankees," Immanuel just put it out there.

"He did, did he? Well, I ain't just a boy, though I am a boy. I work, ya see, and to leave my work would cost me. Which means ultimately, it will cost ya," Jack said.

Immanuel dug into his pouch and put some gold in Jack's hand.

"And what 'bout Nearest, he's gonna hafta do all the work hisself when I'm gone?"

Immanuel looked at Uzziah. Leave it to a boy to hornswoggle both of them.

"Nearest, how much ya want?" Immanuel asked.

"Ya's don't have to pays me, sir, really."

"Nearest!" Jack nearly shouted.

"Sorry, like ya gave the boy, maybe less," Nearest said.

"The same," Jack said.

When they left the distillery, Jack was riding his own horse. Was it unusual for a boy of fifteen to have his own horse in Tennessee? They didn't know, but he sure had one. Jack took a bit to pack up some things and put them in saddlebags. Then, they were on the road that would get them out of Tennessee, and hopefully, out without seeing more Federals.

They did go some circuitous routes. The boy seemed to know every game trail and backway to anywhere. Several times, they saw Federal patrols, but they were so far away, and there were so many ravines between them and the Federals that even if they had been spotted, it would have been impossible for the Federals to catch them.

That night, as Uzziah made supper, Jack got a bottle of sour mash from his saddle bag. It was in a porcelain jug with a cork, and the boy simply passed it to Immanuel and didn't say a thing.

"What's this?" Immanuel asked.

"What do ya think we was doin' back there in that there barn? Making sarsaparilla?"

Immanuel pulled the cork, it made a nice popping sound, and he raised the jug, as had been done since jugs were invented, by putting his index finger through the loop, balancing it on his shoulder, and letting the amber liquid slide down his throat. When he pulled it away from his mouth, he made a face which could only have meant—more!

"Son, whose recipe is this?"

"Mine, well, me and Nearest's," the boy said.

"Uzziah ya gotta try this hooch," Immanuel said, and handed Uzziah the jug.

Uzziah mimicked Immanuel's actions and, bringing it down from his mouth, he smiled.

"Smoothest whiskey I ever tasted," Uzziah said, then added, "Pour us some to sip with supper, will ya?"

Jack took the three tin cups that were sitting out for coffee, and gave three fingers in each. They sat there in the twilight of the Tennessee night, and ate beans, bacon, and biscuits while sipping Jack Daniel's whiskey.

The next morning, Jack took them to the Arkansas/Tennessee border, and the boy told them to just go north and they'd hit St. Louis. Riding their horses all the way to Salt Lake wasn't the easiest thing to do, so they thought they'd try the Missouri River route as far as Omaha.

This was accomplished by a three-day ride up to St. Louis. They stayed off the main roads as they had been doing since leaving Virginia, and when they sat their horses across from St. Louis, they wondered what had changed since the last time they had been there. Was the Growling Catfish still a working bar? Did Charlie Watts still own the place, and how would the old man look now?

Remembering the last time they'd passed through

and the riot they'd almost been a part of, they took a different route to the wharf. Coming around the city, they passed down through the trees to the old Saint Marcus Cemetery. They both knew where it was, and they went there, like metal to a magnet.

They didn't speak, either of them. Charlie had said he would put up a marker for her, and by God, there it was. Both men were taken aback by how he put her name on the gravestone. It read, *Sarah Jones O'Bannon.* As if she had been married to both the men, which, in essence, she had been.

They dismounted and, leaving their blacks ground tied, they wandered over to the gravesite. The horses were happy to chomp grass and wild onions as Uzziah sat down, pulled out his pipe, and began loading it. Immanuel followed suit. They sat, and Immanuel handed the lucifers to his partner, once he'd gotten his bowl going, and the smoke drifted lazily off into the pines and oaks.

Immanuel made a grunting sound, and going to Stygian, he took something from his saddlebags. Uzziah wasn't looking, he just knew the sound that the buckles and straps made when Immanuel got into his horse bags. He came back and had the little jug that Jack Daniel had let them taste the liquor from.

"What the..." Uzziah started to say.

"Hey, we paid that boy and that Nearest negro good for him to guide us safely through Tennessee, and we fed him along the way," Immanuel said, taking the cork from the jug and tilting it into his mouth. He took a sip and then handed it to his partner.

"But when?"

"That morning before we parted, I figured he

wouldn't be pulling that jug out again, so I placed a stone about the same size and weight in his saddlebags," Immanuel admitted, taking another sip.

Uzziah just shook his head. He thought that after all these years, there wasn't anything that his partner, Immanuel, could do that would surprise him. He should have known better. The man had a habit of just doing the damnedest things. The boy, Jack, had been kind, and they really hadn't paid him that much, and sure, the negro, Nearest, he got paid too, but it was worth getting through Tennessee without running into Federals.

He looked over, and Immanuel was staring at the headstone. Maybe he was ciphering the birth date from the death one, Uzziah wasn't sure.

She sure wasn't that old when Undersheriff Hicken tore her from stem to stern. What they had done to the man was awful, but every time he thought back on it, he knew. If it had happened all over again, he would gladly kill that man in the same torturous manner. Some men just deserve what they get, and that was that.

Uzziah wasn't sure how long they had sat there, but the sun had moved a bit when Immanuel gathered up the two horses and came walking back.

"Partner," Immanuel said, and Uzziah realized it was in the sharing of the love from that woman, he couldn't even mentally say her name, but it was in the sharing of that love that their partnership had been sealed. Then, of course, there was the dessert when they gutted and skinned the man who had done it, that, too, bonded them. But really. It was the love that that woman shared that had sealed their deal, it really was.

They rode the same route that the funeral procession had taken that day from the Growling Catfish to the cemetery, and when the old wharf bar came into view, they really weren't surprised when Charlie Watts was standing looking out on the Missouri, smoking.

They rode up behind him, and sat their horses, and slowly Charlie became aware that someone, or someones, were behind him, and he turned, not sure what to make of it.

"Immanuel! Uzziah!" he screamed so loud that some of the whores who worked for him came running out.

They were given the royal welcome. Charlie had aged, of course, and he said the war had been hard on everyone. But the profits, my God! The Federals did have money, and they were willing to spend it, and they got paid regular-like, not like the poor Rebels who were fighting a war on a shoestring!

Uzziah and Immanuel listened as Charlie told his stories of war profiteering, and truthfully, they were glad for the man. If anyone deserved to make a buck over this damned war, it was Charlie Watts.

They had dinner at the Growling Catfish, and two whores, young ones, at that, were given to them for the night.

As they walked back to the back, they saw that Charlie had reinvested his profits. The rooms were really separated now, and they looked like regular hotel rooms with all the accoutrements.

Uzziah had been given a black girl, and he wasn't sure what to make of that, but she was smart and funny, and her way of doing it was just as good, or better, than he'd had it done before. She was indefatigable and wore the old Virginian out.

Immanuel had some Chinese girl who liked to laugh, and all night, it seemed that's all she did. Uzziah wondered if the man ever got his willy wet, or did they just laugh all the time.

The next morning, both mountain men seemed satiated, and they ate breakfast there at the bar, it was actually rather good. Eggs Benedict, which neither had ever had, and the yellow sauce that went over the eggs and the fried potatoes on the side. Charlie Watts may be getting older, but his fare at the Growling Catfish had certainly improved!

They caught the afternoon steamer for Omaha, Charlie saying that was the one with fewer Federal Troops on it, and it did seem mostly to be just regular folks going about their business. Oh, there was the usual gamblers and whores, but they had enough to get a room and be comfortable. They ate supper in the salon and had cold beer with fried Catfish and grits. It was good.

Immanuel amused himself with a game of cards, and Uzziah, loving the way the moon looked on the Missouri, sat out on the deck, and thought about the night that Kate Warne, the Pinkerton woman, had lured him into her trap. He had to smile, thinking of how vulnerable he really had been back then.

"Have ya been this way before?" a voice, a female voice, came from the other side of the doorway where the light spilled.

Uzziah thought for sure, she must be talking to someone sitting beside her, so he just looked away.

"Well, you're not friendly, are you?" she asked.

"I'm sorry, were ya talkin' to me?"

"There's no one else out here," she said.

"It's the light from the salon, can't see nothing on the other side of it," Uzziah said, as he got up with his coffee and walked past the light, and there she was.

"My name's Marianne," she said as she seemed to curtsey with her voice.

"Uzziah O'Bannon, at yer service."

She couldn't have been more than twenty years old, if she were a day and beautiful, my, my! Even that old Virginian knew when he saw a brunette that was as pretty as any roan horse he'd ever seen. She was sitting there with a wrap around her, the night air could get cool on the river, and quite frankly, he couldn't believe that she had started up a conversation with an older mountain man like himself.

"Are ya travelin' alone?" Uzziah asked her.

"Heavens no, what young lady would do that, except, well, surely, you didn't think..."

"No, no, no, didn't think that," Uzziah found himself almost embarrassed.

"My grandfather is with me, and he's tired from all the traveling."

"I see," Uzziah said.

"No, you don't. You don't see at all."

"Well, okay, tell me, then," Uzziah said, quite frankly.

"My grandfather and I recently had a conversion to the Latter-day Saints," she said, looking at him as if she knew he didn't know what she was talking about.

"Really?"

"You don't know what that is, do you?"

"Well, let me just say this, I met Joseph Smith and was married to a Mormon woman," Uzziah said.

"You're funning me, aren't you?" she said, and thought seriously about getting up and walking away.

"No, no, I'm not, actually. My partner, that's him in there at the furthest gambling table," Uzziah said, pointing over his shoulder.

She craned her neck and looked into the salon.

"The one that's dressed like you're twins?" she said, and tried not to giggle.

"Yeah, that's Immanuel, my partner," Uzziah said, then added, "I wasn't joking about Joseph Smith, and I know Brigham Young, too."

She looked at him and cocked her head, not sure what to make of this deerskin-clad pioneer who was professing such things.

"I think it's time I went to our suites and check on grandfather," she said, and he stood up when she did.

"Maybe we'll see each other some other time," Uzziah said.

"Perhaps," was all she said as she left him standing there.

2

When the sun was rising up on the Missouri, Immanuel and Uzziah were in the salon, waiting for the breakfast to be ready. Uzziah looked across the room, and who should he see but the young lady from the night before. She was on the arm of an elderly man, most likely her grandfather. His hair was like spun silk, and it was as white as the driven snow. His posture was good, but the way she held his arm, it looked more like she was supporting him, not the other way around.

"That's the young girl I was tellin' ya 'bout," Uzziah said, tapping Immanuel on the arm.

"And I thought ya were exaggerating," Immanuel said, as he stood, realizing that the young woman was just as beautiful as Uzziah said she was.

Uzziah stood and raised his hand to them across the room. She saw him and said something to her grandfather, and they proceeded toward the other side of the salon.

"Are you the liar my granddaughter met last night?" the cantankerous old man challenged Immanuel.

"No, sir, that was my partner here, Uzziah," Immanuel said, smiling.

"May we sit and have breakfast with you?" Marianne asked.

"Sure," Uzziah said, and both he and Immanuel waited for her to make sure her grandfather was seated, then Immanuel held the chair for her as she sat.

"Such manners in rough men, it's unaccountable," the old man said.

"Well, have ya ever had lobster?" Immanuel asked Marianne's grandfather.

"I have, it's delicious," he said.

"Well, we're like the lobster, sir. Rough exteriors and all sweetness and light inside," Immanuel joked.

The old man laughed, then said, "So, now we know both of you are liars," and he laughed even harder.

Immanuel and Uzziah looked at each other, then Immanuel spoke. "Yer from back east, that's easy to see, and a Northerner to boot. Am I right?"

"Philadelphia, the city of brotherly love," the old man said.

"Well, Philadelphia, let me tell ya somethin'," Immanuel said, "this is the west, and you have called my partner and I both liars. There are men, no matter your age or infirmities, who would be most happy to end yer life, simply for that insult. I suggest ya pull it back a bit, now that ya crossed the Mississippi."

It was then that the waiter walked up and handed out the breakfast menus.

"Coffee?" he asked everyone.

Everyone nodded that coffee was in order. They all took their menus, but the old man was gazing over his at Immanuel. He put his down and pushed his arm across the table.

"Erasmus Timothy Wells," he said. "Please call me, Tim. This is my granddaughter, Marianne Shirley Wells. I believe the other ruffian met her last night," he said as he and Immanuel shook hands.

"Uzziah," he said, as he extended his hand to Tim and they shook.

"Well, you've survived the first barrage. I do hope I wasn't too rough on both of you?"

"We've experienced worse," Uzziah said.

The waiter came back with the coffees, and everyone ordered their breakfasts. Most of the eating was done in silence, except when someone needed salt or pepper, or the biscuits had to be passed. When the plates were cleared away, they sat back and were enjoying their coffees.

"If you smoke, Marianne doesn't mind, do you, dear?"

"No, please," she said.

Before Uzziah or Immanuel could get their pipes going, the old man, Tim, had his going and was blowing smoke across the table.

"So, Uzziah, Marianne told me some things I'm not inclined to believe," he said.

"And what are you inclined to believe?" Uzziah came back.

"Fair enough," Tim said, then added, "What was Joseph Smith like?"

"He was like any other man," Uzziah said.

"Balderdash, the man received a revelation from

God, if the Book of Mormon is to be believed," Tim argued.

"Well, Jesus Christ was like any other man, and he was the Son of God," Uzziah came back.

"Did you meet him once in passing?" the old man asked.

"Jesus, no, he's been my constant companion since I was a boy," Uzziah said.

Erasmus Timothy Wells had himself a good laugh, too good. Marianne had to slap him on the back when he started coughing.

"You're funnier than you look, which, to this old man, is pretty funny. No, of course, I meant Joseph Smith when I said meeting him in passing."

"No, I actually lived in the same town, was a guest at his house, and he conducted the wedding service for my Mormon wife and I," Uzziah said.

Marianne's grandfather looked between the two mountain men and shook his head.

"There is so much misinformation out there about the prophet," he said.

"Well," Immanuel said, "tell ya what. We're goin' to Salt Lake, and ifn yer goin' there, too, we'd be glad to escort the both of ya safely there."

"We have hired a man who will see us through, no need to worry about that," the old man said.

"Is he on this boat?" Uzziah asked, wanting to know if they had made a wise choice.

"No, no, we met him in St. Louis, and he went ahead to make ready everything which needed to be done," Tim said.

"So, he's waiting on ya, where?"

"Omaha, Nebraska. I gave him money enough for

wagons and supplies," Tim said, then turned to his granddaughter. "Shall we, my dear," he said, extending his hand toward her. She got up and helped him from his chair. They were both standing there.

"I hope you didn't expect us to pay for your breakfast," Tim said as he walked over and paid for theirs.

"Nice fella," Immanuel said, smiling.

"Not really," Uzziah said. "I don't think he believed anything I told him."

"I would guess that's an accurate statement."

"No tellin' how much the old geezer paid fer the wagon and supplies," Uzziah said.

"Well, ya can bet it weren't cheap. Partner, I think we need to watch those two, and make sure they ain't robbed blind and the woman sold to Comancheros."

It took three more days of steaming up the Missouri to get to Omaha. When they docked, there was a man waiting for the Wells. He didn't look that rough, but the men who were handling the carriage, and had all the supplies on mules, looked like they had been roughed up a bit before they had been let out in public.

Immanuel and Uzziah watched as the man who had arranged everything bowed and scraped to get them in the carriage, and to make sure Marianne was settled. It was a landau, and had a covering, and a trunk. The man in charge would be driving the carriage, and the other three men would bring the supplies along on the pack mules. It looked like they would be heading right out from Omaha, but it became obvious, the old man wanted to stay a night or two at a hotel before they began their adventure. There seemed to be an argument of sorts, but the old man could give it out as well as take it, and fairly soon, the more polished of what Uzziah thought of as the thieves relented and took them to the Saratoga Springs Hotel located at 24th and Grand Ave in Omaha.

It was a two-story brick structure with a grand porch across the front. It wasn't crowded by any other buildings, but it did have a good restaurant inside, and that's where Uzziah and Immanuel decided to have supper the night before they took off for Salt Lake.

When they were eating, Marianne and Tim Wells came from their room on the first floor, and even though they saw the two mountain men, they sat nowhere near them in the dining room.

"Do ya think we should feel insulted?" Immanuel asked.

"Nah, I can't figure the old man out. He basically called me and you both liars, and now, he's burrowing in with these roughnecks. It don't make sense."

They ate for a while without talking. Uzziah had the meatloaf, something his mother, Rahab, had perfected when she was a young wife, and Uzziah pronounced it edible. Immanuel wasn't sure what sort of recommendation that was. Since there were stockyards in Omaha, Immanuel had the beefsteak, and said it was more tender than a pair of boots, but he wasn't sure the boots wouldn't have tasted better.

All in all, the meal was taken there, just so they could continue to watch the young Marianne, and her obstinate grandfather, who seemed hell bent for leather to jump from what he thought was a frying pan right smack dab into the middle of the fire.

After they had finished their supper, Uzziah and Immanuel walked by the Wells' table.

"Are you two following us?" Tim Wells asked.

"We are goin' to the same town, sort of hard not to be goin' in the same direction," Uzziah said.

"Let me be more open with ya, sir. Those men that ya've hired look like they would probably be able to take everything ya have, and sell yer granddaughter to a bunch of Mexican bandits!" Immanuel said frankly.

Marianne gave an intake of breath as she raised her napkin to her mouth.

"I will ask you not to scare my Marianne!" Tim Wells said loudly, loud enough to get the restaurant manager's attention. He came running over.

"Is everything all right here, Mr. Wells?" he asked.

"No, these gentlemen, and I use the expression loosely, seem to be bent on disturbing my granddaughter," Wells said.

"I will send for J.A. Miller, the City Marshall, if this cannot be resolved," the manager said.

"No need, we were just leavin'," Uzziah said, as he took Immanuel's arm and led him from the restaurant at the Saratoga Springs Hotel.

They, Uzziah and Immanuel, waited on the west side of Omaha, in the Council Bluffs area. Uzziah remembered the Mormon Gunsmith where they had bought harmonica guns—both rifles and pistols—back when they were traveling with the Brigham Young party.

They were ahead of any parties going west, so they planned on spending the morning with the gunsmith.

But Jonathan Browning's shop was deserted, and when they inquired where the gunsmith was, they were told he had migrated to the Salt Lake Valley before the War Between the States.

They left and went up into the hills, which weren't that far away from the trail that most used to get to Cheyenne, then onto the Salt Lake Valley. Both men had been that way before, and as they waited to see if Tim Wells and his granddaughter, Marianne, would come this way. Uzziah couldn't help but think of the last time they had made this particular trip. He had a coffin with the body of his Mormon wife, Hannah, in the back of his wagon, and they were helping lead the Brigham Young expedition to their eventual home. Warm memories flooded back in on Uzziah. Immanuel kept the binoculars trained back and forth on the road that led west.

It was a little past noon when Immanuel nudged Uzziah, who had fallen asleep.

"It's them. The carriage, the mules, and the entourage of bandits," Immanuel said.

It was easy country to follow someone without being noticed. The Injuns had done it for years. They kept their distance, and the undulating hills and valleys allowed them to stay out of sight and check in on the Wells' party when they wanted to. After nearly a week of traveling, Uzziah finally spoke up.

"Ya know not everybody's got to like ya."

"What's that got to do with anythin'?" Immanuel asked.

"Well, ya might be takin' this the wrong way."

"Takin' what the wrong way?" Immanuel asked.

"The fact that the old man don't like us. We've been disliked afore, plenty."

"So?"

"So, maybe the old man is a better judge of character than ya give 'em credit fer, and those bad lookin' hombres, are just that, bad lookin' so no one bothers their customers!" Uzziah said.

"Look, I ain't the one with the ogle-eyes over Marianne, that's you. I just don't like that busk Yankee way of a man sayin' what he thinks and thinkin' it's right, just acause he thinks it!"

"The old man rubbed ya wrong."

"No shite," Immanuel said, then the conversation, or rather the argument, was interrupted by gunfire.

Both men kicked up their mounts and rode to the top of the next hill. From where they stopped, they could see that there was something going on down on the road. They had stayed off the road, just so they wouldn't be spotted.

A man lay in the road, and he wasn't moving. It wasn't the old man, it was one of the mule drivers. There weren't any Injuns around, and no one else seemed to have accosted their party. But there was a lot of moving around down there, and finally, the driver of the landau, the nicest and most respectable of the men the old man had hired, jumped the old man in the landau and took away his pistol.

"The old man had a pistol, think he shot one of the mule men," Immanuel said, handing the binocs to Uzziah.

"What the hell," Uzziah said as he scanned the

scene. "They seem to be startin' back up, but they're leavin' the man in the road."

"Let me see," Immanuel said, and spying through the binocs, swore. "Damn! That don't seem right!"

That night, when the larger party made camp, Uzziah and Immanuel didn't bother to. They hung back until it was early morning, then they tied both their black horses nearby, but down by the creek, and snuck in on foot.

They had left a guard, which was smart, because the boys could only count two bedrolls around the fire and the tent that the old man and the girl stayed in. There had been four hombres, counting the nice-looking one, and the three bandit-looking guys. The dead man back on the trail had been one of them. That meant there was someone around who wasn't in a bedroll and probably awake, carrying a rifle.

They weren't quite sure what to do till they saw a couple Pawnee sneaking toward the camp, who were a bit closer than they were. They hadn't even known that the Pawnee were around.

As the Pawnee got closer, Uzziah and Immanuel decided it would be best to get their horses and ride in when the action started. The Pawnee were on foot, and they didn't know how many there were, so being mobile might be important.

Back at the horses, they checked their weapons and rode back toward the camp when they heard a woman's scream and several shots.

When they rode in, a Pawnee was coming from the

tent with the young girl, Marianne, over his shoulder. Stepping from the tent, the old man, Tim Wells, fired a shot into the Pawnee's back, and he dropped Marianne.

When Immanuel and Uzziah rode in, there were several other Pawnee who had rushed from hiding, and they were shot off their feet, first by the Hawkens, then the Walker Colts were pulled out, and reloading became academic.

Every time Uzziah fired, there seemed to be another Pawnee coming from the bush. He finally threw his Bowie knife, impaling another Injun, then took to using his tomahawk like a saber as he rode and swung long arches, catching them in the head when he could.

He didn't have the time to watch Immanuel, but when it all settled down, Marianne had a rifle, and there were only two of the original party of hombres left, the nice-looking one, and the last of the bad hombres, and he was badly wounded with an arrow in his stomach.

The old man had either passed out or fallen over, no one could be sure.

"What the hell was that all about!?!" Tim Wells asked from the ground, well, he must have fallen over, since he certainly was talking.

"I'm sorry, sir, but we were attacked by some Pawnee," the nice-looking guide said.

"Are ya sure it wasn't them?" Tim Wells said, pointing his pistol at Uzziah and Immanuel.

"Who are you?" the guide asked, still holding his rifle.

"Don't point that thing at me, son," Immanuel said, "Unless, ya intend to use it!"

"They have been following us!" Tim Wells said, still pointing the pistol around.

"Old man," Immanuel said, "Put the pistol down, now!"

"Grandfather, do as he said!" Marianne ordered, and by golly, he obeyed. Well, that was a turn of events.

3

They made an uneasy camp that night, neither of the mountain men sure what the heck was going on. The old man who had, it seemed, ruled the roost, suddenly had backed down just because his granddaughter had told him to. The man who was the guide turned out to be okay. His name was Frank Gear, and he had hired the rough men because he knew it was going to be rough country.

The one who had been killed and left on the road had said something vile to Marianne, in Spanish, and, it just so happened that was a language that she spoke, so she shot him dead. Grandpa had taken the pistol from her after she'd drilled the bad hombre, and that was why it looked like he had done the killing. Now, Uzziah and Immanuel weren't sure what the hell was going on or who the hell to trust?

After Marianne and Grandpa Tim had turned in, and the remaining men—Immanuel, Uzziah, and the guide, Frank Gear—sat around the dwindling fire. They weren't going to build it back up again in case there were more Pawnee out there.

"What'd he say to her?" Immanuel asked the guide.

"Don't know, Mexican ain't one I speak," Frank said.

"Did she hesitate, or just pop him?" Immanuel kept on.

"She took the pistol from her purse with incredible speed and shot him dead," Frank whispered.

"Yeah, don't blame ya, wouldn't want to agitate her any," Immanuel said, smiling at Uzziah.

"I speak a little Spanish, but she probably wouldn't repeat it, right?" Uzziah asked anybody who would answer.

"She has a short fuse, sir. I would let it lie," Frank said.

"Guess the apple didn't fall far from the tree," Immanuel said.

"Sixty years later," added Uzziah.

"Well, done heard it said that grandkids are a lot more like their grandparents than they are their parents," Immanuel said.

"Tip-toeing with her would probably be a good idea," Frank said.

"And I know ya had yer eye on her," Immanuel said to Uzziah, nudging him in the arm. They were fairly close together around the embers of the fire.

"I'm celestial married," Uzziah said.

"Ya a Mormon?" Frank asked.

"Well—" Uzziah started in.

"No, he ain't!" Immanuel finished it off for him.

"How come ya said what ya said?" Frank asked.

"I's married to an LDS girl, once," Uzziah said.

"She let ya go?"

"She died," Immanuel straightened that out right away.

"Oh," Frank said, then added, "Sorry."

"Childbirth," Uzziah said, as an explanation.

"Yeah...what about the kid?"

"It died, too," Immanuel was setting the record straight.

"He...he died," Uzziah said, giving Immanuel a look.

"Okay, I'm gonna turn in," Immanuel said, and he got up and carried his bedroll under the carriage and laid down.

"It's warmer over chere," Frank offered.

"He ain't worried 'bout the cold, but the Pawnee," Uzziah said, pulling his bedroll around him by the fire.

With Immanuel and Uzziah's expertise in traveling this country, and the guide, Frank Gear, helping out, they managed to get to Fort Laramie in a couple weeks. They encountered no more Injuns, but saw various groups of peoples, some travelers on the Oregon Trail, and others just—well, who knew? They began to keep a watch at night, so that if there were bandits or desperadoes around, at least they'd have a fighting chance.

When they pulled into Fort Laramie, it was not without a great deal of relief. Many had gone that route and not made it, and Tim Wells praised God as they entered the gates of the Fort. He stood in the landau and shouted his praises to the sky.

"These galvanized Yankees have seen it all, the old

man could have come ridin' in naked and they wouldn't have said a thing," Frank Gear said.

They took the mules and supplies that they had remaining, set up the tent, and made them a place in the corner of the adobe fort. They were at least safe now from Injun attacks, but the journey to the Salt Lake Valley was another grueling month. They wouldn't be pulling into the Mormon city until early fall, and both the boys figured that's where they'd stay until the spring of 1864.

At the campfire that night, Marianne and her grandpa, Tim, retired early. They were relieved to have made it thus far. Before the old man went into the tent—he always gave his granddaughter time to change—he spoke to Uzziah. "I been listening, and I think I may have misjudged you on several accounts," Tim said.

"What ya mean?" Uzziah asked him.

"Well, when we go in to sleep, I don't always fall asleep fast. Your stories about Joseph Smith and Brigham Young, and your Mormon wife, I'm inclined to believe them now. I apologize for being such a skeptic," the old man said.

"That's fine. Lots of folks have done lots of things ya can't imagine they done. Just 'cause ya don't believe 'em don't mean they didn't do 'em," Uzziah said, giving the old man some Virginia homespun wisdom.

"Well, you and your partner have been quite helpful, and if I make it as far as the Salt Lake Valley, I sure would appreciate an introduction to Mr. Young," the old man said, smiling.

"Sure, I'd be glad to," Uzziah said, and the old man kept smiling as he hailed the tent and went on inside.

The three men were around the fire again, and this

time they didn't have to worry about Indians coming in and trying to kill them. They had relaxed. Immanuel brought the jug of Jack Daniel's out and, taking a sip, passed it to Uzziah, who sipped and handed it to Frank Gear.

"What's this?"

"Well, taste it and ya tell me," Uzziah said.

Frank tilted it up, sipped, then had himself a better sip.

"Damn! That's good whiskey, Tennessee style, ain't it?"

"Sure is," Immanuel said, as he sipped some more, "Me and Uzziah found this kid, Jack Daniel, who worked with this old negro slave, Nearest. We think the kid learned distillin' from the slave man."

"Nearest was his name?" Frank asked as he took the jug.

"Yep," Uzziah said, "they got the damnest names, don't they?"

"Say, what'd ya mean when earlier ya said that 'bout galvanized Yankees?" Immanuel asked.

"Well," Frank started in, "the Federals can't afford with the war on to send regular troops out chere, so they force Confederate prisoners to do the duty, sort of galvanize 'em into it," Frank said.

"Really?" Uzziah asked.

"Ya talk to 'em, y'all see, they almost all got a southern accent."

They relaxed there at Fort Laramie, and the fort welcomed them. They had news of back east, and monies to spend in the little store, and sure enough, Uzziah found a couple of good-ole-boys who hailed from Virginia out there, fighting Indians and not wasting away in some Yankee prison. There was also a little cantina run by some sutler.

The Virginians hated thinking of themselves as Yankees, and they really didn't, but serving and carrying a weapon and actually doing something besides living in a hellhole was better than most of the Confederate prisons.

One night, Marianne was walking the perimeter of the walls, up on the walls themselves. The sun was going down, and the Confederate galvanized Yanks could have cared less about a pretty girl walking along the walls. They welcomed it, in fact. Uzziah saw her up there and went up the ladder to join her for a bit. She saw him coming, and he was surprised when she smiled and waited for him to catch up.

"What ya doin' up chere?" he asked her.

She looked out on the prairie and the way it sloped away from the fort, and the streams that were running well this time of year, the way they were turned golden by the setting sun.

"It's amazingly beautiful, isn't it?" she said, then added, "Looks like someone threw some gold ribbon out there and it just unraveled."

"Beautiful and dangerous," Uzziah added.

"Maybe that's one of the reasons the Indians don't want to share it with us."

"Nah, it's just different, and after all the centuries of them fightin' each other and no one else, they don't want the competition. Besides, we got better weapons, and our diseases kilt 'em off like flies."

"I know, I heard about that. Some say the army actually delivered blankets with smallpox on them to the Indians," she said with a sad face.

"Well, it's certainly cheaper than bullets," Uzziah remarked.

"So, you're against the Indians?"

"No, but when ya have to fight 'em just 'bout every time ya run into 'em, sorta makes ya wary of 'em."

She leaned on the wooden wall and looked out at the last of the sunset. The blues and mauves were gathering further east and taking over the sky, but the last of the colors of red, orange, and pink waned beautifully.

"I have a temper," she said.

"I heard."

"The man I killed. Really, his insult wasn't meant for me, but when you understand, you understand. I didn't even think, just pulled the gun and shot him dead," she said, not looking at Uzziah.

"Well, we all kilt some we wished we hadn't," Uzziah said.

"Oh, don't get me wrong, I would do it all over again. That's what I like about this country, the west. You can do things that would send you to prison back east, and everyone understands." She turned to him with that, and coming closer, she put her hand down on his deerskins and felt his manhood.

"Ma'am!" he blurted out, instinctively backing up.

"Things like that," she said, and walked away from him.

Uzziah waited for her to be helped down the ladder by some galvanized Yanks, then, once she had gone into the tent, he went to the fire.

Uzziah walked up and noticed that Frank had

already turned in, he had taken to sleeping in the landau because of the snakes.

"Saw ya romancin' that gal," Immanuel whispered to his partner.

"Yeah, if ya wanna call it that," Uzziah whispered, not wanting anything he had to say heard by her.

"Whatcha mean?" Immanuel had no idea.

"Take a walk with me," Uzziah said, and Immanuel got what was left of the Jack Daniel's jug from his saddlebags and followed his partner.

They both had a nip while Uzziah was looking over his shoulder at Marianne's tent.

"What happened, partner, ya get yerself a taste?" Immanuel said, his eyes squinting in a knowing way.

"There's something wrong with her," Uzziah said.

"Whatcha mean, she's beautiful. Maybe a little quick on the draw, huh?"

"In more ways than one," Uzziah whispered.

"Ya can talk now, she can't hear ya unless she's a bat," Immanuel remarked.

Uzziah didn't know exactly what to say. She had touched him where he'd want a woman like her to touch him, but it had been in such a strange way with no lead-up to it.

"She held my stuff," was the only way he could think to say it.

"Whatcha mean stuff?" Immanuel asked, stopping right where he stood.

"Ya know," Uzziah said, looking down.

"Didn't ya want her to?" Immanuel asked, confused.

"Not like that," Uzziah said.

"Like what?"

"She gave me no warnin', just was standin' there and reached out and took my stuff in her hand, covered it, I mean."

Immanuel looked back over at the tent. "Just like that, no kiss or nothin'?" he asked.

"Nope, out of the blue," Uzziah said.

"Damn, son, I believe that's an invitation," Immanuel said, and smiled as he took another sip of Jack Daniel's whiskey and started whistling.

Uzziah knew Immanuel wouldn't understand. He probably shouldn't have told him. That woman, Marianne, she was trouble, big trouble, and he decided right then and there to get to the bottom of it. There was a danger to Marianne that he had never experienced with any other woman. And he had seen some stuff, but this young woman. He wasn't sure what it was, but there was something akilter in her. And he wasn't sure that taking advantage of something like that would get him anywhere but killed.

The next day, Immanuel told Tim Wells, the old man, that they would be leaving the next morning. If he, or his granddaughter, needed anything that they hadn't picked up at the sutler's store, then they better get it.

That afternoon, while the sun was going down, Uzziah and Immanuel packed their things and got their horses ready. The guide, Frank Gear, did the same for the Wells.

There was the cantina on the fort property, which was understandable, there being no other place for the soldiers to unwind. It stayed open late, and sometimes, when either Immanuel or Uzziah were relieving themselves, they could hear a guitar from the place or see someone staggering back to the barracks.

The night before they left on the last leg of their journey to the Salt Lake Valley, Uzziah was going back to his bedroll when he saw a woman, it had to be Marianne, there weren't any other women there, but squaws, and she was leaving the little cantina with a soldier. They were arm in arm, and while he stood there watching, they stopped and went into a long kiss.

Well, that surprised him, sort of, but then again, maybe another White woman had traveled into the fort and he just hadn't seen her. He thought no more about it, but he sure wanted to check to see if Marianne was in the tent with her grandpa. He started to look in on them when he was interrupted by Immanuel.

"Psst!" Immanuel said right before Uzziah lifted the tent flap to see if Marianne were still in the tent.

Uzziah turned, and Immanuel was up on one elbow, looking at him strangely. He walked over and Immanuel grabbed him by the boot.

"Not a good idea, young son," Immanuel whispered.

"I was only gonna check on Marianne," Uzziah whispered back.

"Uh-huh, but ifn that old man caught ya, he'd shoot ya fer sure," Immanuel said, then added, "Now, go back to sleep."

Uzziah really wanted to know if Marianne had taken a soldier from the cantina, but he rolled back into his bed and fell asleep.

Behind the stables, back against the stockade fence, a man, the soldier Uzziah had seen and a woman were lying down. She took off her top, and in the moonlight, her breasts bounced nicely as she rode the soldier to his completion. As he laid back, spent and satisfied, the woman pulled a knife and dragged it across his throat. He tried to yell out, but his windpipe only made a hissing sound, sending blood up on the woman's breasts. As he lay there bleeding out, and struggling, trying to keep the blood from running his life out, she rubbed the blood over her breasts, and then plunging her hand down, she brought herself to her own completion as the man jerked in his death.

Immanuel got everyone up at false dawn, and they had eaten and were out the gates of Fort Laramie before reveille had sounded.

As they pulled out, Uzziah looked over at Marianne, who smiled back at him as Frank Gear drove the landau from the fort. He still wondered if that had been her with the soldier as they left the cantina, but he let it drop.

They made good time on the first day, and the second. Everyone seemed to be in high spirits with the thought of finally reaching their destination, the Salt Lake Valley.

The third day, as they were getting ready to pack up after breakfast, Immanuel saw something on the horizon. It was coming from the direction of Fort Laramie, and it was coming fast.

"Someone's riding hard toward us," Immanuel said, his eyes still glued in the binocs.

"Let me see," Uzziah said, and as he adjusted them to his eyes, he saw. It was a lone rider, with a spare horse behind him, and he was riding with some intent. In fact, it was almost as if someone were chasing him.

Uzziah searched his backtrail, but could see no one back there, but still the soldier rode with such urgency!

They all stood there and watched as he got closer and closer. The other horse tied behind him was stretched out, just trying to keep up. He had used both horses to increase his speed without wearing either of them out. What the hell was the hurry all about?

When he was easily within rifle range, Immanuel had both hands on the binocs and even recognized one of the soldiers from Fort Laramie. It was one of the galvanized Yanks from Virginia that Uzziah had befriended.

"It's one of the guards from the Fort," he announced, as they prepared themselves for whatever news he would bring.

"I think it's bad news," Marianne said as she watched with the others.

"Well, he certainly ain't ridin' that hard to tell us they missed us," Immanuel quipped.

It was then that the soldier's horse stepped into a gopher hole. They could hear the snap of the horse's leg from their camp, and when the horse cried out in pain and tumbled, the soldier was thrown on the path in front of the tumbling horse. They could hear the wind being crushed out of him as he was smashed into the ground by the weight of the horse.

Then, all was quiet. The dust settled as Immanuel and Uzziah rode out to where the man lay, perhaps dying, perhaps dead. The screaming horse was certainly not dead, and Immanuel was the first one off his horse as he lowered the Walker Colt and put a bullet right between the eyes of the writhing horse. As the sound of the shot faded out, the scene became a quiet, macabre tableau of death. Then they heard the soldier gasping.

Both men rushed to his aid, but the foamy blood which bubbled at his lips belied the fact that his lungs had been crushed.

"She...she..." the soldier breathed in his Virginia accent.

"She who? She what?!?" Uzziah asked, fearing that he knew the answer.

"He...he..." the cavalryman said as he gasped for air that wouldn't come.

Both Uzziah and Immanuel looked at each other. The man had ridden hard for two days. The dead horse was frothy, and the one that was grazing lazily back of the accident didn't look like the rider had done him any favors, either. There was something desperate about this ride that had ended with what? No message delivered, no warning of whatever—just a dead horse and a dead rider.

"What in God's name?" Uzziah said.

"He was comin' to tell us somethin', pard, I know he was," Immanuel said, and they both looked back at their camp, where everyone stood watching them.

"She done somethin'," Uzziah said.

"Whatcha mean?"

"I saw her, 'member, last night when I was 'bout to go into the old man's tent."

"Yeah, ya damned fool, what the hell were ya gonna do?"

"Nothin'," Uzziah protested.

"Bull."

"Look, I saw this couple come from the cantina on the fort. The woman weren't no squaw, and after what she done when we was on the wall—"

"You jealous, son of a bitch!" Immanuel said, smiling.

"No, no, it ain't like that, honest," Uzziah protested.

"Then tell me, Mr. She Grabbed My Junk, what is it?"

"Don't know," Uzziah said. He couldn't get through to Immanuel when he acted like this. He could understand, yes, she had put her hand directly, making no mistake, on his manhood, and it had literally scared him to death. What woman does that but a whore? And he had seen someone who looked like a White woman walking with a soldier from the cantina. Maybe something had happened? She had killed a man for just insulting her, who knew, maybe she was—well, he didn't know what she was!?!

"Okay, well, we got another horse, we can tie him to the landau, and we gotta bury this Old Dominion buddy of yers," Immanuel said.

Uzziah hefted the dead man, whose body acted as if there wasn't a solid bone in it, up on the second horse. They left the dead horse, but took the army saddle off. It was a McClellan saddle, and neither of the boys thought they'd be using it, but you never could tell.

As they rode back toward their party, everyone was standing there watching except Marianne. She was busy packing things and paying little to no attention to what was going on.

"What was that all about?" asked Tim Wells, the old man.

"Wish we knew, sir," Immanuel said.

"He didn't have anything to say?" Marianne asked from where she was packing her things.

Everyone looked at her.

"No, no," Uzziah finally said, "by the time we got to him, he was dead."

"But," Marianne insisted, "I was looking through the binoculars, and it looked like he was talking."

Both mountain men looked at each other. Had she been looking? And why was she so interested in what the man said, or if he said anything at all?

"Might strange," Frank Gear said, then added, "It sure looked like he was running from something, or maybe to tell us something, didn't ya think?" he looked around, but the old man looked away.

"Who knows, and who cares?" Tim Wells said, and both Immanuel and Uzziah thought that was a bit callous, but in a sense, he was right. The man had tried to speak, but hadn't gotten much out.

"Whatever he said, I wouldn't believe him," Marianne said, out of the blue.

"Granddaughter, shut up!" Tim Wells said with such a force you'd have thought he was forty years younger.

She looked at him and smiled, then went back to packing.

Later that same day, as the sun was losing itself in some cumulus clouds, Immanuel rode over to Uzziah.

"It'll be a beautiful sunset, huh?" Uzziah commented.

"Partner, I think there's something rotten in the state of Denmark," Immanuel said, making one of his Shakespearean allusions.

"Hamlet?"

"Yeah, me thinks the lady doth protest too much," Immanuel said, then added, "I think that's McBeth."

"Just spit it out, will ya?" Uzziah pleaded.

"I got the strangest feelin' that Marianne knew what the messenger soldier had come to tell us, and I am gonna watch her closely tonight."

"Old son, ifn she gets the jump on ya, she won't be the first woman to do so," Uzziah said, chuckling.

"Hey, this ain't funny. Something happened back at the fort, I got this itchin' feelin' 'bout it," Immanuel said, concerned.

"Like maybe I was right and that was her with the soldier leavin' the cantina?"

"Ya shoulda looked in the tent."

"Well, I was gonna, but somebody stopped me," Uzziah said, looking hard at Immanuel.

As they were about to look for a place with both water and some shelter, Uzziah spotted about fifteen wagons off to the south.

"Lookie there," he said to Immanuel.

"I knew we was close to the Oregon Trail," Immanuel said, then added, "Let's camp with 'em tonight."

"Ya think that's a good idea?" Uzziah asked.

"Ya mean..." and Immanuel didn't say her name, he just looked back at the landau.

"Yeah," Uzziah said, but then he pointed. "Well, it may be too late," he added.

A rider from the wagon train was coming up on the two mountain men, and as he pulled rein, they did, too.

"Afternoon," the man said. He was in his fifties and looked like he had seen a lot of action.

"Afternoon," both mountain men said at the same time, and Immanuel looked at Uzziah as if to say, *I hate it when we do that!*

"Would ya like to camp with us tonight, or ya can join us on the trial, ifn yer on yer way to Oregon," the man said, with a slight southern accent.

"Sure," Immanuel said, "when ya plan to circle it up?"

"Right 'bout now, I'd say," he said as he motioned back to the wagons, which were circling next to a river.

As they rode back to inform the others, Uzziah spoke up.

"This is a mistake."

"Hey, the woman is forward, and maybe ya saw her at the fort with a soldier, and maybe ya didn't. Fact is, all we got is her touching yer junk, and then this guy riding out to tell us something, but dead men tell no lies, as they say."

"I still think it's a mistake," Uzziah said, and left it at that.

The others seemed glad this far into Shoshone territory to be camping with a larger group.

Frank Gear was relieved, and so was Immanuel. He had finished off the liquor that he'd stolen from Jack Daniel, and there was always some hooch around a wagon train. Uzziah liked the fact that he probably wouldn't have to cook, since all the women in one of these trains wanted to show off their culinary skills.

They set up camp, right there, pulling the landau up like it was one of the wagons, and as people do in situations like this, everyone was being really friendly.

They ate at the fire of the wagon in front of the landau, and the woman's cooking, she'd wrestled some prairie chickens into a pot and done a fine job on a prairie chicken stew. Uzziah made biscuits and johnny-cakes, and Immanuel thought for sure, one of the young women were going to steal him away so they could, at the least, get the recipe.

Uzziah kept an eye on Marianne, who flirted with a young man who couldn't have been more than seventeen years old. The flirting probably wasn't noticeable to anyone but Uzziah. Immanuel had found a man with a jug, and halfway through the prairie chicken stew, Uzziah knew his partner wasn't going to be much help with anything except crawling into his bedroll when the whiskey ran out. That was one thing with Immanuel, he'd stick around till the whiskey was gone, and then crash.

Someone pulled out a guitar, and someone had a harmonica, which reminded Uzziah of his brother Obadiah, and the music was cheerful into the night as folks danced and caroused as much as the wagon master would let them.

The wagon master was the older man, who had ridden over and asked them to join the camping. He was friendly, but Uzziah suspected that he probably had spotted a group of Shoshone and wanted more guns around if something happened. That was fine, he and Immanuel had had their own run-in with a group of braves when they left the Salt Lake Valley, and if it hadn't been for Hannah's coffin being exposed when the canvas burned off their wagon, well, let's just say, his dead wife had saved his life twice since she'd died.

The young man was dancing with people his age, and he asked Marianne for a dance. She turned him down, then her grandpa said something to her. Uzziah witnessed all that and was glad she hadn't taken up with the boy, but sure wished he knew what the old man had said to her. Fairly soon, the wagon master called the party off, and everyone settled into their tents, wagons, wherever they slept.

Immanuel had seen some clouds earlier and decided to sleep under the landau like Frank Gear, and Uzziah followed suit. The tent that Frank set up for the old man, Tim Wells, and his granddaughter, Marianne, was within the inner circle of the wagons, and Uzziah couldn't see it from where he slept. Just as well, he needed to get some sleep and stop worrying about some gal who was prettier than most.

Uzziah saw Immanuel stumble out of his bedroll and walk far enough away not to be rude, and he did the same, but only once, compared to what Uzziah had thought Immanuel had done. Drinking whiskey can cause you to get up more times than usual if you're not used to it.

In the morning, everything was going along as it did in these situations. People were packing up, fixing breakfast, and gathering the horses when there was a blood-curdling scream that sent chills down both the mountain men's backs. Screams like that usually accompanied a death or two.

Both mountain men ran in the direction of the scream, only to find the mother of the teenage boy, standing waist-deep in the river, holding her son's dead body.

They liked to never get the body away from the mother of the boy, but the wagon master pulled her aside while Uzziah and Immanuel took the body from the river.

"Ya see any marks on the boy?" Uzziah whispered.

"What ya mean? The boy drowned," Immanuel said, his eyes blurry from the whiskey the night before.

"Just check him over without being obvious," Uzziah asked Immanuel.

As they pulled him out of the river and up to where his parents' wagon was, they moved their hands all over that boy. He wasn't bleeding anywhere, and there were no bumps on his head, and all in all, it looked like a simple drowning.

"No, no!" the mother wailed, "I told 'im not to go for no midnight swim, I told 'im no!"

Neither of the boys could help it, but their heads slowly moved in the direction of Marianne and her grandpa, Timothy Wells. Again, she was paying no attention whatsoever to what was going on, she was busy packing up her and her grandpa's stuff. Finally, when she did look at the woman who had just lost her son, her expression was one of boredom, or so Uzziah thought.

Uzziah decided it was no good trying to talk to Marianne, but after breakfast, such as it was, with the discovery of the drowned teenage boy, he sauntered over to old man Wells.

"Awful 'bout the boy, huh?"

The old man looked at Uzziah and frowned. "Yes, young men should not swim at night," he said.

"Can Marianne swim?" Uzziah asked.

Old man Wells looked at Uzziah as if he'd asked him if his granddaughter was in league with Satan.

"Certainly not! Who teaches a young woman to swim in this time and era?" he said and walked away from Uzziah.

They stuck around for the funeral. The mother of the drowned boy was inconsolable. There was a preacher with the wagon train, and he did a fine service, but when they'd packed up and the wagons were ready to roll, the woman would not leave the gravesite.

"Don't she have other kids?" Immanuel asked Uzziah as they both sat their horses, and were watching the wagons roll away, and the woman was adamant about staying.

"Evidently, it was her first and oldest," Uzziah said.

"I saw ya talkin' to the old man."

"Yeah, so?"

"What'd ya say to him? He seemed fairly upset with yer conversation," Immanuel whispered.

"I just asked him if Marianne could swim?"

"Ya did what!?!" Immanuel nearly shouted.

"Ya heard me."

"Ya think, my God, yer not thinkin' that, are ya?"

"Death seems to be followin' this young lady, Immanuel," Uzziah said, looking over to the landau, which was pulling away from the wagon train. After all, they weren't going to Oregon, but the Salt Lake Valley.

"So, what did she do, huh? Lure the boy into the river, and drowned him? He was as strong as an ox, he woulda fought her off, right?"

"Unless she had some of what ya used on Hanna?"

Immanuel just looked at Uzziah with his mouth open. He couldn't believe his ears. The man was basically accusing the young girl of luring the teenage boy into the river, chloroforming him, then pushing him beneath the stream. If she had done it, it would have been a calculated murder worthy of a mad person.

"I can't think like that, I just can't," Immanuel said.

"Yer lucky she didn't take no shine to ya, old son," Uzziah said as well as warned.

4

By the time they got to the Salt Lake Valley, much of what had happened on the trail, the death of the messenger from Fort Laramie, and the drowning of the young boy with the wagon train, much of that had simply been forgotten. But it was all tucked away in the back of Uzziah's mind, and he had every intention of talking to Porter Rockwell about it. He certainly did.

The temple, whose sight had been picked out by Brigham Young soon after the saints got to the Salt Lake Valley, was still not constructed. The site was the site, but when the US Army was rumored to be coming to Salt Lake shortly before the beginning of the Civil War, the foundation that had been dug and the sandstones that had been laid in place were all covered up by dirt to keep outsiders from seeing what plans were in the works. The fact that the US Army didn't show because of the commencement of firing on Fort Sumter relaxed the Mormon militia.

When Uzziah, Immanuel, and the Wells, Timothy

and Marianne, plus their guide, started down into the Salt Lake Valley, the population of the area was around forty thousand people. Most of them were emigrants who had gladly come to the valley, either to escape the persecution of the saints being done in various parts of the country, or to be with saints, since they had converted.

When Uzziah had had the opportunity to talk to Timothy Wells, he got the impression that since he and his granddaughter had converted to the Mormon Church, their desire to be in the Salt Lake area coincided with those of other converts.

Yet as Uzziah sat Shadow and they made their way into the valley of the Salt Lake, Uzziah could only imagine what would happen if, in fact, Marianne Wells were someone who took advantage of her sex and preyed on men. He, Uzziah, hadn't heard of such a thing, but that didn't mean that it couldn't, or didn't happen. Women were, in essence, much the same as men, and the desire to kill for pleasure could, Uzziah imagined, be found in both sexes. He had known men, Injuns and whites alike, who were off-center enough to enjoy the act of killing another human being.

Uzziah knew that Porter Rockwell was the Deputy Marshall in Salt Lake, and once they were in the city, they traveled toward its center, where he imagined Porter's Office would be. Finally, when they could find no Marshall's Office, Uzziah stopped at a store and went inside.

There was a man in the mercantile store who was sweeping the floor. He was dressed nicely, almost too nice to be a store clerk.

"Pardon me," Uzziah said.

"Yes, sir, how can I help you?" the man said as he put the broom aside.

"I'm looking for Deputy US Marshall Porter Rockwell," Uzziah said.

"Why would ya think he was here?" the man asked, puzzled.

"Well, I had no notion atall that Porter was here, I simply can't find his Marshall's Office."

"He don't have one. The man wouldn't be caught in such a position ifn his life depended upon it, which it probably does," the man said, coming closer.

"I don't understand?"

"Look, ifn you was a deputy US Marshall, would ya sit in an office with a sign out front that advertises the fact that yer in there?"

"Well, guess, I never thought of it thataway," Uzziah said.

"Well, believe you me, Mr. Rockwell thinks that very way, and that's probably one of the reasons he says he'll die of old age, not a bullet," the man said, smiling.

"Well, how does one go about findin' the man?" Uzziah finally asked.

"He owns the Pony Express Station, and even though the express has been discontinued with the telegraph, he had a Hot Springs and Brewery at Point of the Mountain. That's directly south of Salt Lake. Ifn ya stay on the main road outta town, ya can't miss it," he said as he took up his broom and leaned on it.

"Thank ye, sir, 'preciate it," Uzziah said and went back outside.

They rode south of the main city toward Point of the Mountain, and sure enough, there the brewery was. This whole time, the Wells had stayed with Uzziah and Immanuel, and so had their guide, Frank Gear. The point of getting to Salt Lake for the old man, Timothy Wells, was to meet and talk with Brigham Young. Uzziah wasn't sure why, but he suspected it had something to do with his granddaughter's malady, which Uzziah thought was just simply being murderous.

When they pulled up in front of the Hot Springs and Brewery, they noticed that it was also an inn. There was a man outside who put their carriage up in the barn and was tipped for doing so. All five of them walked into the lobby of the Hot Springs and Inn.

"Welcome to the Porter Hot Springs, Brewery and Inn," a young woman said behind the counter. She was familiar to Uzziah because the last time he'd seen her, she was only seven years old.

"Emily?!?" Uzziah said as he stood there holding out his arms.

The woman squealed and ran around the counter and into Uzziah's arms. He picked her up and spun her around.

"Emily, Emily, Emily, I can't believe it! You look just as ya did when ya was a wee girl," Uzziah said, setting her back on the ground.

"Uzziah, I could never forget you. Why, it must be over twenty years since we've seen ya?"

"Close to it. Where's yer pa?"

"He's in the brewery. I'll send someone to get him," Emily said as she looked around at the other guests. "You'll need rooms, yes?"

"Of course," Uzziah said, but he felt he was putting

Porter's family at risk having Marianne stay there, but what could he do?

The rooms were assigned, and Uzziah and Immanuel decided to share a big room, while the old man, Timothy, and Marianne went off to their rooms on the second floor. Before they left, Frank Gear had some words with Marianne's grandfather, and Uzziah saw the old man counting some bills into Gear's hand. Uzziah figured that would be the last they would see of the guide.

"Would ya be the man looking for the Deputy Marshall?" a man asked Uzziah.

"Yes, sir, that'd be me," Uzziah said.

"Come with me," the man said, and Uzziah handed Immanuel the key to the room he'd gotten from Emily and started to follow the man.

"I need to talk with my partner for a moment," Uzziah told the man.

Uzziah turned to Immanuel, who was watching Marianne and her grandfather disappear up the stairs.

"Do not go anywhere with that woman," Uzziah warned Immanuel.

Immanuel looked at him oddly, then smiled.

"Afraid fer me, are ya?" Immanuel said, winking. "'Fraid I'll get my wanker squeezed?"

"Just be careful," Uzziah said as he motioned to the man who was going to take him to the brewery.

They walked out of the inn and to the back of the property, where there were smells that Uzziah recognized from his days of trying to brew beer with his brothers back in the woods. They went into an unpainted building, and then the man took him down a set of stairs to a basement where there were three large vats that had various stages of beer being brewed.

Porter was standing next to one of the vats and stirring it.

Porter looked about the same as he had many years ago, a bit heavier around the middle, but his smile when he saw his old friend was infectious.

"Uzziah! Uzziah!" he had said his name in just about the same state of elation that Emily had said it, which made Uzziah feel that his memory had not been forgotten in this family.

The two men met on the floor of the brewery, and instead of grabbing each other, they sized each other up, as if they were wrestlers about to grapple.

"Ya are a sight fer sore eyes, my brother," Porter said, and then they embraced, but it was tender with great affection, each man holding the other, each man a bit teary-eyed.

"Porter, how good to see ya," Uzziah said, as he pulled back from the hug.

"And ya are the last person on this earth that I expected to see when I woke up this mornin'," Porter said, laughing his deep laugh.

The two men went back upstairs to the brewery office, where Porter poured them each a mug of beer, and they sat at the large desk in the room.

"Here's to ya, my friend," Porter said, as the two men touched mugs.

"And to ya, my great Mormon friend," Uzziah said, and the two men drank deeply.

They talked family and chitchat for most of an hour, then Porter's head turned as he looked at Uzziah.

"There is something else of import which is on yer mind, ain't there, my friend?"

"There is," Uzziah said, accepting another mug of beer.

"Spit it out."

"I've brought some people with me—"

"New friends?"

"Not exactly, we met in St. Louis, and I have to tell ya, I wish we hadn't."

"Do tell," Porter said as he leaned in toward his old friend.

Uzziah related the meeting in St. Louis and how it had not initially been friendly. Then, he told about him and Immanuel following the odd couple, the old grandfather and his beautiful granddaughter, then witnessing the shooting on the road, and her nonchalance at shooting a man who had only insulted her in a different language.

He told Porter about their arrival at Fort Laramie and then leaving, and how on the night before they'd left, he'd seen what he thought was a White woman coming from the little cantina, and his wanting to look into the old man's tent, but then, he didn't. And how three days later the rider from the Fort and his accident, and how he'd tried to tell Immanuel and Uzziah something, but died. Then, the meeting up with the wagon train and the drowning of the young man whom Marianne had flirted with, and when he was through trying to explain himself, he shrugged and looked at Porter.

"What's yer impression of her?" Porter asked, then Uzziah told of their time on the fort wall when she grabbed his manhood without warning, and then walked off.

"So...she's dangerous, then?" Porter said.

"Yes, I think so, and I've brought her to your doorstep," Uzziah admitted.

"Listen, I think you've got one active imagination. Sounds to me that she is too forward fer yer mountain man ways. What does Immanuel think?"

"He sorta falls into that same category that ya do, I guess."

"Why don't ya take me to meet her? I'm a fairly good judge of character. What harm can it do?"

"Okay, but don't let her beauty blind ya," Uzziah said.

"Blinded by beauty, sounds interestin'," Porter said, laughing.

Uzziah went to the door of the rooms that Timothy Wells and his granddaughter were staying in. He knocked, and the old man opened the door.

"Yeah?" he said, none too friendly-like.

Uzziah could see into the rooms, and Marianne was reading in a rocking chair by the window. She hadn't looked up.

"Porter Rockwell and I have been talkin'," Uzziah started in.

"Smells like you been drinking," the old man said.

"That, too," Uzziah admitted.

"And what brilliant ideas did the drink give you?"

"Since he's the bodyguard of Brigham Young, the Prophet of the Church, thought the both of ya would want to meet the prophet, guess I was wrong," Uzziah said, turning around and starting to go back downstairs.

"Wait," Tim Wells said, and he shut the door partway, and murmured something to Marianne.

The door opened back up, and Wells was smiling and Marianne was grabbing her wrap and hat.

"We'd like to go," Wells said.

"Well, ain't like he waitin' fer us now, ya know," Uzziah said.

"Then, when!?!" old man Wells spat out, again none too friendly-like.

"After breakfast tomorrow, that's when Porter is setting the meeting up," Uzziah explained.

"Fine," the old man said and slammed the door in Uzziah's face.

Uzziah went back to tell Porter, who was still messing with the brewing of the beer.

"Can ya set up a meeting tomorrow?" Uzziah asked.

"Sure, we could go now, if ya like?" Porter offered.

"Nah, tomorrow will be fine," he said, then stopped before he left the basement, "I sure hope this is a good idea," he said.

"What harm could it do?" Porter said, still stirring the concoction that would wind up as beer.

Well, that's what Uzziah was worried about, the harm it could do. He wasn't exactly a Mormon anymore, unless he could be considered a Jack Mormon, which he supposed he was. But that didn't make any difference. He felt bad about introducing the woman who might be dangerous to the prophet. He was beginning to think that maybe Immanuel was right, and she was just at the wrong place at the wrong time, and he was letting his imagination run away with him. But then, the image of the drowned young man from the wagon train would flip into his brain, and he knew, he just knew, Marianne had had something to do with that!

That night, as Uzziah was getting ready for bed, he thought about talking to Immanuel about what he had said to Porter, but didn't. He did tell him about their breakfast, though.

"Hey, old son?" Uzziah said.

"What is it, partner?"

"Porter and some of his family are gonna have breakfast with us in the morning."

"Sounds good."

"That's not all," Uzziah said, pushing himself up on the headboard of the single bed.

Immanuel turned over and looked at his partner. "What'd ya do, now?"

"What's that supposed to mean?" Uzziah asked.

"Usually, when ya say something like, *that's not all*, there's some trouble comin' our way."

"I set this up so that Porter could check out Marianne," Uzziah said sheepishly.

"What!? Hey, if Luana finds out ya did this, it ain't gonna go well," Immanuel warned.

"Not check her out in that way, I mean, ya know... don't ya?"

"What have ya told him?"

"I think that young lady is dangerous," Uzziah said flatly.

"Dangerous to whom, men who ain't forward 'nough to take her up on her invitation?"

"That ain't fair!" Uzziah said a bit too loud.

"Well, young son, ifn she had grabbed my manhood, I do believe I would have taken it and put it where it belonged—inside her!"

"You're impossible!"

"No, old woman, yer the one that's missin' some social cues. Ifn a gal kicks ya up, ya better start trottin', or get left behind," Immanuel said, blowing out the lamp and laughing to himself.

That didn't sit well with Uzziah. He had this feeling about Timothy Wells's granddaughter, and he couldn't shake it. Maybe he'd get some support from Porter in the morning at breakfast. He'd wait and find out.

They were all at the breakfast table, having coffee. Luana and her youngest, Orin, who was—Uzziah couldn't believe it—twenty-four years old. He was a strapping young man and handsome in a rough way, the way his father was.

The conversation around the table was going nicely when Marianne and Timothy Wells walked into the dining room, and what Uzziah saw in Orin Jr.'s eyes scared him. The boy—well, he was a man now—he could not take his eyes off Marianne. In fact, he stood up and pulled out a chair right beside him, and his mother, Luana, made some comment about bringing up a boy in the right way, and everyone laughed. But

Uzziah saw the whole business as an invitation for disaster.

Marianne immediately started talking to Orin, Jr., and it was mostly in whispers, but when he started laughing, he let everybody know how he felt. The boy was smitten, and that had not been the reason that Uzziah had arranged this breakfast. Porter was supposed to be checking out the dangerous Marianne, not her ingratiating herself to his boy!

"This woman is amazing, she may be the funniest young woman I've ever met," Orin Jr. said as she put her hand on top of his.

"Where's this bodyguard of Brigham Young you were going to introduce us to?" the old man said, getting right to the point as far as he was concerned.

"Well," Luana started in, trying to be as tactful as she could with the belligerent old man, "Porter was called out early this morning. It seems there was an incident on the Mountain Point Road, and the services of the Deputy Marshall were required." She then added, "But, he's been gone since just after three a.m., so I suspect he'll be here shortly."

"Well, I should hope so. I want that man to introduce me and my granddaughter to the Prophet Brigham Young," Mr. Wells said matter-of-factly.

"Are you LDS?" Luana asked.

"Yes, my granddaughter and I converted back before we began this journey. You know, there are so many perils that I wanted us both to get right with the Lord Jesus before we made the trip," he said, but his tone was still pugilistic and didn't exactly fit the words he was speaking.

"How did ya hear 'bout the church?" Uzziah asked. He had been wanting to ask that question for some time.

"It was Marianne's notion. She heard about a meeting in our hometown, and she literally dragged me to it!" the old man said as he sipped his coffee.

So, thought Uzziah, it wasn't the old man who had started the process, it was his granddaughter. Why did she convert? What possible reason would there be for the old man to want to meet Brigham Young? Though he was president of the church and the only prophet since Joseph Smith, he couldn't help but be suspicious of Marianne's motivation in all this.

The conversations around the table went on, especially the one between Orin Jr. and Marianne. Uzziah was trying to figure out a way to curtail that when who should walk in but Porter, he seemed tired, well, the man had been up all night.

Porter's eyes went directly to Marianne Wells, and Uzziah knew at that moment that any suspicions he had managed to put in Porter's mind had instantly been erased—just like that!

"Porter," Immanuel said, "I'd like to introduce you to Mr. Timothy Wells and his granddaughter, Marianne."

Porter came around the table to where they were seated. Wells tried to get up, but Porter put his hand on the old man's shoulder, and they shook with him seated. His full attention, then, turned to Marianne, whom it seemed, turned her charm up to the fullest degree. If she had shown his son, Orin Jr., any attention at all, it was all eclipsed in the attention she was now paying Porter Rockwell. Uzziah could see Porter's chest swelling like he was a bantam rooster, about to preen around for the hens.

"You must be the man that Uzziah has told us about, Porter Rockwell. Well, Uzziah," she said, looking right at him, and his heart turned ice-cold, when she did so, "You certainly did not tell us that this mountain of man was the epitome of masculinity. Sir, it is a great pleasure to meet you." She stood, and Porter made no effort whatsoever to keep her seated.

They actually hugged, and Uzziah looked at Luana, who reacted by stiffening. Marianne had just met the man. He had just met her, but they hugged as if they were long-lost friends. Uzziah watched to see if she would secretly grab his manhood, but nothing that obvious happened. It was just that the length of the hug went on a tad too long, and Uzziah swore Marianne whispered something in the ear closest to her mouth.

The hug was broken, and Luana relaxed, and it seemed the moment was not as special for her as it was for Porter. Uzziah thought that Porter would hear about that hug later, if not sooner than later.

"Porter, come sit!" Luana veritably ordered her husband, and she was on the opposite side of the table away from Marianne.

He obeyed without the least hesitation, and the girl showed up, and everyone got into ordering what they wanted for breakfast, and even as Uzziah kept an eagle eye on Marianne, nothing else untoward happened.

Halfway through their repast, Uzziah spoke up.

"So, what was the emergency that called out the Deputy Marshall so early this morning?"

Porter was chewing, and he continued to do so till he swallowed.

"I really don't want to talk about it in mixed company, let's just say, it was a death, and like all deaths, grizzly," Porter said, and everyone at the table was glad that the discussion was over, at least everyone, but Uzziah.

"Can ya at least tell us, who was kilt?" Uzziah asked, and the entire table turned to him as if he had just broke wind.

"A stranger, out of towner, nobody, really, anybody knew," Porter said, then he changed the subject. "Say, a little birdy told me that you, Mr. Wells, and the delightful Miss Marianne Wells, would like to meet the Prophet Brigham Young?"

The old man's eyes lit up, and he looked at his granddaughter.

"I told you not to say anything," he said, mildly scolding her.

"But Pop Pop," she said, calling the old man a nickname which Uzziah had never heard before, and getting grins around the table for it, "If you don't ask for what you want, no one will ever know you want it!"

There was a general laughter around the table at that comment, and the old man blushed, which got everyone laughing again.

So, thought Uzziah, that's what the whispering was all about in Porter's ear when they hugged.

"It can be easily arranged," Porter said, "I'm meeting with the prophet today, and it will be taken care of."

Luana looked at Porter as if he had broken some sort of rule about people meeting Brigham, but maybe Uzziah was reading something into her look that wasn't there?

Breakfast was over, and Orin Jr. volunteered to give the old man and his granddaughter a tour of the brewery and the stables. They left, and Porter walked with them as far as the door.

"Do you think that's a good idea?" Luana asked Porter without caring who heard.

"What?" he asked innocently.

"Brigham is a busy man, and you're supposed to be his bodyguard, and you're going to arrange a meeting between this old man and his granddaughter? You don't even really know them."

"And?" he asked, not liking this line of questioning.

"She's right," Uzziah said, and both Immanuel and Porter looked at Uzziah as if he were interfering in a husband-and-wife squabble.

"Ya see, even Uzziah thinks it's unseemly," Luana said, looking at Uzziah and smiling wanly.

"I'm gonna see 'bout the horses," Immanuel said, as he looked at Uzziah, expecting him to also get up, but he poured himself more coffee from the pot left on the table.

Immanuel walked out, and Luana went back toward the lobby of the inn. Porter looked at Uzziah and shrugged.

"Tell me about the death," Uzziah said flatly.

"Some guy who nobody can place met a terrible end. It was robbery, I'm sure. His pockets were turned inside out, and everything of value was taken."

"How was he kilt?" Uzziah pressed.

"I told ya, it was grizzly!"

"Tell me the details, please?" Uzziah asked.

Porter got a flask from his inside coat pocket and poured some into a coffee cup, tilting the flask toward Uzziah, who shook his head *no*.

Porter sat down and, in a sotto voce voice, began talking. "He'd been pulled off the highway. We ain't found his horse, or carriage, or whatever he was travelin' on, yet. He was mutilated, Uzziah, mutilated."

"How?"

"His dern pants was down, and his pecker had been —well, removed."

"Cut off?"

"Yeah, and yeah, and ya know where we found it?"

Uzziah shook his head, *no*, again.

"In his dab blame jacket pocket."

Both men sat there for a moment, as Porter drank the whiskey he'd poured himself, and Uzziah shifted his coffee mug over in front of Porter.

"No shite!" Porter said as he poured two fingers into Uzziah's cup and gave himself another shot.

"Where's the body?"

"The icehouse, that's where we take all the bodies who aren't known."

"I wanna see 'em," Uzziah said.

"Really, why?" Porter asked, sincerely wanting to know.

"What did Marianne whisper in yer ear?"

"What?"

"The young lady, Marianne, she whispered something in yer ear, when she hugged ya, didn't she?"

"Yeah, yeah, sure, it was her Pop Pop's request to see the prophet."

"That's all?"

"Ya sound like Luana, glad she didn't notice," Porter said, sipping the whiskey.

"I think she did, as a matter of fact," Uzziah said.

"Ya think so?"

"Yeah, I do."

"Shite! I'll sure as hell hear 'bout that later."

5

Immanuel and the Wells went somewhere that morning. Uzziah wasn't sure where. Didn't matter, if Uzziah was right, Immanuel was safe as long as he wasn't alone with Marianne. He knew that what he was thinking was sort of crazy, and he decided to do some soothing on his own, without telling anyone.

He and Porter were to meet up near the Temple Square, which, at this time, only had a foundation for the new Salt Lake City Temple. Uzziah went extra early and stopped by the telegraph office in the downtown area. He tied up Shadow and walked on inside.

The office smelled of electricity and oil for some reason. The man behind the counter was receiving a message and was busy taking it all down. At one point, the message languished, and he turned to Uzziah.

"Fill the form out, ifn yer sendin' a message, otherwise, I'll be right with ya," he said, then the key started clicking, and he went back to transcribing.

Uzziah moved over to the little standup table the

man had pointed to, and sure enough, there were telegraph sheets ready to be filled out. The amount you paid was listed above the sheets. Uzziah took one of them, flattened it out really good, and printed with the pencil.

When the telegraph man was through with his transcription, he got up and, walking over to the counter, he read the message to Uzziah.

"Just wanna make sure I got this right, okay. *City Sheriff, St. Louis, Missouri—stop. Am interested in murders occurring before this date—stop.* Then ya put the date. *Please advise sooner than later—stop. Porter Rockwell, Salt Lake City, US Deputy Marshall—stop.*"

The man looked up and sort of smiled.

"Ya ain't Porter Rockwell. I know brother Rockwell," he said apologetically.

"Sorry, I'm Uzziah Ferguson O'Bannon, and Porter and I were law enforcement officers back in the Midwest a few years back. He said ya do this fer me, as a courtesy," Uzziah said, and he slipped a coin across the counter to the man.

"Well," the operator, who had on a visor to shield his eyes from the light, said, "Guess, that'll be okay," as he slipped the coin into his pocket, then he added, "Ya still gotta pay fer the telegram."

"Sure," Uzziah said, and he counted out in coins the requisite amount.

As Uzziah rode down the street outside the telegraph office, he couldn't help but notice how much the town had grown. It was no longer a muddy place where sections divided things, but there were gravel streets, and some brick buildings. It really was coming right along. He rode down to where Porter told him the icehouse was and tied up Shadow. Porter was standing outside the icehouse, smiling.

"Ya sure ya wanna see this, partner?" he asked, still smiling.

"Yep," Uzziah said, and the two men walked inside.

The man who ran the icehouse nodded when he saw Porter, and the two men walked all the way to the back, where Uzziah guessed they kept the bodies. No need to scare off ice business just because someone was murdered.

There was a coffin back there, and the victim was in it.

"This ain't purty, ya know, and he ain't dressed," Porter said as he grabbed the coffin top and removed it.

It took a lot for Uzziah to be—what could he say—troubled, but he'd be damned if what he saw, that naked man with no scrotum or penis, well, even the stuff that he'd seen Injuns do, couldn't top the sight. And yet, he could not look away. Porter tried to put the top back on, but Uzziah stayed his hand.

"Were his pants up or down when ya found him?"

"Well, I didn't find him, a farmer did," Porter said.

"Do ya know the farmer?"

"Sure, he's one of the Larues," Porter said.

"Hannah's family?"

"Yeah, those Larues."

"I need to talk to the farmer," Uzziah said, letting go of Porter's arm and allowing him to return the coffin top. "Ya say ya found his penis?" Uzziah asked.

Porter slid his hand into the coffin and pulled out a paper sack. He handed it to Uzziah, who carefully opened the bag and peeked inside.

"My God!" Uzziah said.

"And mine, too," Porter said.

The penis must have been cut when it was engorged, whoever did it got the whole thing. Uzziah stuck his Bowie into the bag and moved the penis.

"Where's his scrotum?"

"We didn't find that," Porter said as he reached over and placed the sack back into the coffin.

"Ever see anything like that?" Uzziah asked him.

"Can't say I have, you?"

"Hell no, not even in fightin' Injuns."

"Well, this stranger met with a world of hurt, didn't he?"

"He ain't no stranger, I know the man," Uzziah admitted.

"What!? How!?"

"He's the guide that old man Wells hired to bring them to Salt Lake."

"Really, ya sure?"

"Yep, and I saw the old man pay him, and it weren't a bit of money."

"It were a lot?"

"Yep."

"Well, then it was robbery," Porter said.

"Why the mutilation then?" Uzziah asked.

"Who knows," was all Porter could say.

"I might. Hey, does Fort Laramie have the telegraph?"

"Nah, just runs between St. Joseph, Missouri, and San Francisco—coming through here a course. Why? What'd ya do?" Porter asked.

"Ya might get asked about something I did," Uzziah admitted, but he wanted to keep everything above board with Porter, he had always been honest with Uzziah.

"Which is?"

"I sent a telegram and signed yer name," Uzziah said, looking at his old friend.

"That's okay. Who'd ya telegram?"

"Sheriff of Saint Louis."

"What'd ya say?"

"Checking on unsolved murders, gruesome or otherwise, in the city."

"Ya think it's that young girl. Marianne?"

"Maybe?"

"Uzziah. I can tell ya that I've met a lot of murderers in my time, and she don't fit the bill, period."

"Then, there won't be any harm in checking. Ya still gonna let her and her Pop Pop see Brigham?"

"Uh-huh, come on, let's get outta here," Porter said as he shivered, walking to the front with Uzziah following him.

"How long ya keep his body?"

"Well, we was going to chunk him into Porter's field, but now we know who he is, I don't know."

"I'll pay for his funeral," Uzziah said.

Porter took a pencil and pad from his coat. "What was his name?"

"Frank Gear, that's what he said his name was," Uzziah said.

"Okay, well, we'll get a marker made with his date of death, don't happen to know how old he was, do ya?"

"Nah."

"Okay, I got work to do," Porter said.

"Can I come with ya, when ya introduce Marianne Wells and her grandfather?"

"Sure, Brigham would love to see ya, I'm sure. Ya know where all the big houses are?" Porter asked as he walked out with Uzziah behind him.

"Yeah, I saw the area when I rode into town."

"Meet me, and hopefully them, there at around three in the afternoon, okay?"

Porter got on his horse and rode off toward the downtown area. Uzziah stood there, wondering if the telegraph was as fast as they said it was. He thought he'd stop by and see if he had gotten an answer from the sheriff of St. Louis. First, he opened his chronometer and checked the time. It was only half past eleven in the morning. He'd check on the telegraph, then go back to the Brewery and Inn at the end of Mountain Point Road.

"You again?" the telegraph operator said. "Ain't got an answer, ifn that's what yer lookin' fer," he said.

Uzziah tipped his hat and went back out to Shadow and rode fairly quickly back to the Brewery and Inn. The day was beautiful, and the Uinta Mountains still had a bit of snow in them.

When he got to the Brewery and Inn, Emily, Porter's oldest daughter, was behind the counter.

"Hey, Uzziah," she said all friendly-like.

"Darlin', is Immanuel around?"

"No, he and old man Wells and his granddaughter went up into the hills."

"Why?"

"I guess 'cause she wanted to, there ain't much up there," Emily said.

"They took the landau?"

"Don't know," she admitted.

Uzziah went to the stables, and Stygian wasn't there, but the landau was. A young boy, looking a lot like Emily, was mucking stalls.

"Son, did some people leave from here to go into the mountains?"

"Ya must be Uzziah?" the boy said, coming over and extending his hand.

"Yeah, you are?"

"Emily's oldest, Benjamin."

"Glad to meet ya, Benjamin," Uzziah said as they shook.

"Same here," Benjamin said, then added, "Ya talkin' 'bout the beauty with the dark hair?"

"That's the one."

"She's hard to miss, she and I believe the man who is yer partner—"

"Immanuel?"

"Yeah, that's his name. They left about an hour ago."

"Old man Wells with 'em?"

"Yeah, I was a bit worried 'bout the old boy, but he sat a horse like he was born on one."

"They say where they was goin'?"

"Nah, ya ever see a woman that beautiful, Uzziah?"

Uzziah could see how a young man would be enticed into trusting the beauty that Marianne showed on the outside, but he had a feeling that there was a darker and more horrific side to her, which she managed to keep hidden. Uzziah thought that if anyone ever saw that side, it would probably be the last time they saw anything. He wondered how much of her secret her grandfather shared, or if he were entirely in the dark about her darkness.

"Uzziah?" The boy's question had gone unanswered as the mountain man was lost in thought.

"What?"

"Her beauty, it's exceptional, ain't it?"

Uzziah realized that Emily's son was about the same age as the boy who had drowned from the wagon train.

"Look, ya know the devil makes himself look good so he can fool ya, don't ya?"

Benjamin hadn't expected a question like that, but being a good Mormon, he knew all about the devil.

"Why yes, we was talkin' 'bout that in Sunday School just this past Sabbath, why ya askin'?"

"Don't go anywhere with that woman alone. Do ya understand?"

"Yer tryin' to save me from my sinful self, ain't ya?" Benjamin asked, smiling big.

"There ain't nothin' to smile 'bout when it comes to that woman, understand?" Uzziah said very seriously.

"Yeah," the boy said, a bit disappointed Uzziah didn't want to kid with him about a beautiful young woman, "I understand."

Uzziah figured there couldn't be that many ways into the mountains, so he tracked Immanuel's horse, Stygian. He knew the hoofprints of the horse like they were his own. They went down the main road into town for a bit, then turned west. The Uintas were the only mountain range in the northern hemisphere that were set east to west, and that's the way they run. Uzziah took the trail that led into the greenness of the foothills, and then he saw where they had stopped to water their horses, and the good news was, all three of them were still together.

He thought Immanuel was safe as long as the woman couldn't get him alone. There was something of the Black Widow in Marianne, and he was fairly sure that her Pop Pop didn't know. It would be an unthinkable evil if the old man knew and was somehow participating. Uzziah drove that thought from his mind.

It took him the better part of an hour or more to find where they finally stopped. There was a little valley that just appeared there in the foothills, and there was a brook running through it, and the horses were tied up, and old man Wells was lying on a blanket, and it looked like they had had a picnic lunch, and then who knew?

As he walked up, the old man got up on one elbow and, shielding his eyes, looked at the man who was approaching.

"Uzziah, what a pleasant surprise," Timothy Wells said.

"Hey, Tim, where are the others?"

"There's only Immanuel and Marianne. They took a hike up the hill, Immanuel said he thought there was a waterfall there that he wanted to show her."

What the hell would Immanuel know about a waterfall? All he wanted was to get Marianne alone and have her grab his manhood. What he didn't realize was, it might be the very last time that anything ever touched it ever again.

"Thanks, think I'll catch up with them," Uzziah said.

"I wouldn't worry, Immanuel seems a perfectly capable man. He'll take care of her," Wells said as Uzziah scurried off, and the old man turned his head and looked after him. "I wonder what's gotten into him?" he asked no one in particular.

Uzziah had not been hiking in quite some time, and these hills were not exactly unhilly. He was out of breath when he heard two voices, one a woman's and the other unmistakably his partner, Immanuel.

As he came up on them, they couldn't see him. They were lying under a big old spruce, and the spackled shade that dotted their forms made them look as if they were in a painting by one of those French masters—Impressionistic, Uzziah thought they called it.

He hid himself and listened.

"How ever did you decide to go into the mountains and forsake humanity?" she said in her best girlish wonder voice.

"Well, I ain't exactly forsaken humanity, I mean, I almost got married once," he said.

Uzziah couldn't believe it, Immanuel was swallowing her bait, hook, line, and sinker.

"No, you, married?!?," she said, acting astonished.

"Yeah, I been around," Immanuel said, and Uzziah felt embarrassed for him.

"Well," she said as she reached over and untied his deerskin pants, "I'd like ya to show me how around you've been."

Well, Immanuel was staring at her hands like they were the cobra snake that get enchanted from the baskets in India. She was playing the tune, and his snake was about to arise.

"I do so love big, strong men," she said, as she

fumbled artfully with his manhood, and the ugly snake began to raise its head.

She was reaching behind her, and Uzziah wasn't gonna wait for her to pull the boning knife that would take Immanuel's manhood.

He came crashing from the brush, and both of them sort of scrambled away from one another, she annoyed as all get out, and he, trying like the devil to put things away and tie up his deerskins.

"There ya are!" Uzziah said, and the look on Immanuel's face was one of vast disappointment. The man had no idea what his partner had just saved him from.

"What the hell are ya doin' chere!?!" he asked, none too friendly-like.

"Thought I'd see what y'all were up to," Uzziah said, watching the girl like she was the viper he thought she was. Could she ever think that she could take two of them at the same time? He thought he could see in her face that very thought, so he put an end to it.

"Tim ain't doin' so good. I think the sun's got to him," Uzziah said, and before he could say another word, the young woman was off and running back down the hill.

Immanuel stood and looked at Uzziah.

"What's up?" Uzziah asked.

"Well, there was something, but it seems to have gone away," Immanuel said wistfully.

"Come on, we don't want her to have to handle the old man by herself."

They walked back toward where they'd had the picnic, or as Uzziah was thinking, where Immanuel had had his last meal, if his partner hadn't shown up.

"Why exactly did ya come looking for us?" Immanuel asked as they made the clearing where old man Wells was being badgered by his granddaughter.

"We've been invited to see Brigham this afternoon, us and them, I didn't want them to miss the opportunity, if y'all lollygagged in the mountains," Uzziah explained.

"What time is this meetin'?"

"Three this afternoon."

"Good God, Uzziah, it's only one o'clock!" Immanuel said, exasperated.

"What's this about, Brigham?" the old man asked. Well, one thing was for sure, his hearing was great.

"We're gonna meet him this afternoon," Uzziah said, as if he were announcing Santa Claus's arrival.

They rode back down through the verdant canyons and streams, stopping once to water the horses, and Immanuel got to flirt some with Marianne, who was letting him know that he just missed the best piece of prime that existed. Immanuel was like a puppy in her hands, and once again, Uzziah thought about Proverbs 30:18-19.

These three things amaze me, no, four are a wonder to me, the way of an eagle on the wind, the way of a snake on a flat rock, the way of a ship on the high seas, and the way of a man with a maiden.

He felt sorry for his partner, and his partner just wanted to kick him all over creation. Immanuel actually thought that he had kept him from something wet and wonderful, when Uzziah imagined that was exactly what Frank Gear had thought when she had seduced him into the bushes and cut his scrotum and penis from his body. It was wet, but wonderful only to the devil of a girl who got her rocks off doing such evil things.

They made it down to the barn in plenty of time for everyone to get spiffed up to see the prophet. Benjamin ogled Marianne, and Uzziah thought he'd better talk to Emily about her son before they found the boy having been eunicid by Marianne.

6

Marianne looked like she was going to see the King of England when she appeared from her rooms. The old man, Timothy Wells, was dressed to the nines also, and Uzziah wished that these two were going to be a blessing to the prophet, but he feared that something else was in the making.

He and Immanuel rode side by side in the back of the carriage, and Immanuel couldn't get his eyes off Marianne. He tried to chat with his partner, Uzziah did, but each time he said something, Immanuel just looked at him like he was a bug.

The ride into town didn't take but about forty minutes, and when they turned down the street that had all the best homes in Salt Lake City lining it, it was fairly obvious which one was the prophet's.

It wasn't auspicious, but it was massive, and Uzziah wryly thought, well, the man did have quite a few wives, and he wasn't sure how many, but to keep peace in a household with that many women, he'd have to have some room to grouse in.

Porter drove the landau for Mr. Wells, and Marianne, and Uzziah couldn't hear what was being said, but it seemed Marianne was keeping up a steady stream of conversation with Porter. He'd have to ask him later what they talked about. Uzziah felt bad about bringing this viper into the prophet's home, and he certainly hoped that the man's ability to read people would come into play, otherwise, who knew what would happen.

Both sets of reins were taken by young Mormon men who seemed delighted to be working for the prophet, and why shouldn't they be?

They were shown into the foyer of the home and asked to wait, the prophet would be with them momentarily.

Through a set of double sliding doors, Uzziah could hear voices. He remembered that Brigham had a deep voice, and one of them was certainly his. After about a twenty-minute wait, the sliding doors came open, and several men with long beards but no mustaches, typical of Mormon men, left the library, and behind them was Brigham.

When he saw Immanuel and Uzziah, his smile was bigger than Uzziah figured it would be. He seemed genuinely glad that the two mountain men were there.

"Porter told me all about your arrival," he said as he hugged first Immanuel, then Uzziah. "And I have to tell you, it has been some time since you were with us. Have you visited the Larues, yet?" he asked, thinking of the family that Uzziah had married into, and being thoughtful about it.

"No, Prophet, I haven't, but I have every intention," Uzziah said.

"Ah, yes," Brigham said, "the road to hell, I hear, is

paved with those." He laughed. "By the way, to you and your partner, Immanuel, I shall always be Brigham. We've fought Indians together, and we will always be friends," the prophet said as his eyes wandered over to Marianne Wells, and Uzziah could have been mistaken, but they lit up at that very moment.

"And who is this ravishing young woman?" he asked as he walked the short distance to her.

"This is my granddaughter, Prophet Marianne Wells," Timothy Wells said.

And Brigham showed excellent taste when he stopped short of greeting Marianne and turned to Timothy Wells.

"And you are?" Brigham asked.

"Timothy Wells, sir, and at your service." The old man bowed like he was meeting an oriental potentate.

Brigham reached down and grabbed Timothy's hand and brought the man to a standing position.

"Please, sir, I am but a servant of the Lord Jesus Christ, and it is I who am at your service."

"We are new to the LDS Church, and it has been my granddaughter's fervent desire to meet you, sir," Timothy said.

It was then that Brigham turned to Marianne, and Uzziah knew there was going to be trouble. For no matter what she was, or what she had done, her charm, her beauty, and that smile, well, it rendered most men idiots!

"I am delighted to hear that, my dear," he said as he took her hand, and surprisingly, she pulled herself to him and hugged him for quite some time.

"It's an honor, sir, and I do hope this is the beginning of a long and fruitful relationship," Marianne said.

Well, everyone was astonished at her boldness, but where does lying back and being a mouse get one—nowhere. Brigham was delighted with her forwardness, and Uzziah noted a woman, older, more Brigham's age was standing in the hallway, and she frowned openly at this affront, or at least Uzziah was sure that's what she considered it.

"Please, won't you all come into my study," Brigham said, not letting go of Marianne's hand.

Uzziah looked over at the frowning woman, who took off like she was about to report a fire, and maybe she was?

Brigham sat behind his desk, and Uzziah wouldn't have been surprised if Marianne had sat on his lap, but instead, he pulled a straight-back chair over to her and placed it behind his desk, while the rest of the party sat opposite.

"Well," Brigham said, "you couldn't have come at a more auspicious time. We're having a dance, a ball if you will, and half the city will be there. We may not have built the temple yet, but we do have a rather large community center, where we hold services until the temple is built, and the ball, if you will, will be there. It's this coming weekend, and"—Brigham turned and looked at Marianne—"I'm certainly hoping, as new members of the Latter-day Saints, that you and your grandfather can attend."

"I didn't know Mormons danced," Marianne said more than asked.

"I have encountered teachings that suggest that fiddle music and the dance, especially, can enlarge and enlighten the soul," Brigham said.

Marianne clapped as if she were six years old, and Brigham blushed, of all things.

"Why, Brigham," Porter said, "I do believe you're blushing!"

"Well, and why shouldn't I? This young lady had brought a sense of fun and play here today, and I am quite enjoying it," he said as he reached over and squeezed her hand. She took the opportunity to take his hand and hold it. He blushed again, and everyone had a good laugh, everyone but Uzziah. He hid his non-amusement by putting his hand to his mouth and looking at Immanuel, who was really enjoying the merriment.

There was more chatter as they sat there. Brigham got his hand back when he got out the plans for the Mormon Temple and spread them on his desk. Uzziah couldn't help but think back to when he and Hannah had visited Joseph Smith, and he had done something very similar with the Nauvoo Temple plans.

Brigham leaned on the desk, and Marianne leaned in, putting her hand on top of his, and he looked briefly at her and continued his explanations of the plans.

All in all, it was a very good meeting for two new converts to the church, but Uzziah's fears grew as he realized this young woman, this Marianne Wells, might just be able to worm her way into being the prophet's newest, youngest, and certainly, from what Uzziah had seen, most beautiful of wives. That thought scared Uzziah to death.

If a murderess were to become part of Brigham's household, she would be forever safe from prosecution, much less even being thought a murderess. If she could ply her wares, as Brigham's newest wife, she could decimate the young men of Salt Lake, and they would never know where to look. He made a mental note to go by the telegraph office on the way back to the Brewery and Inn at the Point of the Mountain Road.

All in all, Brigham looked like he didn't want the afternoon to wind down, but a woman, one of his wives, certainly, came into the room. He was frowning at her the whole time. She whispered something into his ear that displeased him, then she left.

"I'm afraid Eliza has reminded me that I have other duties that need to be attended to," he said as he hastily scribbled something on a piece of paper and handed it to none other than Marianne Wells. She took the note, and it disappeared into her reticule.

They left, saying their goodbyes, and some hugs were exchanged, but none so noticeable as the one which Brigham and the young Miss Wells exchanged.

The carriage was brought around by the same two young Mormon men, and Marianne flirted audaciously with them. They got in, and the young men brought Uzziah and Immanuel's horses out to them. They took off together, going back to Point of the Mountain Road and the Brewery and Inn, but Uzziah turned to Immanuel before they were out of the city.

"Got to check on something, see ya back at the Inn," Uzziah said.

"Okay," Immanuel said, not taking his eyes off Marianne.

"And promise me something," Uzziah said.

"What's that?"

"Don't be alone with her, okay?" Uzziah asked, tilting his head in Marianne's direction.

"Yes, Mother," Immanuel said, because he knew it would get under Uzziah's skin, but it really didn't.

Uzziah pulled up to the telegraph office and went inside. The telegraph operator was busy taking down some of the jerked lightning, and Uzziah waited. When he finally got through, the man got up, and reaching beneath the counter, pulled up a telegraph, but he didn't hand it to Uzziah.

"I checked with Porter, ya know?" he said, holding the telegraph like it was a ransom.

"Figured ya would," Uzziah said, and looked at the man till he handed him the telegraph.

It read: *Per your inquiry—stop Three men mutilated —stop No arrests, no leads—stop Do you have leads?— stop*

"You read this, right?"

"Well, yeah," the man said, like it was the dumbest thing he'd ever heard.

"Do me and Marshall Rockwell a favor, okay?"

"Within limits."

"Do not go repeatin' any of this, okay?"

The man looked at Uzziah like he wanted to hit him, then he took in Uzziah's size and, deciding better on that, he puffed up and got indignant. "Who in God's name do ya think ya are, mister?"

"Someone who will come back and thrash ya if this gets out," Uzziah said without smiling.

"Okay, just wonderin', we're straight now, I'm sure," he said as some more jerked lightning started coming through and he walked over to transcribe.

As Uzziah rode out by himself to the Brewery and Inn at the end of Mountain Point Road, he tried to think of what he could do to forestall any more death. Clearly, the woman, Marianne, was a direct and present threat to Porter, Luana, and their family. By the time he'd gotten there, he knew exactly what he was going to do.

"Where's Porter?" he asked Orin Porter Jr. as he walked from the stables.

"He ain't got back from the city, yet," Orin said. "Is there anything I can help ya with?"

"Is yer ma here?"

"Yeah, she's at the front desk."

When he walked into the lobby, she and Emily were cleaning up. They had mops and buckets, and dusting reachers, and were going to town on the lobby.

"Luana, can I speak with ya a moment?" he asked her while smiling at Emily.

"Sure, Uzziah, what is it?"

"Privately, please?"

She took him back into the office off the front desk and she sat down heavily.

"I am gettin' too old fer this chere work," she said, sighing.

"I need to ask ya a favor."

"Uzziah, fer you, anything."

"Tell Mr. Wells and his granddaughter that ya got reservations comin' in and they'll have to find other accommodations," Uzziah said, looking right into Luana's eyes.

"And why would I do that?" Luana asked.

"I really can't say, but I'll make up whatever ya lose on their rooms," Uzziah said as he pulled out his pouch.

"There's something wrong with that young lady, ain't there?" Luana said, sitting up in the chair and staring at Uzziah.

"Well..."

"I knew it from the first time I laid eyes on her. Don't tell me, I don't wanna know, but they's outta here today," Luana said.

"I can't thank ya enough," Uzziah said.

Luana stood and walked over to Uzziah, "Sometimes," she said conspiratorially, "a woman gets a feelin' 'bout 'nother woman and she can't explain it, but I'm glad ya confirmed my suspicions, truly," she said. As they walked from the office, she said to Emily, "Make up a bill for the Wells."

"They leavin'?" Emily asked.

"They sure is."

Uzziah felt somewhat vindicated. He had his suspicions about Marianne, but when another woman, namely Luana, had similar suspicions, well, it all began to fall into place.

Uzziah went into the café at the Inn, and Immanuel was sitting there.

"Havin' some lunch?" Uzziah asked.

"Yeah, wanna join me, since I ain't supposed to fraternize with certain individuals?"

"By the way, where is she?" Uzziah asked.

"Floatin' on a cloud, the last time I saw her. She's so excited about the Mormon Ball, can't even believe there is such a thing, that her grandpappy had Porter turn the carriage around and take her to a millenary."

One of the young Mormon girls who worked for Porter came out.

"What ya want?"

"What ya got?"

"I'm havin' the special," Immanuel said.

"Yeah, give me that, too," Uzziah said.

"Ya don't even know what it is," the girl said.

"Ifn it's good enough for him, it's good enough fer me," Uzziah said, noticing the beer in front of Immanuel, "And bring me one of those, too," he said, pointing to the beer.

She left, and Uzziah looked at Immanuel, and Immanuel took a draw from the beer, wiped the foam mustache off on his sleeve, and sighed deeply.

"Okay, what's up?"

"That Marianne, she ain't right," Uzziah began.

"Yer just sayin' that 'cause she's chosen me," Immanuel argued.

"Yer lucky I found you up there in the hills, ya was 'bout to lose yer balls."

"Look, just because she's too forward fer ya, don't mean she's too forward fer me, understand?"

"'Member Frank Gear?"

"Yeah."

"He's dead."

"What?"

"And that ain't the bad part," Uzziah said, leaning nearer to his partner.

"Well?" Immanuel coaxed him.

"They can't find his scrotum," Uzziah whispered.

"What the hell's a scrotum? Part of his shootin' mechanism?"

"Ya might say that. It's his ball sack," Uzziah whispered as the girl came up with the beer for Uzziah.

Immanuel looked at Uzziah as he took his first sip of beer. "Mmm, good and cold."

"What 'bout the rest of him?" Immanuel asked.

"Oh, his johnson was in his coat pocket."

"What?!?"

"Yeah, they found him out on Mountain Point Road, well, off the road, with his pants around his ankles, his johnson in his coat pocket, and his ball sack missing."

"What 'bout the money they paid him for the trip?"

"Gone with the ball sack," Uzziah said, taking another appreciative sip of the cold beer.

"Good God, who'd want a man's ball sack?"

Uzziah just looked at Immanuel, and the two mountain men had been partners for so long that Immanuel could literally read his mind.

"Marianne!" he whispered to Uzziah, who, smiling, nodded his head.

"You're nuts," Immanuel whispered.

"Well, they could have been yer nuts, ifn I hadn't showed up in the hills when I did," Uzziah said, nodding his head up and down.

"You've absolutely gone crazy," Immanuel said.

Uzziah handed him the folded yellow telegraph message.

"What's this?"

"Read it," Uzziah said.

Immanuel read it, looked back down, read it again, then looked up at Uzziah.

"This is from the Sheriff in St. Louis," he asked.

"Yep."

"The same sheriff's office where we took one of the undersheriffs and cut his you know what off, then flayed him?"

"Yeah, so?"

"Uzziah, yer lettin' yer imagination run away with ya, young son, really. St. Louis got more than 150,000 people, and what we done is probably nothin' compared to what's happenin' now. I'm surprised there ain't more dead and mutilated men lying 'round," he said, finishing off his beer, and the Mormon girl brought the specials.

"What's this?" Uzziah asked, looking down at his plate.

"It's a salmagundi," she said.

He looked over, and Immanuel was digging into whatever was sitting there.

"Thanks," Uzziah said as she walked off.

"Immanuel, there seems to be everything but the kitchen sink in this mess," Uzziah said.

"It's basically lettuce and a bunch of things to make ya eat it. It's good fer ya," he said as he continued to eat.

"Are ya trying to lose weight?"

"Maybe?" Immanuel said as he kept crunching away at the mass of greens, pickled pig's feet, fruit, nuts, and vinegar.

"Did she say something 'bout yer weight?"

"She who?" Immanuel asked, his lips slimy with oil, and lettuce hanging from his mouth.

Uzziah got the girl to take the salmagundi away and bring him a slab of lamb with mint sauce, gravy, and potatoes. There were a few green beans on the side.

The two men ate in silence, if you can call chomping on all that lettuce silence. Uzziah just shook his head and realized he'd have to solve this whole business on his own. If Immanuel was eating salad, he was ready to sacrifice his balls sack, too, if necessary. That Marianne was a loose cannon, and Uzziah vowed he'd tie her down.

7

There was some fallout from what Uzziah had requested of Luana. But Uzziah had to give her credit, she stuck to her guns. Old man Wells was none too gracious, and Marianne showed a side of herself that even Immanuel said was rather dark. The old man demanded the money that they'd paid back, saying that if they weren't going to let them stay there, then, the whole thing was off, whatever that meant. When they finally left, the room that they had stayed in had been totally vandalized. And not just a tad here and there. The curtains were shredded, and the furniture was broken up like kindling.

Emily started crying when she tried to clean the room, and finally, Orin Jr. and Porter had to get in there. They burned the broken furniture, and Orin hired a few of his friends to help him paint the walls back to their pristine condition.

"I should say something to Brigham about this," Porter said. "It's absolutely pagan, the way the room was left."

He and Uzziah were talking in the brewery.

"I wish ya wouldn't," Uzziah said, not sure why he was sort of standing up for the Wells.

"Really?" Porter asked.

"Look, I think there's something darker at work here than simply somebody's rage," Uzziah said.

"Like?"

Uzziah had tried to tell Immanuel about his suspicions and had failed miserably. He wondered if perhaps, now that this darker side of the woman had been seen, Porter would listen.

"Look at this," Uzziah said as he pulled the telegraph out of his vest pocket and handed it to Porter.

Porter read it and looked at Uzziah.

"Ya think she did the man on Mountain Point Road, don't ya?"

"Yeah, I do," Uzziah said, "and that's not all. There was a boy of seventeen who drowned on our way down here."

"What?"

"We joined a wagon train for just one night, and this strapping young man was found the next morning, drowned in the river."

"But she'd have to struggle with some strappin' youth, wouldn't she? Were there signs of a struggle?"

"Well, I got a theory on that," Uzziah said, then he told Porter about how he and Immanuel had taken Hanna O'Bannon from the battlefield at Fredericksburg by chloroforming her.

"So, ya think she's luring these men into compromising situations and knocking them out somehow and then...what?"

"Castrating them, when she feels like it, or otherwise, leaving them dead by drowning, or whatever method she can concoct that won't point in her direction."

"What did her grandpa do before he became an old man?" Porter asked.

"Don't know," Uzziah said.

"Maybe he was a doctor, that would explain her use of the knockout drops and her use of something besides a Bowie knife," Porter said.

"Has there ever been a woman like this?" Uzziah asked.

"Look, my friend, my thoughts have always been, if ya can imagine it, it's probably happened. Bloodlust is not only among men. Women must feel it, somewhat, but are ya sure 'bout Marianne? She seems so lovely, and I have to tell ya, Brigham has talked about nothin' else since he met the young woman," Porter said.

"Well, what's he been sayin'?" Uzziah asked.

"He's attracted to her, and thinks maybe she is to him," Porter said. "Where did they come from? Do ya know that?" Porter asked.

"No, 'fraid not," Uzziah said. "Where did they go after Luana had 'em leave?"

"Not sure, I'll check into it," Porter said, "but seriously, I'm havin' trouble thinkin' 'bout her like this, especially when I think of the nature of the way that Frank Gear was kilt."

"Well, it sure weren't the old man who tore up the room," Uzziah said, and Porter shook his head in agreement, or maybe it was frustration.

Porter found out that the Wells had moved to a boarding house in downtown Salt Lake. It was owned by a Yankee woman who wasn't a Mormon. But there had never been any trouble there, so Porter and Uzziah decided to sit outside the boarding house and wait for the odd couple to leave. When they did, he went straight to the lady who ran the place, showed his badge, and she let both men—Uzziah posed as Porter's deputy—into the room.

They searched through their stuff, making sure not to leave a mess, and put things back the way they were found. They hadn't found anything of import, and the landlady ran up and said that the Wells had returned. Just as they were about to leave, Uzziah saw the end of a small black bag under one of the beds. He pulled it out, and it had a name written on it in gold letters, *Dr. E. T. Wells, MD*. They opened it up, and, sure enough, it was a doctor's bag.

Just as they were leaving by the back door of the boarding house, Tim Wells and his granddaughter were coming in the front.

Uzziah and Porter went to a café and had some lunch. At least Porter didn't order a salad.

"Well, he's a doctor, or was a doctor," Porter said.

"Yeah, wish I'd had time to check to see if there was a scalpel in the bag," Uzziah said.

"The Mormon Ball is this coming weekend," Uzziah said.

"Yeah, I know, but how do we keep Brigham from allowing the Wells to come to the party?" Porter said.

"Don't think that's gonna happen," Uzziah said.

"Let me tell ya, the last time I saw Brigham so interested in a young woman, she ended up married to him," Porter said, digging into the steak he'd ordered.

"Ya think that's what he's got in mind fer her?" Uzziah asked.

"Yeah, I do, and even if she never kills again, and if she's the one, well, her bloodlust won't allow that, but even if she did stop, what would happen to the Church if it was found out that one of the prophet's wives was a murderess?"

These questions were questions that neither of the men could answer. They both had their suspicions, and Porter probably wouldn't have given Uzziah's theories any credit at all if the two men hadn't faced down the Chinese mob in a Missouri city together. Still, what could they do until the next victim showed up?

Not far from the boarding house where the now-known Dr. E. Timothy Wells and his granddaughter were staying, there was a bar called the Salt Palace Bar. It was further down Main Street, toward the Salt Lake itself.

The very night in which Uzziah and Porter had found the doctor's bag under the bed, Marianne waited till her grandfather was sound asleep. She knew he would sleep well, because he had taken a sleeping potion, and hardly ever awoke before morning.

She slipped out the back door of the boarding house, the same exit that Uzziah and Porter had used when they avoided running into the odd couple. She walked down to the Salt Palace and, going inside, took a corner seat at the bar. It was still that time in history when any woman who went into a bar was considered a loose woman. Marianne had been smart and worn a hat she'd gotten from the millers that was black and had a black veil that covered enough of her face that no one would be able to recognize her. She wasn't worried, she knew she wouldn't be back ever!

The first man who walked to her table and started speaking to her would be the last man.

"Hey, sweetheart, never seen ya in here before," he said, then took a seat.

They had a couple drinks, then the barkeep told Porter the next day that was the last she saw of them. The barkeep was a part-owner, and she didn't like the fact that her place had been used for nefarious purposes.

What no one knew was that the couple walked toward the pier that stretched out over the Salt Lake. It was a popular spot for families during the summer, but at night, the only ones who came down this far were looking for a private place to do private things.

"When did ya move to town?" the man asked. He was slender, but strong, and his voice reminded Marianne of someone who could probably sing well. He was most likely a tenor.

"You sing, don't ya?" she asked him, as they shared a bottle that he had in his jacket.

"Well, at church I can belt it out," he said, smiling, thinking that this was his lucky day.

"What's yer favorite hymn?" she asked him. He told her, and she did not recognize it, probably because it was a Mormon hymn. She figured that after she married Brigham, if it went that far, she would know all the hymns and wouldn't be at a loss.

He sang a few bars, and when she laughed, he shut

up, but it was beautiful. She almost felt sorry for what she was about to do, but doing it made her so excited in a way that usually only happened when men and women did things together.

They sat at the end of the pier, and when she guided his hand to her breast, which was just under a slip of a blouse, he let her unbutton his pants, and as she was holding his manhood, he leaned back and moaned, then there was a cloth placed across his face, but when he tried to fight, he found himself without strength. He fell back, but his manhood stayed engorged with blood, as she drew it and his scrotum from his long johns, and taking the doctor's tool from her reticule, she circled the whole of his manhood, and blood gushing, it literally fell into her other hand. That was when she had her termination of excitement, and hefting the bloody mess in both hands, she tossed it into the lake, where, instead of sinking, it floated due to all the salt in the water.

The man, what was left of him, was found floating in Salt Lake. It was first ventured that he had wandered down there and fallen in off the pier, but when his body was examined and he was found to be missing some rather private parts, the theories changed.

There was blood found on the pier, and no signs of a struggle, which reinforced Uzziah and Porter's idea that she had used chloroform to subdue her victims before emasculating them.

As they looked around, Uzziah saw something floating further out than the man, and getting into a nearby rowboat, they oared themselves out to what remained of the man's scrotum and penis. The fish had enjoyed some of it, but it could only have belonged to the dead man, who, again, showed no signs of struggle.

When they took the body and its parts to the icehouse, they passed the boarding house, and sitting on the front porch drinking his morning coffee was Dr. Wells and his granddaughter, Marianne. He did not see either of them, but she saw both Porter and Uzziah, and when she waved at them, they made no attempt to wave back.

"If she done it, she's as cold-blooded as they come," Porter said.

"Oh, I'm fairly sure she's a black widow, I just can't figure how her grandpa don't know."

"People know what they wanna know," Porter said, and Uzziah took a look back over his shoulder, and she was still following their progress, and of all things, smiling.

The Mormon dance was to be at the community center that very night, and part of Uzziah felt good that she had killed before the dance, perhaps she would have satiated her bloodlust and could control herself at the dance.

Uzziah rode Shadow back to the Brewery and Inn, and when he showed up, Immanuel was just coming from their rooms.

"Where ya been?"

"Porter—helping Porter with a case," Uzziah said, not wanting to get into it.

"Another murder done by our lovely Marianne?" Immanuel quipped.

Uzziah just looked at his partner, thinking how they might have found his remains there in the foothills, bled out before he could come to consciousness, his exsanguinated body white in the afternoon sun. It was the things that people thought were impossible that would eventually sneak up on them and take their lives. What we feared was the obvious, but it was the not so obvious, the mundane, or even the beautiful that would saddle up to us, and when we least expected it, remove whatever they wanted and, in doing so, extinguish our life.

Immanuel looked at Uzziah, they were on the way to the café at the brewery.

"I was just kiddin' with ya, young son, ya know that, right?" Immanuel said, trying to make light of something that Uzziah had just witnessed, which was anything but goodness and light, and certainly didn't need to be kidded about.

"I'm thinkin' of gettin' proper clothes for the dance," Uzziah said to Immanuel.

"Really?" Immanuel hadn't really thought about it, but he supposed dressing better for the prophet would probably be a good idea.

"Yeah, ya wanna come with me?" Uzziah asked.

"Yeah, let's do it, and let's buy it outta our Yankee fund," Immanuel said.

"That would be totally appropriate," Uzziah said, thinking that wearing a fine three-piece matching sack suit with the money they'd taken off the dead blue belly would be appropriate, considering the fact that he was sure they would be apprehending a cold-blooded murderess.

They rode down to a men's tailoring shop that Porter had suggested, and they both were able to buy off the rack exactly the three-piece sack suit that Uzziah had thought about and seen a couple of times on the paddleboats.

Immanuel went with the black wool, but Uzziah decided he wanted to stand out a bit. Perhaps it was because he knew he was after a killer who thought she was safe from all scrutiny. Perhaps, he wanted to stick out and remind her he was watching. It would be harder for her to ignore him when he was wearing a light tan sack suit. They tried them on and had a laugh or two when the man whistled when they came from the dressing rooms. When they looked at themselves in the three-way mirror, both thought they looked as good as they ever had. Immanuel paid, and they rode back to the Brewery and Inn at end of Point of the Mountain Road.

The morning of the Mormon Ball, Brigham Young woke with a renewed spirit. He knew why, he really did. It was the young woman whom Porter and Uzziah and his partner had brought to see him. He loved it when there were new converts to Mormonism, after all, that was what was going to keep the movement, and he knew it was a movement, going someplace important.

As he bathed, he thought of her, and to his surprise, he emerged from his bathwater a bit more a man than when he had entered it. There was nothing wrong with that, since procreation was a gift from the Lord, and when beautiful women inspired a man's thoughts, among other things, and he managed to achieve himself more readily, then there was simply nothing wrong with that, either.

He got dressed and was about to start his day when there came a knock on his door. He wasn't surprised when he opened it, and it was one of his wives, Eliza.

"Good morning," she said.

"And this couldn't have waited until I was at the breakfast table?"

"No, Brigham, it couldn't have," she said as she closed the door behind her.

"Oh, we are in a conspiratorial mood, are we?" He knew she was always looking out for his best interest, but sometimes, he found it taxing to put up with some of the things she brought to his attention.

"There's nothing conspiratorial about what I have to say, and I do hope, through the grace of our Lord Jesus Christ, that you will not only listen, but take heed," she said as she straightened his tie. He was sure it was straight when she started fiddling with it, but he let that go.

"Please," he said, which was his way of inviting her to speak openly.

"I noticed the other day when Mr. Wells and his granddaughter, Marianne, were here, that you took an inordinate interest in the young woman," she said, trying not to mince her words.

"And by inordinate, you mean?"

"Brigham, she was nearly sitting in your lap when I came into the room, and neither of you could take your eyes off the other."

"I like her breeding," he said.

"Well, you've used one appropriate word," she sniped.

"I will not have you insinuating things, do you understand?"

"Perfectly, but even though she may be beautiful, and of course, if able to bear children, she would make handsome babies, but we know nothing of her, her grandfather, or any of her kin. You know how vital it is to know a genealogy, I know you do."

"All right, I'll slow down if that will make you feel safer, better, or whatever you're driving at. But they will be at the ball tonight, and I, personally, am looking forward to it."

"As you should. This ball will be the capstone of the social calendar for all Mormons, and enjoying it will be simple. I just don't want you to get lost in all the falderal and end up doing something that you shall ultimately regret."

He put his arm around her and turned her as he opened the door. They walked out together. He knew how to treat women, after all, he had innumerable wives. How could a man who had so many wives not know how to treat women? King Solomon, whom he liked to think of as a great, great man, had 300 wives and 700 concubines. Why, the man couldn't have serviced all of them in three years, much less one. But there was no record of any rebellion among either his wives or his concubines. He did, Solomon, drift from the true faith as he grew older by putting up shrines to his foreign wives' deities, but Brigham knew he wasn't about to commit that atrocity.

"You have always had my best interest in mind, Eliza, and if I live to be a hundred years old, I shall never be in a position to give you enough thanks," he said as they made the landing at the bottom of the steps and she, smiling at him, led the way into the dining room.

8

It was the night of the Mormon Ball, and the community center, which also substituted for a house of worship for the Mormons, had been decorated lavishly. Streamers hung from the rafters, flowers in vases were situated everywhere, and the crowning achievement was the table decorations. Each table had a Book of Mormon on it, but it was really made of pottery, and flowering from the book were sprays of roses, red, white, and blue. The red and whites were natural, but the blue ones had been white before their stems were placed in vases with blue food coloring in the water.

It was a symbol of how much the state, Utah, wanted to be admitted into the precious Union. The state had tried three times without success to enter the Union. Each time, the reason had basically been the same, the plurality of marriages that were sanctioned within the LDS Church. And yet, the territory had been governed mostly by outsiders, and the residents of the state wished to put an end to that. So, it wasn't without merit that they displayed the Union colors, since many who would attend would be representatives of the US government.

As the carriages started arriving, the band struck up a celebratory note. Brigham Young and his entourage made a grand entrance.

Brigham loved the attention, and yet, Porter knew that it wasn't just Marianne Wells that he had to worry about. As the primary bodyguard for the prophet, he knew there were factions within the state itself that wished to derail the LDS attempts to control the territory. Porter was especially glad to have Uzziah and Immanuel with him in his attempts at security. It was, and had been, well known that if someone wanted to exchange his life for that of the prophet, then there would be no stopping him, or her, for that matter. And yet the firepower that was hidden during that dance would have been enough to stop a small revolution.

The tables were all open seating except for the dignitaries and special guests. And yet, when Brigham entered the ball, the first thing he did was make sure that he found Mr. Timothy Wells and his granddaughter, Marianne. When he did, he swept them over to where his table was and had the waiters insert two more chairs and two more place settings so that they could be there to celebrate with him.

It was a great honor, and many who saw this wondered what was going on. Who were these people? This older man and the young woman. Surely, they weren't a married couple. Then, as the gossip made the rounds, it was discovered that they were recent converts to Mormonism, and that Brigham had taken an especial interest in Marianne Wells and her grandfather.

Anyone who knew the prophet knew that he had an eye for the ladies, and no one doubted that this newcomer would not escape his net of interest.

The band played while the dinners were brought out, and keeping with the cuisine of the west, the main entrée was beef. It was prime rib, and the slabs that appeared on Immanuel and Uzziah's plates were nothing short of grand.

"Now this is a piece of meat," Immanuel said, "and they even brought the horseradish and the sour cream."

Baked potatoes and a green salad rounded out the meal, and except for the playing of the band, there was little conversation around the tables as the meal was enjoyed.

As soon as the plates were cleared, desserts were brought out, and coffee served. Then, the dancing began. And who should lead off the dancing festivities but the couple of Brigham Young and the lovely Miss Marianne Wells. They danced divinely together. There was no doubt that both of them knew all the dances and that Brigham was leading the young lady expertly.

"Whatcha think?" Porter said as he sat down at Uzziah's table. Immanuel had already spied a lovely older woman, whom some said was a widow, and they were turning circles in a waltz.

"I think we'd better keep an eye on the old man and watch her every move," Uzziah said.

"It ain't hard to watch her move, that's a fer sure!" Porter said, knowing the double meaning.

"Yeah, well, just remember, it's her charm that gets her into range, and her skill that finishes the job," Uzziah commented.

The evening wore on, and Marianne made no moves to do anything but dance, flirt with Brigham's friends, and drink punch. The boys had danced some, mostly Immanuel and his charming widow, and when the evening was winding down, Immanuel walked over to where Uzziah was standing at the table with the punch bowl.

"I think, I'm leavin'," Immanuel said.

"What 'bout Brigham?" Uzziah asked, referring to the fact that he had hardly danced with anyone but the beautiful Marianne the whole evening.

"Hey, he don't need my help. I just hope I can do as well with the widder, over there," Immanuel said, as he indicated the charming widow who looked older, but was certainly still a striking beauty.

"Fine, Porter and I can watch him," Uzziah said.

Well, since it was a Mormon Ball, the president and prophet of the church was more or less obligated to stay and say his goodbyes to all the guests. It became obvious to those remaining that it was time to leave or be rude to the prophet, so the hall emptied out fairly quickly.

When it came time for Brigham to leave, his carriage pulled up in front of the hall, and when he came out, the only other person with him was Marianne Wells.

Porter walked up to Brigham once he'd helped Marianne into the carriage.

"Sir, are ya takin' her back to yer house?" Porter asked, concerned.

"No, she suggested we go on a moonlight drive," he

said, indicating the nearly full moon that hung over the desert.

"And yer gonna do just that, now?" Porter said, a bit sarcastically.

"I do not need yer protection from the wiles of this woman, Porter, now, go home to Luana, whom, I might add, looked beautiful tonight, and do what the Lord has decreed, *Be fruitful and multiply.*"

Porter stepped back from the carriage, and as he was walking toward Uzziah, they heard the driver step-up the horses, and the carriage disappeared down the street.

"Yer lettin' him go with her, just like that?" Uzziah said, shrugging his shoulders in disbelief.

"Maybe we're wrong 'bout this, Uzziah, huh?" Porter said, seeming out of options.

"I'll get our horses, at least we can be at the home if he takes her back there," Uzziah said.

They had their horses and were mounted up in no time at all. They rode hard down the city streets, probably too fast for the city, but it was late at night. There was hardly anyone out and about, and besides, the moon lit everything up as if it were day.

When they got to Brigham's house, the carriage was nowhere to be seen.

"Where's the carriage!?!" Porter asked, and there was fear in his voice.

"Obviously, it's somewhere else. What did he say to you, exactly?" Uzziah asked.

"He said, '*She suggested we go on a moonlight drive,*'" Porter said.

"But she doesn't know the city, or the area," Uzziah mused, then he remembered the trail that was big enough for a buggy that she had taken Immanuel up, the place near the falls where she had almost killed his partner.

"Come on!" Uzziah said, "I think I know exactly where they're going!" and he kicked Shadow up into a gallop and headed for Point of the Mountain Road.

Porter rode up alongside Uzziah and shouted over the hoofbeats.

"She's takin' him to the brewery?"

"No, to the waterfall," Uzziah yelled back.

"What waterfall?" Porter asked.

"Just follow me," Uzziah said, and nudged Shadow in a higher gear. He looked, and Porter was having trouble keeping his horse up. Well, that would just be what it would be.

By the time Uzziah made the trail that led to the meadow and the waterfall beyond, it was obvious that a carriage had been up this way. There were wagon marks in the soft soil, and they were new.

As they made the meadow, they could both see the carriage parked, and when they dismounted and ran up to it, a dead body lay across the driver's seat. It had been stabbed, there was blood everywhere.

"My God, Brigham may already be dead," Porter said, as he drew his gun.

"Not yet," came a voice off in the brush.

They both turned to see Timothy Wells with a Greener pointed directly at them. When they made him out, he emphasized his advantage by pulling back both hammers on the Greener.

"What the—" Porter said, but stopped.

"Dr. Wells, how nice to see you," Uzziah said as he took a step toward the man.

"Stop right there, I got two barrels, one for each of you," Dr. Wells said.

"I thought there was such a thing as a Hippocratic oath, and the first words are: *First, do no harm!*" Uzziah reminded the good doctor.

"Yeah, well, the first has passed, and harm was done, that's what this is all about," he said.

"Where's Brigham?" Porter asked.

"Right where he needs to be, sitting peacefully under the moon, not suspecting a thing in the world," Dr. Wells said.

"She's gonna kill 'im?" Porter went on.

"We can only hope," the doctor said.

"Ya can't let this happen, Dr. Wells. Marianne needs help," Uzziah pleaded.

"Yes, yes, she's needed help for some time now, but there's only one thing that she wants, and that's blood," Dr. Wells said, a sick smile on his face.

"Drop it!" came a voice behind Wells. It was Immanuel's voice, and the sweetest sound that either Porter or Uzziah had ever heard.

"Maybe I'll just kill them," Dr. Wells said, right before Immanuel's Walker Colt barrel cracked him across the noggin. Wells, being the old man that he was, went down like a sack of potatoes.

"I'll stay and cover 'im," Immanuel said as the two men ran off like they were late for something important.

The moonlight lit the scene like it was the theater, a full moon will do that at times.

Marianne Wells had Brigham Young's manhood in

her hands and was moving in for, well, the kill. As they watched, she moved close to him like she was going to kiss him, then slipped the powerful chloroform-soaked cloth over Brigham's face. He jerked at the smell, but before he could muster a move, he was laid back on his back, and she still had his manhood in her grasp.

As she reached for the scalpel, Uzziah shouted out.

"Don't!" It was a single word, but she still grabbed the surgical instrument and went for the prize. Then a shot rang out, and her head flopped to one side, and the prophet was sprayed with her brains.

Porter looked at Uzziah, whose Colt was smoking.

"Son, that was a hell of a shot," was all Porter said.

Back at the carriage, Immanuel heard the shot and hoped that something right had been done among all the mistakes he'd made. Dr. Wells awakened, moaning.

"Oh, oh, my head," he said, putting his hand on the goose egg he had. "What the hell happened?" he asked no one in particular.

"Something good, I hope," Immanuel said.

From the direction of the waterfall, Uzziah and Porter came walking, each with his own burden.

Uzziah carried the body of Marianne, her head drooped and bloody.

"Nooo!" Dr. Wells screamed, and he tried to run to the body, but Immanuel grabbed his shoulder.

"Uh-uh," Immanuel said.

As they got closer, Brigham, in Porter's arms, began to awaken.

"What?! Huh!?" he mumbled. "Where's Marianne?" he asked, actually concerned about the woman who had come within seconds of making the Prophet and President of the Mormon Church a eunuch.

Uzziah laid her body down on the ground, and as Brigham regained his feet and gazed at her in the moonlight, he realized she'd basically had her head blown off.

"Why!?" he screamed.

"She had this," Porter said, and showed the scalpel to him.

"What's that?" he asked.

"That's what she was gonna nut ya with," Immanuel put it so eloquently.

"My God!" Brigham said.

"And mine," Uzziah said.

9

It was the territory of Utah. The territory that so desperately wanted to become a state. There couldn't be a trial, but there certainly was a hearing, a closed hearing within the Mormon Church, held in the home of Brigham Young, in his study, and those admitted to it were sworn to secrecy. The story would never see the light of day, ever!

It seemed back in 1857, Dr. Wells and his entire family, including his beautiful granddaughter, Marianne, were on their way to California and had traveled through the southern part of Utah after going through Salt Lake City. It was early in September of that year, and they hoped to get to the foot of the Rockies before winter came, and maybe even beyond.

The Baker-Fancher wagon train was seen by a lot of Mormons as it made its way south. A woman whose husband had been martyred by Missourians thought she saw one of his murderers on the wagon train, and that information got to the southern Mormons, who were in a hysteria created by rumors that Joseph Smith had said Jesus was coming soon.

Add to that the fact that eleven miners and plainsmen were among the wagon train, and they were known as the Missouri Wildcats. Some of these supposedly taunted, vandalized, and caused trouble for Mormons along their route. Some even claimed that these Wildcats had bragged that *they shot the guts out of old Joe Smith.*

Dr. Wells was brought into Brigham's study for questioning. It was decided that it would be best if a non-Mormon would question him, and Immanuel James Jones was appointed to do the questioning.

Dr. Wells was asked to place his hand on the Bible and swear that what he told was the truth and nothing but the truth, so help him God.

"I do swear so," Dr. Wells said.

"Who exactly were you and your granddaughter, Dr. Wells?" Immanuel asked.

"We were a part of the Baker-Fancher wagon train. All was going well. We passed through Salt Lake and resupplied there. There didn't seem to be any trouble, but some of the men on the wagon train did get into a sort of shouting match with some Mormons, but nothing came of it, so we thought it meant nothing."

"After you passed through the Salt Lake area, where did the wagon train go?"

"We went directly south and were within less than a hundred miles of being out of the Utah territory when we were beset by Paiute Indians, and it would be revealed not long after that that some of the Indians were actually White men disguised as Paiutes."

"What was the purpose of that disguise, Dr. Wells?" Immanuel asked.

"First let me tell you, we held off the attack for five days, then under a flag of peace, a white flag, these men, not Indians, not Paiutes, showed themselves and told us that there had been a mistake, that the Paiutes thought we were another party, and if we handed our weapons over to them, that we would be allowed safe passage the rest of the way."

"And then, what happened?"

"Well, I didn't trust those White men, and when the group took their weapons with them to surrender, Marianne and I stayed back. We hid there in the meadow. It wasn't a very good hiding place, and after the White men had massacred everyone who surrendered, they found us. They had some wounded, and when they found out I was a doctor, I was allowed to go and patch their friends up."

"What happened to Marianne?"

"Well, they told me they would take her to safety while I did my doctoring, but it turned out that anything that came out of their mouths was lies. They took Marianne to a wagon, and there they raped her, repeatedly. She wasn't sure how long they did it, but when I found her, they thought she was dead. It was days later. She was just thrown out in the meadow for the varmints to find and eat."

"But she lived?"

"Well, yes, until Uzziah killed her, she did."

"What happened after the raping and you and her went back east?"

"Well, I started noticing that when she gave me my sleeping potion that sometimes, she gave me so much that it was hard to awaken the next day. On those occasions, I'd found some of her clothes in the burn barrel out back, and they were covered with blood. When I asked her about them, she said she had killed a chicken for supper and it had bled all over her."

"But ya suspected otherwise?" Immanuel coaxed the doctor.

"I did, and once when she seemed particularly restless, I didn't take the sleep medication she gave me, but waited up for her, and when she returned, she was covered in blood. I was fairly sure it was human blood."

"Then, what did you determine?"

"That she was killing men for what men had done to her," the doctor said.

"Why didn't you turn her in to the authorities once you'd discovered this?"

"I confronted her, and she admitted most of what she had done, but how could I blame her? Then, she came up with this plan of killing Brigham Young, whom she thought was personally responsible for the Meadow Massacre. I thought she could fight her bloodlust against men if she could find and kill this last victim. A sort of take the head of the snake idea."

"But?"

"It was something she couldn't control."

"So, you allowed her to go on killing, is that right, doctor?"

"Yes, I did, but we were so close to her bagging her last kill, Brigham Young," Dr. Wells said, and he looked at Brigham. "And we almost bagged you, didn't we!?!" the doctor asked.

"Doctor, just one last question. As a doctor and one who had taken an oath to do no harm, how could you have allowed yourself to become involved with all this killing?" Uzziah admired Immanuel for asking that last question. The answer didn't satisfy anyone.

"She was so beautiful, and when she wasn't killing, so kind and generous. What they had done to her had changed her forever, and if there was just one chance in a million that she might stop and change back to what she was before the Meadow Massacre, well, I was willing to take it."

When Uzziah and Immanuel continued on their way to their mountain home, they rode for quite a spell before either one of them spoke.

"That ain't the first woman ya kilt, was it?" Immanuel asked.

"Maybe, maybe not, can't rightly remember," Uzziah said.

"Well, she was certainly the most beautiful woman ya ever kilt."

"Yep, she was."

The weather wasn't looking good for them to make it all the way to the Rockies, and who knew, they might have to stop somewhere short.

EPILOGUE

The doctor was allowed to leave Salt Lake City because, even though he knew about her murderous ways, he had not participated actively in any of them, except the last, when he thought the killing of Brigham Young would possibly cure her.

As Dr. Erasmus Timothy Wells left Salt Lake and made his way back east, he was, to say the least, surprised that the Mormons had let him go. They had even offered to bury his granddaughter, which he took them up on. The service was not well attended, even the mountain men, who had accompanied him and his daughter from St. Louis, were not there.

At a waystation on the stage line, Dr. Wells ate lunch. Afterward, he went back outside to board the stage that was leaving shortly. He pulled his pipe from his jacket pocket and lit up.

As he blew the smoke from his pipe, he realized how invigorating the mountain air was, and as the doctor looked around, he thought perhaps when he got to Denver across the Rockies, he might just put out a shingle and enjoy this fine air for the rest of his life.

A woman had come out, and as she watched the old man, his head exploded, then he collapsed to the ground. Right after this, a shot rang out. She screamed, and then was joined by others who wouldn't go near the body of the doctor till they were certain that no more shooting was going to take place.

Back up in the hills surrounding the waystation, a single man put his rifle with a sight on it back in the scabbard on his horse. He then mounted up and rode away.

A LOOK AT BOOK NINE: THE HANGING TREE
A UZZIAH MOUNTAIN MAN WESTERN DOUBLE

Justice follows close. Trouble never rides alone.

After leaving the Salt Lake Valley, Uzziah O'Bannon and Immanuel Jones aim for the quiet of their Rocky Mountain cabins. A stop at a trading post changes everything when a U.S. deputy marshal arrests Uzziah for the long-range shooting death of Dr. Erastus Timothy Wells. Though Uzziah insists the shot came from a Winchester—not his Hawken—he's jailed anyway. Immanuel breaks him out, and the two flee into the high country with a posse and a Shoshone tracker in pursuit. Even an avalanche on Mt. Elbert fails to stop the chase.

In Oro, a midnight robbery and a rigged trial deepen the trouble. The mountain men prevent Deputy Marshal Vergil Higgins from hanging, but he refuses to let them go. From Denver City to the settlement, Higgins presses the chase until his obsession leads to the kidnapping of Standing Bear's adopted son, drawing the Crow into a violent clash with the Blackfeet.

When the fighting ends, winter closes in. Uzziah rides back to the cabins alone, while Immanuel remains at the settlement, facing choices that could change both their lives.

This two-book bundle includes the nineteenth and twentieth novels in the *Uzziah Mountain Man* series.

AVAILABLE APRIL 2026

THANK YOU

Thank you for taking the time to read *Death to Deserters: A Western Double*. If you enjoyed it, please consider telling your friends or posting a short review. Word of mouth is an author's best friend and much appreciated.

Thank you.
J.J. Bonham

ABOUT THE AUTHORS

He was good looking and could sell ice to eskimos. But ... writing asked something else from him. He would have to corral his interest in being free. Writing would take him to a place where he was tamed, but also able to actually tell a story.

After the first two weeks at the Yale School of Drama, he called the head of the playwriting department, Milan Stitt and told him he was quitting. Milan invited him to lunch at a nearby Mexican restaurant in New Haven. He told the man who had had plays on Broadway that he wanted to be a free writer. Milan smiled, then explained the way to freedom was always through discipline.

Something in him clicked and it all began to make sense.

Three years later, when he received his MFA in playwriting, he received the much coveted Cole Porter Prize for Excellence in Writing.

Enter a woman, years later, when the first 'J' in J.J. Bonham, Jack Bonham, had written thirty screenplays in 7 years and had one optioned which looked like it actually might be done.

Unlike Milan Stitt, this woman had no plays on Broadway, but was a divorced mother of four grown children. She loved soaps, and was an ardent watcher of the same. In the years of her devotion to watching she developed an uncanny ability to discern plot and analyze character. Uncanny, really better than any of his teachers at Yale.

They, Jack & Judy, the other 'J' in J.J. Bonham, married in Buffalo Springs, Colorado. While teaching elementary school in Denver they read the same novella and looking up and into each other's eyes, realizing something. They could do that.

Thirteen years later they had written nearly 200 novels. Westerns mostly because that was who they were – a misplaced couple from the 19th Century who saw life in a western justice sort of way. They danced in Virgina City, Montana. Dances from a different time and place, but still their time and place.

Now, they live in the Bitterroot Valley on five acres and looking out the office window as he puts this together for them, he can see the thunderstorm marching across the Sapphire Mountains. Earlier, sitting on the porch, she had said something about the crack of lightning years before as they said vows of love in Buffalo Springs. He remembered.

www.ingramcontent.com/pod-product-compliance
Lightning Source LLC
La Vergne TN
LVHW040216110826
845146LV00005B/1307

9798895673614